ZACK
JACKSON
& THE RUINS OF ATHOS

I0552758

For Tink, without whom this would not have been possible.

Learn more about this and other works by the author at:
https://HansCummings.com

Edited by Amanda Y. Valentine

Cover Art by Maria Damianou

Interior Art by Hanae Ko

Electronic editions available through all major platforms.

For Tink, without whom this would not have been possible.

Dedicated To
The men and woman of the Mercury, Gemini, and Apollo space programs. Your spirit of discovery and sacrifice will fuel dreams of exploration for countless generations.

Dr. Stephen Hawking, Dr. Carl Sagan, Dr. Brian Cox, Dr. Phil Plait (The Bad Astronomer), Dr. Neil deGrasse Tyson and Bill Nye (The Science Guy). You taught me that the real universe can be just as wonderous as that of our imaginations.

Gene Roddenberry, George Lucas, the cast and crew of Doctor Who, Bioware, Steve Winter & the TSR Staff who created Star Frontiers, and Posthuman Studios. You created fantastic worlds in which to play that grew my imagination in more ways than I can count.

Inspired By
The universe of Zack Jackson was inspired by
numerous sources:
Star Trek
Star Wars
Doctor Who
Mass Effect
Star Frontiers
Eclipse Phase
The Honorverse
Through the Wormhole
Firefly

The Zack Jackson Series
Zack Jackson & The Cult of Athos
Zack Jackson & The Cytherean Academy
Zack Jackson & The Hives of Valtra
Zack Jackson & The Secret of Venus
Zack Jackson & The Ruins of Athos

SPECIES OF THE GALAXY

Devorans

Homeworld: Devorus
Lifespan: 1,000+ Standard Years
One of the older space-faring species and members of the Galactic Confederation, Devorans possess a reptilian appearance and lay eggs but are warm-blooded. The Devoran homeworld is at the heart of the largest conglomeration of planets in the galaxy, the Devoran Union.

Ersidians

Homeworld: Ersid
Lifespan: 150+ Standard Years
A hulking, bear-like member species of the Galactic Confederation, Ersidians believe strongly in honor and that their ancestors watch over and guide them. They have colonized many systems in their local space.Their home planet is the capital of a small network of colony worlds. The current President of the Galactic Confederation is Ersidian.

Humans

Homeworld: Earth
Lifespan: 125+ Standard Years
Humans are the dominant species in the Earth-Alpha Centauri Alliance (EAC). They're more or less like you and me. Thanks to the marvels of modern medicine, humans can remain active well past their one hundredth birthday. Human civilization has expanded to included colonies on most of the inhabitable planets within ten light years of Earth.

Kerrolians

Homeworld: Kerrola
Lifespan: 100+ Standard Years
Kerrolians, close relatives of Traxians, average shorter in height than humans and are covered with fur, have pointed, upright ears (like a wolf or cat), digitigrade locomotion, have elongated snouts and prominent canines (though most don't protrude), and bushy tails. Their homeworld is part of the Traxian Domain and is not a member of the Galactic Confederation.

Ryll
Homeworld: μ (Mu) Arae
Lifespan: 65+ Standard Years
Ryll are an amorphous species resembling giant amoebas. They typically wear bulky environ-mental suits as they are unable to interact with most technology otherwise, though they do possess contact telepathy. Their suit translators are unable to identify emotion or inflection in their thoughts, so they preface their monotone proclamations to ensure clarity. Despite this, they are friendly and have a good sense of humor. Their homeworld is a member of the Traxian Domain.

Uurts
Homeworld: Ersid
Lifespan: 100+ Standard Years
Resembling centaurs from Earth mythology, Uurts share Ersid with their cousins, the Ersidians. Where the Ersidians historically dwell in the mountains, Uurts roam the plains of their homeworld living as nomads. Of course, in the modern era, they share cities all over the planet and on their colony worlds. There are still some Uurt tribes who live a nomadic life, though they are comfortable with technology.

Valtraxians
Homeworld: Valtra
Lifespan: 35+ Standard Years
Valtraxians are an eight-legged insect-like species often described as a cross between a grasshopper and a praying mantis. Their species possess four genders: male, female, drone, and incubator, and they live in communal hives,much like bees or ants. Despite their short lifespan, many become brilliant engineers. Valtra is a member of the Galactic Confederation.

Chapter 1

"Watch out!" Jenny yanked Zack's arm, pulling him down behind a boulder. A wave the size of a small vehicle smashed into the reef, showering them with briny water. As the surge receded, strands of black algae clung to them and the surrounding rocks, leaving greasy black stains where it touched their skin and clothing. Zack clutched Jenny, bracing against the undertow that threatened to drag them into open water.

Zack lifted his head to look back toward the Athosian ship. The top of the bulbous, pickle-shaped ship remained concealed behind jagged stones jutting above the surface of the sea. "Can you see a way back?"

Jenny shook her head. "The water filled the gaps. We might have to swim for it."

Another wave crashed into their rock, soaking them in a deluge of warmth. His hand closed around his communication device, his C7, now forming a block-like protrusion through his sodden pants. *At least it's waterproof.*

"I'm sorry, Zack. I didn't expect the tide to come in so quickly." Jenny squeezed Zack's hand.

"How much higher do you think it will get?" Zack stared into the churning water, its dark color obscuring his view of the rocks that lay below. Opposite the rising sun, three moons low in the sky gazed down upon them with passive indifference.

"I don't know." Jenny stared toward the island where they had made camp. "When the tide goes out, make for the nearest rocks. We have to hurry."

Zack released her, then pulled himself hand-over-hand along the reef closer to their camp. The receding sea revealed the tops of the boulders bridging the gap between the island and the mainland.

"Go, now!" Jenny leapt toward the first rock, Zack hot on her heels. She slipped on some slick black algae draped over the boulder and fell forward. Zack seized her waist, but he failed to gain a foothold on the sea-soaked algae and followed her into the water. Upon impact, bitter, salty liquid entered his nose and mouth before he surfaced sputtering and coughing. He felt Jenny pull him by his collar through the water toward another rock.

The island seemed so far away, though Zack knew it lay less than a hundred meters from the mainland. Given the truck-size waves that battered them, a hundred meters might as well be a hundred kilometers. They clung to the reef as the tide rolled in, until it raised them above the slick, wet surface.

Holding hands, they kicked their legs and swam for the shore ahead. Inward rushing water pushed them parallel to the shore until the tide ebbed and the undertow dragged them backward. Desperate to avoid being pulled into the open sea, they redoubled their efforts to swim across the current.

The current ripped their hands from each other before it slammed Zack into another rock. He cried out in pain, sputtering and spitting as more nasty water rushed into his mouth. Fortunately, he maintained his grip on the reef. As the tide threatened to drag her past him, Zack seized Jenny's hand, holding it tightly. They allowed themselves a short respite before kicking off the rock and continuing their swim toward the island's shore.

Halfway there, the tide rolled in again. Despite linking arms and kicking with all their might, the incoming waves pushed them farther sideways than they had progressed forward. To Zack, the island appeared no closer, despite their efforts.

Zack felt something slither up his leg. Yelping, he kicked wildly and thrashed, breaking his arm lock with Jenny.

"What are you..." The sea splashed into Jenny's face, drowning her words. Zack reached for her to link up again, but an oncoming wave crashed into him, separating them further. He saw Jenny twist around and swim toward him.

The outgoing current pulled Zack away from the shore, and his legs slammed into another rock. Bracing himself against it, he wedged his foot into a crack to gain leverage. Jenny managed to swim over to him when another wave pushed her toward the island.

They strained to maintain their hold on the rock as the waves bashed them. Blinking to clear his vision, he coughed. "We're almost there!"

Jenny gasped for breath. "Look there!" She pointed toward an outcropping. From their vantage point, it appeared to connect to the island.

When the tide seemed at its lowest point, they pushed off. They swam toward the next protruding reef, reaching it just as incoming waves threatened to push them past it. Its jagged surface proved sufficient for them to cling to when the water rose high, so they rested, waiting for the tide to ebb before following it ashore.

Upon reaching the shore first, Jenny seized Zack's arm to pull him out of the water. Gasping for breath, they collapsed onto the moss-covered rocks where they lay with their soaked clothes clinging to them.

Zack rolled over to look at Jenny. "Let's not do that again."

—— 《》 — 《》 — 《》 — 《》 — 《》 — 《》 ——

"I'm glad my parents made me take swimming lessons in grammar school on Messier Habitat." At the time, Jenny had considered it a waste of time. Nevertheless, her mother had insisted, and now as she lay shivering on the rocky shore in dripping wet clothes, Jenny thanked her for that useless activity.

Jenny stood and helped Zack to his feet. His skin felt oily and slimy. She hoped the water was free from toxins or parasites that like human stomachs. "Let's get back to camp and find towels or something."

"Good idea."

Running back to camp seemed like a better way to mitigate shivering than merely walking. When they arrived, they spotted Major Jericho and the other adults, Sergeant Montgomery Coulson and Lieutenant Elizabeth Herd, working to erect a canopy tent at the center of their camp. Coulson and Herd stopped working when they saw the soaked pair.

"I take it your trip to the mainland didn't work out? At least the Athosians have fast fabricators. We made enough materials for a decent camp already." Major Jericho glanced up from his work. Jenny noticed he had his leg resting on a sealed black pack.

"The trip there was fine. The tide came in while we were out." Jenny's teeth chattered as she spoke. "Getting back was trouble."

"It came in so fast." Zack shivered, rubbing his arms.

Lieutenant Herd put her hands on Jenny's shoulders. "Come on, let's get you out of those wet clothes." She looked back at the men. "We'll go into the ship; you guys can take care of Zack out here."

"Where's Ix?" Zack started to remove his shirt as Coulson stood by with a towel.

Jenny didn't wait around for the answer and walked back to the Athosian ship with Lieutenant Herd. They passed through the entry room into the conference chamber. After they landed, the Athosians had darkened the bubble-shaped window overlooking the half-moon table to give the chamber some modicum of privacy. Jenny stripped off her Junior Ranger uniform and tossed it in a pile before taking the towel from Lieutenant Herd.

"You look miserable." Liz gathered up Jenny's wet clothes while the young woman dried off.

"The water felt warm while we were in it, but as soon as we were out, I felt really cold." Jenny scrubbed her skin with the towel. The black, military-issue towel lacked the plush softness to which she had grown accustomed at home and the Cytherean Academy. "It feels a little oily, too."

"According to our readings, it's full of microorganisms and other compounds that our equipment can't identify. The Athosians assure us our purifiers will make it potable." Liz turned to leave before holding up the wad of wet clothes and glancing back at Jenny, "It looks like we're close to the same size. I'll bring you some dry clothes. They're not fashionable, but they'll do until these dry."

"All right." Jenny continued to dry herself until the door slid shut behind Liz. Upon wrapping the towel around herself, Jenny plopped into one of the conference chairs. The hard plastic material provided no comfort to her battered muscles. Squeezing her eyes shut, she clenched her jaw. *We're not stranded here. We're not stranded here. The Athosians will get us home. They will. Zack believes them. I believe Zack. I am not going to cry. Not here. Not now.*

Chapter 2

Once Zack dried off, he put on his old clothes, still covered in grime and android fluids from their last night on Cytherea. Both Coulson and Major Jericho brought spare uniforms in their packs, but adult uniforms were much too large for Zack. Now that he no longer dripped with water, he felt the heat of the sun on his skin.

Major Jericho tossed him a cup. "Get some water from the purifier. You need to stay hydrated, especially after a workout like you just had. When you're finished, refill the purifiers, and check the traps."

Zack took a moment to gaze at the alien sky before he headed to the drinking station. Athos's midday sun, closer than Earth's, shone brightly, making for a hot and humid day.

Trudging across the fragrant patches of grass covering the island, Zack found the absence of insect life unnerving. At home Zack took for granted the backdrop of nearby animal calls and the buzzing of insects. Here with no noise, save for the gentle wind, the silence stood a stark contrast.

The gray canopy covering the drinking station flapped in the breeze. The purifiers, a trio of steel cylinders each about half-a-meter tall, sat nestled in a hollow that Major Jericho had dug into the uneven terrain. It reminded Zack of a cafeteria drink dispenser, though beverages the school provided were much more palatable.

Zack twisted the handle on the dispenser spout and waited for his cup to fill. Major Jericho's team only had their personal purifiers with them when the Athosian ship had been forced to flee Cytherea, so keeping them filled remained a constant struggle. Their testing equipment indicated the water surrounding them was filled with unknown microorganisms and no one wanted to take the risk of alien diseases or infections.

Grimacing, he sipped the water. The purifier imparted a metallic aftertaste to all the food they re-hydrated in it, and drinking the water straight tasted even worse. As Sergeant Coulson pointed out the first time he and Jenny complained about it, though, it was better than dying of thirst. He looked into the buckets of fetid water sitting alongside the purifier, curious about how the device made the nasty water within potable.

"Is there enough left for me?" Jenny approached, cup in hand. Her hair, though tied back, lay flat, plastered to her head, still damp from their ocean misadventure.

Zack stepped aside and nodded. "How's the real purifier coming along?"

Sergeant Coulson and Lieutenant Herd worked on assembling a larger purifier as quickly as the Athosians on the ship could fabricate parts, but between the ship repairs and their power conservation strategy, there was only so much that could be done each day.

"Liz and Coulson are getting ready to go out to find more raw materials for the Athosians. Maybe a couple more days. What are you doing?"

Zack finished his water before collapsing the cup and stowing it in a pocket. "I have to refill all the purifiers, then check on the traps."

Major Jericho, with help of the Athosian fabricators, sank some fish traps around the island's perimeter over the last several days. Finding fresh food would stretch their rations further and allow them to avoid food fabricated by the Athosians ship. Although technically edible, fabricated food tasted unpalatable because Athosian systems weren't calibrated for humans.

"Did you find Ix?" Jenny looked around for the Valtraxian.

"It's helping the major set up a cooking station." Zack looked over his shoulder toward their base camp. "I guess they're counting on actually finding some fresh food."

Jenny turned away, nodding. "I'll go help Ix. Staying busy keeps my mind off things."

"At least you and Liz are close to the same size." He gestured at his filthy shirt. "This is all that fits me other than my Junior Ranger uniform. It still has Rio's blood all over it."

"This is blood? It doesn't look like blood. What exactly happened to her? Things happened so fast. You just said she was hurt." Jenny stared at the stains on his shirt.

Zack grimaced. Although he knew he could trust Jenny with Rio's secret, it still felt like a betrayal to reveal it without her explicit permission. "Yeah, umm, artificial legs. So, the accident didn't *hurt her* hurt her, but she couldn't walk anymore." He shrugged. "That's probably why she told me to go ahead without her. She knew she'd be all right."

Jenny narrowed her eyes and pursed her lips as she regarded Zack. He felt a cold bead of sweat run down his neck.

She shook her head. "When your uniform dries, you should wash the clothes you're wearing."

Zack glanced in the nearby bucket of water. "You think the water around here will clean anything? It's so nasty looking."

"It's better than nothing, Zack. Maybe." Jenny waved before trotting off. "See you later."

He watched her hurry away, grateful she either believed his story about Rio or didn't care enough to keep digging. Their arrival two nights ago remained a bit of a shock to everyone. Major Jericho, Lieutenant Herd, and Sergeant Coulson stayed calm and set about establishing a base camp and enacting basic survival practices. For his part, Zack was thrilled to be on an alien world no human ever visited before, but Jenny...

Jenny did what she was told, worked quietly, and offered no opinions on their situation. Zack couldn't remember her even cracking a smile when Ix tried to lighten the mood the first morning with a joke.

Granted, the joke wasn't funny, but Zack enjoyed his friend's attempt at humor. He unscrewed the top of the purifier and removed the water reservoir before checking the levels on the second and third units. After filling the reservoir and starting the purifying cycle, Zack headed toward the shore. He located the stake to which the line securing the trap was tied, then followed it down the rocks to the water line. Climbing over the slippery rocks, Zack moved with slow and deliberate actions. He had no desire to get his only other set of clothes wet. According to the Athosians, the three moons orbiting Athos created a complex tidal cycle which caused the water level to fluctuate dramatically over the course of several months.

Upon reaching a level surface, Zack grabbed the rope securing the trap and hauled it hand-over-hand until the trap itself was just visible beneath the surface of the water. He saw the bait floating inside but saw no sign of potential meals. He released the rope and let the trap sink down, watching it disappear into the blue-green depths before making his return to base camp.

—— 《》 — 《》 — 《》 — 《》 — 《》 — 《》 ——

Lieutenant Herd greeted Jenny when she returned from her water break. Jenny nodded in acknowledgment, kneeling next to the crate of purifier parts. To her untrained eyes, the contents of the crate looked like a box of scrap metal, a puzzle with no pattern to the pieces. As Jenny studied the schematic on her implants, the lieutenant crouched next to her.

"I know it looks like a mess, but these things practically assemble themselves."

Jenny lifted a piece of honeycomb mesh out of the crate. "Do you know when we'll have all of the parts?"

Liz gestured at the box. "These are all the guts. They're fabricating the outer shell now. By the time we get this assembled and operational, it should be done. I'll get you started, then you should be able to handle the rest if you follow the instructions. Hand me the intake base, please."

Jenny returned the mesh to the crate before rummaging around for the part Liz wanted. Jenny referenced the schematics to guide her to the proper piece, then handed it to the lieutenant. Liz showed her how to assemble the pieces and how to properly tighten the fittings to form a complete seal that wouldn't rupture while under pressure.

Once Liz left to go scavenging with Coulson, Jenny concentrated on assembling the purifier core. Though she lacked an engineering background like her girlfriend Hiri or even Ix, she found the instructions easy enough to follow. Once completed, the purifier could draw water directly from a nearby source and remove all impurities on demand, without having to be periodically refilled. It would also greatly improve the taste.

She hoped her and Zack's little swim today would bring his head back down to the planet and he'd realize the seriousness of their situation. The adults didn't talk about it, but Jenny saw the charts when they arrived. Even if the Athosians could get them back tomorrow, with the effects of time dilation, several years would have passed back home. She glanced up at the alien sky overhead. Tears rolled down her cheeks as she thought of her parents and her friends back home who would have spent the last couple of years, at least, believing she was dead or lost in space forever.

Her tears blurred her view of the crate of parts, though the schematics she viewed in her implants remained clear. She wiped her eyes, then returned to work. *Enough of that. Crying about it won't help.*

Once she finished assembling the purifier core, she picked up the crate and returned to camp. She cringed at the grimy feeling in her hair and suspected shampoo and conditioner were luxuries she should not expect anytime soon. *I wonder if Liz has a brush*?

She tossed the crate onto the Athosian ship to be filled overnight with more fabricated parts, then she climbed the hill to base camp. The island on which they camped seemed about the size of Ishtar Plaza on Cytherea, though oblong. It lacked anything by way of trees, but it seemed safe enough considering they still had the option of retreating to the ship if the weather became dangerous.

Liz and Coulson showed Major Jericho several specimens of foliage they brought back from their scavenging mission. She found Zack and Ix sitting near the cooking station. Military-grade cooking stations, such as the one set up in their camp, took organic raw materials and processed them into a nutritive paste. S packets could be used to add seasonings to the otherwise bland substance. The cooking station even removed toxins, though that added to the processing time.

Both Ix and Zack sat watching the progress indicator like puppies waiting for feeding time.

"Don't you two have something better to do? It doesn't process any faster if you watch it, you know." Jenny sat on the ground between them.

"Our chores for the day have been completed, Jenny." Ix cocked its head, chittering. "Major Jericho specifically told us to 'relax.'"

"Since we don't have any games to play or holovids to watch, this is the only thing there is to do." Zack pointed at the progress meter. "Sometimes it jumps up ten or fifteen percent."

"Often, it only progresses one percent at a time." Ix chittered while it peered at the device.

"There it goes again!" Zack smacked his leg. "Sixty-three percent complete. What flavoring packet did you put in, Ix?"

The Valtraxian clicked its fingers together. "I was not given any to add. It will be the default flavor."

"Wet cardboard. Yum." Jenny rubbed her stomach. "I can't wait."

"I was not aware you enjoyed the taste of wet cardboard, Jenny." Ix cocked its head. "I will make a note of that for future reference."

Zack laughed. "I think she was being sarcastic, Ix."

Ix peered around Jenny at Zack. "Are you certain?" The Valtraxian looked up at Jenny. "Should I not make a note of that?"

"I don't like it, Ix." Jenny patted the Valtraxian on the shoulder. "Next time, add a flavoring packet to the processor."

The Valtraxian returned to a sitting position on six of its legs. "That, I will make a note of."

Chapter 3

Zack, Coulson, Ix, and Major Jericho slept on one side of the camp, while Jenny and Liz slept on the other. They'd tried sleeping in the ship the first night, but metal floors proved much less comfortable than the loamy dirt of the island. Even the constant crinkling of their emergency blankets seemed quieter away from the close walls of the ship.

Sleeping under the stars reminded Zack of summers at home in Wyoming. Granted, he now gazed up at an alien sky dominated by the great whirlpool of the Milky Way. He tried to pick out patterns of stars while he wondered if Athosians developed stories and characters based on star patterns in the night sky. Light from the galaxy above blotted out many of the stars, rendering the night sky somewhat less cluttered than Zack was used to at home.

Next to him, Ix clicked and chittered. From its level of activity, Zack knew his friend was not sleeping. He turned over, mindful of the noise his blanket made at the slightest motion.

"Ix?" Zack tried to keep his voice low. He hoped only Ix would hear him. "What are you doing?"

The Valtraxian lowered itself so its head lay near Zack's. "Attempting to calculate how long we have been gone."

Zack chuckled. "Gosh, Ix. It's only been two days."

"The elapsed time on Cytherea and Earth, Zack. Not our time. It has been two days for us, but due to relativity and the effects of time dilation, a much greater length of time has passed back home."

Recalling how his mother freaked out when the trip to Bestic took a week of time from his parents' point of view before he could reply to their messages, he furrowed his brow. "Well, this was farther, so we disappeared for longer, right? What, maybe two weeks or so?"

Ix chittered, but no words came out of its translator unit. Waves crashing against the rocks remained the main source of noise in the camp. Zack missed the buzzing of nocturnal insects, and the calls of owls and other birds.

Zack propped himself on his elbow as he regarded the Valtraxian. "What, longer? A month?"

"Assuming their drives are equal to the best technology in the Confederation, I estimate our elapsed travel time, to an outside observer, from Cytherea to Athos, is approximately five years."

"Five years?" Zack chuckled. "Five years... yeah... that's..." A heavy weight settled on his shoulders, and he felt his heart pound in his chest. "Seriously? Five years? If we left tomorrow, we'll get back ten years from now?"

"Yes. Ten years from two days ago. Assuming their drive technology is equivalent to ours. If it is superior, they may have solved certain problems we have yet to surmount. The translation felt different to me, though I have been unable to reconcile the sensations with my previous experiences." Ix reached out and stroked Zack's arm. "We will get home, Zack."

Zack rolled onto his back and stared up at the Milky Way. "I'm like, eighteen now. I'll be twenty-three when we get home, but everyone will still treat me like a kid."

"You have not aged five years in the last two days."

Zack bit his lip. "Do you think they think we're dead?"

"I cannot say. I am curious to know if there were any repercussions for the Devorans firing on the ship while it was docked to Cytherea. That could be considered an act of war against the Earth-Alpha Centauri Alliance."

"A war? Because of us?" Zack felt nutrient paste creeping up his esophagus. He squeezed his eyes shut and concentrated on not vomiting.

"I do not know, Zack." Ix withdrew its hand from Zack's arm. "My calculations could be wrong."

Zack turned away from his friend to wipe his eyes. *You're never wrong.*

—— 《》— 《》— 《》— 《》— 《》— 《》——

After breakfast the next morning, Jenny went back to the ship with Liz and found the crate full of purifier parts, as well as the parts they needed for a camp shower. The shower unit would siphon water from the ocean surrounding them and pump it through a filter before collecting it in a reservoir heated by solar thermal collectors. The system couldn't desalinate or purify the water, but everyone agreed whatever filtration it provided would be superior to not bathing at all.

Liz gathered up the shower parts and pushed the crates toward Jenny. "Feel up to finishing the purifier?"

"I might need Ix's help." Jenny lifted the crate. "I'm not an engineer, and setting it up looks tricky."

"Assembling the core is the hardest part. You'll do fine if you keep following the schematics. Just think, when we're done, hot showers." Liz shrugged. "Well, warm showers. Maybe lukewarm. Definitely not cold."

"Do you have a brush I could borrow?" Jenny followed Liz out of the ship. "Maybe shampoo and conditioner?"

"I have a brush and a comb, but I didn't put any product in my kit before we left. It's all back in my quarters on Cytherea." Liz paused at the point where they had to go separate ways. "If only we'd known we were taking a trip, huh?"

"I would have stayed in bed."

"Ha! I hear that." Liz glanced over her shoulder as she walked away. "Come get me if you have any trouble. The major is having me set this up behind that jagged rock behind the cooking station. Maybe we can get another canopy set up, or a tent or something."

Faced with never returning home again, privacy ranked least among Jenny's worries at the moment, although she appreciated Major Jericho's diligence. When she reached the spot where they'd begun building the purifier, she set the crate down and pulled up the schematics on her implants. Once she found her stopping point from the day prior, she dug through the box of fabricated parts. She felt her stomach twist in knots as she discovered multitudes of tiny fittings and connectors. She sent a quick message to Ix, requesting the Valtraxian's help.

Among the many benefits of her implants, having a power source guaranteed to last longer than she would live meant she didn't have to ration usage of them the way Zack did with his handheld devices. It didn't take long for Ix to arrive.

"Can you share the schematics with me, Jenny?" Ix sorted through the crate of parts while Jenny forwarded the plans through her implants. "I believe I distressed Zack last night. May I ask for your advice?"

Jenny couldn't imagine Zack upset at Ix. "You can ask, but I don't think I have any advice to give."

As it continued sorting through the parts, Ix piled like items together on the ground. "I simply explained to him how much elapsed time had passed back home since we left. He stopped speaking to me and eventually fell asleep."

At the mention of elapsed time, Jenny's eyes became unfocused, and she stared at the incomplete purifier. "Years. We've been gone years, haven't we?"

"Unless my calculations are wrong, or the Athosians possess drive technology far more advanced than our own." Ix finished sorting the parts and moved to the purifier, looking over it as it chittered to itself.

"Has anyone asked the Athosians?" Jenny worked on assembling the siphon that would draw water from the ocean into the purifier.

"No one has seen them since we landed." With four hands available, Ix joined the exterior cladding to the purifier much faster than Jenny would have. "They have been busy repairing the ship. Major Jericho feels having them fabricate parts for our survival needs is enough of a distraction that he doesn't want to disturb them for anything else."

"Do you think they can repair the ship, Ix?" Jenny hoped she wasn't the only person who wondered whether they'd be stranded here for the rest of their lives.

Ix chittered, cocking its head. "Of course they can. We didn't crash. The ship sustained no damage in the landing, and it was space worthy when we translated away from the Sol system. While I acknowledge the translation did not have the expected effects and was, in fact, quite... rough, I believe that was due to the damage caused by the Devorans firing upon us." Ix put down its work before skittering over to Jenny.

It stroked her arm. "We will get home, Jenny. Of that, I have no doubt."

Chapter 4

After several days of moping and hard work, the camp finally felt almost cozy. The cooking station worked flawlessly, the shower actually provided hot water, and the purifier provided them with potable water, though it still maintained an aftertaste that reminded Zack of metallic, wet grass, albeit more subtle now. Zack supposed he could learn to ignore it.

Major Jericho had them sit in a circle with their bowls of nutrient paste. He used the odd, sealed pack as a sort of table for himself. Tonight, Ix selected a flavoring packet that purported to taste like beef stew, although Zack thought it tasted more like stale jerky, albeit in paste form. The setup reminded Zack of a camping trip; however, since the island lacked woody vegetation, they had no campfire. Not that they needed supplemental heat; the warm humid air served that up in spades, and the military-issued flashlights the adults possessed provided all the extra light they needed.

"All right, people. I know it's been tough, but you've all done excellent work getting the camp up and running." Major Jericho rubbed the top of his cropped hair. "Don't think I haven't noticed the moping about. Your anxiety is justified, and I know some of you think you know how much time elapsed back home during our translation."

Ix chittered while Coulson and Liz eyed each other. Zack looked at Jenny, who sat stony-faced, staring into the distance. Zack raised his hand.

"We're not at school, Zack." Major Jericho raised his eyebrow. "What is it?"

"It's like five years right?"

Coulson's eyes widened and he reached for Liz's leg. Shoving his hand away, she bit her lip.

Major Jericho sighed and rubbed his nose. "Based on the distance traveled, that's about right for an EAC ship." The major raised a finger in the air. "I caution you, though. This is not an EAC ship. Our intelligence indicates Athosians use an entirely different drive technology. I don't think we should assume it has the same limitations. At any rate, Alpha Primus is coming out shortly to update us on their repairs, and I will ask them."

He took a bite of his nutrient paste. "Look, however long we've been gone is irrelevant to our current situation. I understand that it's difficult not to think about everyone back home and how worried they must be. We don't know what they saw when we left and we don't know what they've been told. You have to put that out of your mind for now. We're on an alien world that no human has ever been to. There are unknown dangers here, and you all have to stay focused on the here and now. I want everyone safe. I want everyone going home when the time comes. Understand?"

"Yes, sir," Coulson and Liz answered in unison. Major Jericho looked around the circle to Zack, Ix, and Jenny.

"I'll try, Major." Zack didn't know how the major could remain as calm as he was. Ix and Jenny acknowledged their understanding as well.

"There are a lot of things we don't know. There are just as many things over which we have no control. Worrying about any of them is counterproductive in a survival situation." Major Jericho paused as his eyes lingered on Zack, Ix, and Jenny. "None of us were ready for this. Least of all, you three. Surely, you've learned something in the Junior Rangers that can help you here?"

Zack glanced at Jenny and Ix, then nodded. "We crashed on Bestic a couple of years ago. We just had our escape pod, no adults. Our ship exploded."

"Yes." Ix clicked its fingers together. "We were forced to travel through the partially terraformed wilderness to the nearest city."

Liz chuckled. "So you were the kids that went missing on that trip. I thought there were four."

Jenny looked up at the pilot. "An Ersidian, Mungus. He doesn't go to Cytherean Academy."

"You heard about that?" Ix cocked its head toward Liz.

Zack jumped up, pointing at Lieutenant Herd. "Lizard! I knew I knew you! You were the pilot of the *Baden-Powell* who sat next to me on the shuttle from Earth."

Liz laughed. "Took you long enough, Zack. I was wondering if you'd ever remember me." She ran her fingers through her short hair. "Must be the haircut."

"You two know each other?" Major Jericho raised his eyebrows, regarding the lieutenant.

"Know? No. We sat next to each other on a shuttle before those wackos blew up the *Baden-Powell*. We heard one of the escape pods got off course and crashed in the wilderness, but I haven't seen Zack since *Goddard Station*. I hadn't met the other two before this little misadventure."

"Well, then you kids should have this well in hand." Major Jericho stood. "It's humid, but the temperature's comfortable, even at night, and there don't seem to be any predators to worry about. I haven't even seen any bugs. I'm going to have a shower, then turn in for the evening. I know there isn't a lot to do, but try not to stay up too late."

Coulson glanced at Liz. "I didn't even bring a pack of cards. Got anything on your implants?"

The pilot shook her head. "Nothing multiplayer."

Ix chittered. "I have a substantial library of games. What did you want to play, Sergeant?"

"It doesn't matter what you pick, Sarge." Zack chuckled, recalling the games he played with the Valtraxian. "Ix always wins."

—— ⟪⟩ — ⟪⟩ — ⟪⟩ — ⟪⟩ — ⟪⟩ — ⟪⟩ ——

While Ix and Coulson decided on a game to play together via their implants, Liz left to meditate, and Jenny remained under the canopy tent with Zack. She stared into space as she pushed the last bit of nutrient paste around her bowl with a spoon.

She imagined, by now, her parents had returned to work, fully recovered from their near-fatal shuttle accident during the Junior Ranger trip to Valtra last year. She gave thanks that her last conversation with them was positive, at least. Before their accident, hardly a call ended without her being angry with them for some reason.

They often spoke about how Jenny was the only child they wanted, but she wondered if they would have a new baby to replace her when she returned. Ten years was a long time to wait, and she wouldn't blame them if they gave up and had another child.

Jenny wondered if Hiri would wait for her. *Why should she? We only went out a few times. She's a grown woman now and will be even older by the time we return. I hope she found someone nice.*

"Jenny? Jenny?"

Zack's voice shook her out of her thoughts. She turned to him, grateful for the interruption. Her thoughts threatened to spiral into a pit of doom and despair. "What?"

"What are you going to do for the rest of the night?" Zack leaned back and stretched out his legs. "I don't want to just sit here staring at the grass and dirt."

"Until you said something, I was probably going to stare at the grass until I got too tired to be bored, then just go to bed." She offered her friend a smile. "Some evening, huh?"

"Yeah." Zack furrowed his brow as he met her gaze. "There's not a lot to do, huh?"

"Even less than a Junior Ranger trip." She chuckled. "You know, when we left, my parents were still recovering from their accident. I was just getting to know Hiri." She bit her lip. "I miss them."

"Yeah." Zack scratched at the dirt. "I don't know if my parents will be happy or angry when they see me again. They weren't going to let me go on another Junior Ranger trip because they think they're too dangerous. Now I end up in a different galaxy just from being at school."

Jenny nudged him. "They'll be happy to see you, of course. You'll probably look just like they remembered, too. They'll probably be old and gray, though."

Zack's eyes widened. "All our friends will be grown up. They'll have jobs and everything. We'll still have to go back to school."

Shrugging, Jenny looked away. "If we're lucky, Headmaster Troughton will be retired, and Cytherean Academy will have someone who isn't too busy sucking up to the Devorans to teach us properly."

"Maybe Major Jericho will let us go back to the mainland tomorrow."

Crossing the hundred-meter gap between the island and the mainland again did not appeal to Jenny after the last time they tried it. Going during low tide proved easy enough, but they still didn't have a handle on the tidal cycle, and she didn't want to get stuck again.

"Unless the Athosians can help us build a bridge, I really don't feel like crossing that water again."

Zack couldn't argue with that. He rolled over onto his back, looking up at the sky from under the canopy. "Don't you think it's weird we haven't seen any bugs or animals or anything?"

"There has to be something, Zack. We saw flowers on the mainland. They need bugs to reproduce." Jenny did think it odd they hadn't seen any life yet, except for a few blob-like creatures caught in their traps that ended up as part of the nutrient paste.

Zack sat up. "What if they're meat-eating plants? Like Venus flytraps?"

Jenny studied carnivorous plants in her botany classes, but since Cytherean Academy didn't have any in their gardens, nor did Messier Habitat, she'd never seen specimens in person. "They'd still need to eat. No insects mean the plants have to rely on other methods for pollination, like the wind. But, what's the point in having flowers if they're not there to attract insects?"

Zack scrunched up his face as he thought about it. "Maybe the bugs are invisible?"

"That would be something." Jenny didn't think invisible insects existed, but she couldn't prove it to Zack. "There's probably another explanation, but hopefully, we won't be here long enough to find out."

"We gotta find something to do, Jenny. I thought it would be exciting here, but just sitting around waiting for them to fix the ship is boring."

"Maybe we'll find something tomorrow." Jenny sympathized with Zack. Sitting around waiting on other people felt frustrating. Being stranded in an unfamiliar, untamed wilderness exacerbated that feeling. She yawned and stood. "I'm going to bed. See you in the morning."

She returned to her side of the camp. Liz had not yet returned from her meditation; Jenny assumed she used the conference room inside the ship for that since it remained the most private spot on or around the island anyone knew of. She crawled under her emergency blanket and stared upward into space. Seeing the Milky Way dominating the sky reminded her just how far they'd come, and how her life would never be the same.

Why did I help Zack? When has it ever worked out for me? She banished the thoughts from her mind. She knew exactly why she helped Zack, because that's what friends do for each other.

Chapter 5

As Zack feared, the next day, Major Jericho had nothing for them to do.

"I'm sorry, Zack." The major reclined against a rock, with his fingers laced behind his head watching the waves, his feet resting on the sealed pack never far from his side. "All we can do is wait for the Athosians to fix the ship now. Anything I give you will be pointless busy work, and I'm not a fan of that. Never have been. We have a word for it in the military... which I probably shouldn't say in front of you."

Zack shuffled his feet and thought about the Athosian who hatched from the iron star fragment Professor Gladstone gave him before he transferred, the one who started all this mess. He thrust his hands in his pockets. "Can I see that baby Athosian, Squishy? Maybe talk to some of the other Athosians? I have a lot of questions about stuff."

Ever since that first trip to Bestic, encounters involving the Athosians seemed to find a way to complicate Zack's life. Between the cult on Bestic, the tiny stasis pod Professor Gladstone gave him, the research facility on Valtra, and Squishy, Zack felt like half his life revolved around a supposedly dead species.

Major Jericho shook his head. "They made it pretty clear they don't want to be disturbed while they're repairing the ship. I get the sense they're just as lost as we are right now."

Zack thought for a moment. "Well, can Jenny, Ix, and I go across to the mainland again? The tide's just gone out and we know what to watch for now."

"I appreciate how boring this is for you, but I guarantee you, if you join the military, which you'll have to do if you want to be a Galaxy Ranger, you need to get used to it."

Liz approached, then saluted Major Jericho. "Everything is still operational, Major. No changes from last night. How long until your meeting with the Athosians?"

He returned the salute. "They said they'd let me know, so I just have to hang out here and wait."

She raised an eyebrow. "Well, that certainly sounds fun."

"Yeah, yeah. Everyone wants to do something except me. You know, when you've had the career I've had, you relish these moments of nothing."

Liz glanced at Zack. "We should all be so lucky, sir."

"I have an idea." Major Jericho sat up. "Lieutenant, you will accompany our Junior Rangers to the mainland. Take your rifle and scout. See if you can find anything salvageable. See if there's any animal life larger than a microbe, maybe edible plants, too."

Zack bounced on his heels and grinned. "That'll be great. I'll go get Jenny and Ix."

"Coulson and I have already done that, sir. There's nothing there."

"You always kept the island in sight, yes?" The Major gestured for Zack to stay.

"Yes, sir."

"These Junior Rangers have experience in unexplored wilderness areas. More so than you or Coulson, I'll bet. Take them over the ridge, just stay in communicator range."

Liz failed to conceal the exasperation from her sigh. "You're joking, right? This is just to give us something to do, isn't it, sir?"

"You might think that." Major Jericho looked up at her. "But it's exercise more varied than push-ups and jogging around the island, and you could actually find something. Your other options are to sit around in quiet contemplation or to clean the cooking station. Again."

"I see your point, sir." After saluting, Liz turned to Zack. "Get your friends and meet me by the ford."

Zack ran off to find Ix and Jenny. He found Ix lying on the ground by itself, staring across the ocean. "Hey, Ix? Are you awake?"

The Valtraxian sat up. "I am, Zack. I was compiling my observations thus far."

"Major Jericho said we could go over to the mainland and go exploring. Liz is going with us." Zack took Ix's hand and tugged until the Valtraxian stood. "It'll be like Bestic, except safer."

"That sounds interesting. Is Jenny coming?"

They walked toward camp where Zack last saw Jenny. "If she wants. I haven't asked her yet."

"Oh good. It will be just like Bestic. Without Mungus." Ix clicked its mandibles together. "Hopefully, I will not be forced to flee a predator and be separated from you again."

"We'll be fine. Liz is bringing her rifle. She can just shoot anything that wants to eat us." Zack pantomimed holding a rifle. "Blam! Then we can eat it instead."

They found Jenny by the water purifier she helped assemble, getting a drink with Coulson. After greeting Zack and Ix, he left to check in with Major Jericho. Jenny narrowed her eyes as she looked at Zack and Ix.

"You two are up to something. I can tell by your expressions."

Ix cocked its head. "My exoskeleton prevents me emoting in such a way that one would describe as an expression, Jenny."

"Major Jericho said we could go exploring, Jenny. Liz is coming with us for protection." Zack took her hand. "Come on, it'll be fun."

Jenny shook off his grip. "Every time you go exploring, bad things happen, Zack."

"What?" Zack recoiled from his friend. He felt like she'd just punched him in the stomach. "Jenny, I..."

Jenny shut her eyes and turned away. "I'm sorry, Zack. I didn't mean to say it like that."

The three friends stood in silence for a moment. The hum of the purifier pump was barely audible over the sound of waves crashing on the shore and misting saltwater into the air behind the machine.

Jenny turned to face Zack and hugged him. "I'm sorry. It's not your fault."

"We are all scared, Jenny." Ix reached out and rubbed Jenny's arm. "This may give us something else to concentrate on."

"Something to distract us, you mean." Jenny released Zack and stepped back.

Zack stuck his hands in his pockets and looked at the ground. "Yeah, I just don't want to sit around doing nothing anymore. It makes me miss home too much."

"All right, then." Jenny put her hands on Ix's and Zack's shoulders. "Let's go see what's out there."

—— 《》— 《》— 《》— 《》— 《》— 《》——

Jenny and her friends found Liz standing at the tip of the island, looking across the hundred-meter gap at the mainland. She hefted a bulging backpack and slung her rifle over her shoulder. After she finished adjusting the strap on her pack, she gestured toward the exposed rocks. "Looks like the tide is lower today."

Ix peered over the edge at the waves licking the rocks below. "I have been attempting to build a tide schedule. It is difficult with three moons. They make the tides erratic. I also lack the proper instruments for certain measurements, so some of my calculations have proceeded from guesses."

"What instruments do you need?" Liz knelt, set her rifle on the ground so that she was between it and the kids, then removed her pack, and opened it. "We have some things in our kits. Not much, we weren't equipped for a planetary excursion, but some things are standard in all kits."

"I am uncertain." Ix clicked its fingers together. "I have never taken oceanography classes. My education has primarily been in social skills and astronautical engineering."

"Oh." Liz dug through her pack. "I have a toxicity tester."

Zack peered into the pack. "Hey, we used those on our trip to Valtra last summer."

"Great." Liz handed the instrument to Zack. "You get to carry it then. Just don't go wild testing everything. We're not desperate enough to eat grass. Yet."

After closing her pack and slinging it back over her shoulders, Liz looked across the ford at the mainland. "The sun did a good job of drying out the rocks, it looks like. Go on across. I'll be right behind you."

Zack wasted no time climbing down to the first rock. He then hopped from stone to stone until he crossed the gap. Ix followed behind him. Jenny took her time, waiting until Liz checked her rifle and slung it over her shoulder before starting across. Crossing dry rocks during low tide proved much less challenging than when they battled the incoming tide a few days ago.

They waited for Liz on the far side. When she finished crossing, she put her hands on her hips and looked up and down the shoreline. "Coulson and I didn't stray far from the shore." She pointed up the coast. "We went that way, then up the ridge and back. On our next trip, we did the same thing, except in the opposite direction."

Jenny shielded her eyes from the sun with her hand and peered in the direction Liz indicated. "We went that way, too, but we didn't climb to the top."

"Let's just go straight this time." Zack pointed toward the crest.

They walked single file in the direction Zack indicated. Liz led the way, Zack and Jenny followed her, and Ix brought up the rear. The Athosian sun beat down on them without mercy, and though it didn't feel particularly hot, the humidity and thick atmosphere made the climb feel twice as long. Sweat plastered Jenny's hair to her head, and by the time they reached the summit, she felt the back of her shirt clinging to her skin.

Looking back from the top of the ridge, they could see the entire island on which they made camp, along with the Athosian vessel bobbing in the water beside it. Beyond the ship and island lay open sea as far as they could see. In the opposite direction, the mainland curved away from them, lying mostly bare, save for scrub brush and grasses. Farther down the coast toward some hills, they noticed what looked like an inlet. With the tide out and the water level lower than it had been since their arrival, they observed the tops of several domed, circular stones standing above the water in the inlet.

"Those must have been underwater when Coulson and I were up here the other day." Liz tapped the side of her pack. "Someone grab the binoculars out of the side pouch of my pack."

Jenny reached up and unlatched the clip holding the pouch closed. She removed the compact field glasses from the pack, then handed them to Liz. Using her ocular implants, Jenny viewed the domed rocks. Although the zoom function of her implants did not provide the same clarity or magnification as the binoculars, she saw enough detail to determine the rocks, in fact, may not be rocks at all.

"Are you using your implants, Jenny?" Ix chittered. "Those look like the tops of buildings to me."

"They're definitely not rocks." Liz lowered the binoculars.

Jenny agreed. "They look like metal to me."

"Aw man, do you have a spare pair?" Zack fiddled with the toxicity tester. "I don't have implants."

"Knock yourself out." Liz handed the field glasses to him. "I say we head that way, what do you kids think?"

"There may be something salvageable within those structures." Ix raised itself up on two legs to get a different perspective on the inlet.

"It would be easier to salvage if the Athosians would tell us what they need. It doesn't look like there's a way into the structures from here." Liz closed her pack and slung it over her shoulders.

"How long has it been since the Athosians lived here?" Jenny continued examining the structures in the distance. "Will there be anything usable left?"

A shadow passed over the area Jenny examined. After returning her implants back to normal display, she viewed a group of large puffy clouds moving overhead and intermittently blocking the sun.

Liz gestured for the group to start walking again. "Even if everything we find is broken, the Athosians can still break down what we salvage into raw materials, assuming their fabricators work like ours. I haven't seen any indication that they don't."

As they made their way down the ridge toward the inlet, Jenny noticed a patch of undulating violet flowers in the distance. Dancing with the wind, the field of flowers reminded her they still had not encountered any insect life or other pollinators. "Aren't there any animals here? What pollinates the plants?"

They stopped to regard the distant field of flowers. The cool breeze coming in from the coast made the heat of midday a bit more bearable, though it did little to lessen the effect of the stifling humidity. As they approached, Jenny noticed that the flowers covered a swath of the island abutting a stream before crossing the land to a second inlet in the distance, a lush purple carpet over the otherwise barren landscape.

"Shall we go there instead?" Liz shielded her eyes from the sun with her hand. "We're not going to get any closer to those buildings than the shore anyway."

Jenny didn't wait for her friends' response before she changed course and descended the ridge. Behind her, she heard Zack grumble that flowers were less interesting than the buildings, but she chose to ignore him.

Chapter 6

Zack scuffed his feet on the ground as he trailed after the group heading toward the flowery field, casting a wistful look back at the round metal rooftops protruding from the surf. "I don't see what's so great about flowers." When he saw how far ahead the rest of the group had traveled, Zack increased his pace. He descended the hill toward the field of flowers, barely maintaining his footing as he jogged down the hill. He joined up with Liz and his friends at the edge of the field.

The colors on the blossoms shifted from the monochrome coloration Zack perceived from farther away to an iridescent hue as they fluttered in the breeze . The flowers turned toward the group, unfurling their petals like opalescent banners catching the wind.

Liz thrust out her arm to prevent Jenny from moving closer. "Step back everyone."

Ix chittered as it moved away from the blooms. "I have never seen flowers behave this way."

"They're beautiful." Jenny's whisper barely rose above the breeze.

"I think we should give them a wide berth." Liz gestured for her younger companions to follow her as she skirted the edge of the field. "Flowers shouldn't move like that."

Twisting in the breeze, the flowers kept their faces pointed toward the group of explorers.

A chill ran down Zack's spine as he passed them. "It looks like they're watching us, doesn't it?"

"That's creepy." Liz looked over her shoulder at Zack, Ix, and Jenny. "Let's keep moving."

Leaving the animated flowers behind, they climbed a low hill. They followed the ridge line for a short while, arriving at a rock-filled gully that stretched away from the coast. Glistening reflections at the bottom indicated pooling water among the rocks. Liz paused for a moment, then turned to her charges.

"Let's check out that water down there. It might not be as brackish and gross as the stuff we're filtering at camp." They descended the ridge. Ix helped Jenny and Zack scramble down the uneven terrain. When they reached the bottom, Liz crouched on a rock and scooped some of the water into her testing device. It pinged red.

"It's worse than what we've been getting." She stood, shaking water off her instrument. "Well, that's no help."

While Liz complained aloud to no one in particular about their situation, Zack approached Jenny. Shielding her eyes from the sun with one hand and restraining her wind-blown ponytail with the other, she gazed down the gully. After bringing the binoculars up to his face, Zack focused in the same direction.

"Do those look like buildings to you, Zack?"

Zack scanned the area through the binoculars. Though overgrown and crumbling, the shapes at the far end of the gully did, indeed, resemble buildings, or at least, what remained of them.

"Could be. We should go check them out." Zack called out for Liz.

The lieutenant stopped her grousing long enough to join Zack and Jenny. Ix skittered along behind her. "What's up, kids?"

"Buildings." Jenny pointed down the gully. "Just there, see them? Either buildings or what's left of them."

Liz squinted as her ocular implant adjusted to the new view and zoomed in. "You might be right."

"We should go check it out." Zack glanced up at her.

Shrugging, the lieutenant motioned to Zack and Jenny. "Lead the way, you two."

—— 《》 — 《》 — 《》 — 《》 — 《》 — 《》 ——

Despite her reservations about exploring Athos in general, Jenny led the group down into the gully with Zack by her side. Smooth rocks lay strewn about. Though not a particularly hot day, walking under the blazing sun with no shade from trees reminded Jenny why she preferred the controlled environs of Cytherea and Messier Habitat. She glanced up at the brilliant orb overhead and wondered how long they'd last before their skin burned.

With the reminder of home, the weight of their situation slammed into Jenny like a meteor. Tears welled in her eyes. She wiped her face and bit the inside of her cheek as she repeated to herself in a whisper: "We're going to get home. We're going to get home."

If... no, when we get home. I'm going to concentrate on my studies. No more Junior Rangers, no more helping Zack with crazy schemes. Just school, Hiri, and home. That's it. Stay safe, stay sane, and put all this behind me. No more adventures.

As they drew closer, they saw a desolate expanse of deteriorating buildings, an entire city worn down to the foundations by harsh, scouring wind and unrelenting weather. Liz stopped them short of entering the ruins at the end of the gully.

"Athosians are aquatic." Liz took in the enormity of the rubble. "Who lived here?"

Zack climbed a nearby rock to gain a better vantage. "Maybe this used to be all underwater?"

"These look like buildings you'd find on Earth or Ersid. No one living underwater would build structures like these." Liz pointed to the ground-level gaps in walls that suggested entryways.

"Clearly, the Athosians did not live alone on this world," Ix chittered. "Perhaps slaves?"

Jenny shook her head. "These ruins must stretch for dozens of square kilometers, and they're so far away from the water. How would the Athosians control them?"

"They have those environmental suits. They could easily come ashore in them. They—" A high-pitched whine sounded above them. They looked to the sky to see a sleek, three-pronged angular vessel streak overhead. For a moment, they stared at each other, the silence among them broken only by Ix's clicking.

"Was that"—Zack stared into the sky, although the ship had long vanished from sight—"Was that a ship?"

"It was." Liz gestured for the three Junior Rangers to follow her as she jogged back up the gully. "But whose?"

"A shuttle from our ship?" Jenny already knew the answer, but thoughts of the alternative sent shivers down her spine.

"I doubt that very much." Liz looked back at them over her shoulder. "Come on, keep up. We need to get back to camp."

They scrabbled along the rocky bottom of the gully until they reached a spot where Liz could help them up onto the ridge. Ix climbed on all sixes while Liz helped Jenny, then Zack up the incline. Once they all exited the gully, Liz pushed them to pick up the pace. They raced back to camp, only slowing to cross the watery gap between the mainland and the island. Fortunately, with the tide still out, the crossing was merely challenging, rather than treacherous. Coulson and Major Jericho stood near the hatch of the Athosian ship, conversing with Alpha Primus.

Liz held up her hand signaling the three Junior Rangers to wait where they stood. They weren't so far away, though, that Zack, Jenny, and Ix couldn't overhear.

"I take it that ship wasn't Athosian, sir?" Liz saluted Major Jericho as she approached.

Alpha Primus answered, "It was not. It does not match any known ships in our database, though, admittedly, they are a millennium out-of-date."

Major Jericho returned Liz's salute. "There's no chance they didn't see the Athosian ship here. No one leaves the camp until further notice."

"Understood,   sir."
Upon seeing Zack's puckered lips and furrowed brow, Jenny understood he would not like being confined to the island. *At least it'll keep him out of trouble.* She guessed Major Jericho implemented the restriction out of concern for their safety. Suddenly, Jenny felt a brief twinge in her stomach, but it passed quickly.

Zack's eyes widened for a moment. Jenny noticed his pale complexion and the beads of sweat forming on his forehead. "Uh-oh." He turned and ran, taking half-a-dozen steps before doubling over and retching. Jenny turned away and bit her lip to distract herself from the sounds of Zack emptying his stomach.

Liz and Ix tended to Zack. Major Jericho took Jenny aside. "Why don't you get him some water?"

Nodding, she jogged to the purifiers. By the time she returned with a jugful of clean water, she felt a twinge in her stomach. She handed Zack the jug, noting his green pallor.

"I don't feel so good. I'm cold." He sipped at the water, then gagged and returned the jug to her.

Jenny felt cold sweat roll down her back. "I think I have it, too. Right before you got sick, I started feeling weird." She looked up at Major Jericho standing over them.

He frowned. "You two look terrible."

He crouched, then pressed his hands against their foreheads. "You're burning up. How long have you felt ill?"

Zack shook his head. "It just hit me, just now when we got back to camp."

"Me too." Jenny wrapped her arms around herself, shivering.

"Fantastic." Major Jericho sighed. "I'll check the med kits, see what we have. In the meantime, go to bed and try to stay hydrated. I'll have Coulson get you more water."

After Jenny helped Zack to his feet, they shuffled to their bedrolls.

"Do you think this is some sort of alien flu?" Zack crawled under his blanket and clutched it around his chin. Jenny fought to keep her teeth from chattering.

"I don't know." Jenny's stomach knotted and her face flushed. She knew what was coming. "I have to go."

Jenny sprinted for a secluded spot, reaching it just in time to keep her vomiting relatively private. When she finished, she returned to her bedroll. A canteen of water waited for her. She crawled under the blanket and shut her eyes, hoping the twisting knots in her stomach would calm before she tried the water.

She dozed intermittently for the next few hours. She awoke when Major Jericho crouched next to her and touched her shoulder. He handed her a couple of pills, along with the water.

"Obviously, we don't have a cure for whatever this is, so hopefully, your bodies will fight it off with a little help. This should help with the fever. Zack said you both drank unfiltered water a few days ago?"

Jenny gagged down the pills and water and shook her head. "We didn't drink. But maybe we swallowed some sea water when we got caught in the tide."

"All right, that makes sense. There're all kinds of pathogens in this water. Get some rest. One of us will check back later to see if you feel like eating. Would you be more comfortable in the ship?"

Jenny shook her head and clenched her jaw as another shiver passed through her body. She felt like she'd only be comfortable if she were unconscious. Her stomach knotted again and she curled up, trying to focus her mind on anything other than her discomfort.

Chapter 7

Zack awoke in Ishtar Plaza. As he lay on the grass, the buildings looming over him curled inward, like talons. As he climbed to his feet, the plaza spun, whirling around him.

Squeezing his eyes shut, Zack reached out for a solid object to steady himself. His hands grabbed empty air and he stumbled, fighting against the constant spinning sensation.

Finally, his hands closed around a supple surface, like a leather-covered pole. Daring to open his eyes, he saw Dravs. The blue-scaled Devoran seized Zack by the shoulders.

"Zack! You're back!" His friend's tongue lolled when he leaned forward. "Mm... you look delicious."

Molten goop slid over Zack's hands, burning them. The Devoran's scales sloughed off, revealing red and stringy white bubbles. Dravs grew and grew until he towered over Zack, his shoulders broadening until he resembled a slice of pepperoni pizza.

"You've eaten me so many times, Zack, it's only fair that I eat you now!" Pizza-Dravs reached downward, dripping molten cheese from his slavering maw.

Screaming, Zack backpedaled. He stumbled over a log-sized breadstick before falling into a bed of crunchy lettuce leaves.

"No, not salad!" Zack flailed at the leafy greens clutching at and covering him. "It's just filler!" After freeing himself from the roughage, he rolled over to a bench. He pulled himself to his feet and fled just as Pizza-Dravs took another swipe at him.

As he ran, Zack scanned the area, seeking a hiding place where the colossal pizza abomination couldn't reach him.

Pizza-Dravs roared a wet, sauce-bubbling-through-molten-cheese sound at the loss of his quarry. Zack passed a cafe, dashing around the corner into the stairwell that led to the upper level. He paused to catch his breath on the landing.

What is going on? Zack stood on his tiptoes to peer over the railing at the top of the stairs. Pizza-Dravs raged, ripping a tree—no, not a tree, a tree-sized breadstick—out of the greenspace. Using it as a club, he bashed the bistro Zack just passed. Zack heard the crash of shattering glass as the assault demolished the façade of the cafe.

A distorted announcement crackled over the plaza's sound system. "Attention Cytherea Residents: students are arriving."

Pizza-Dravs cheered. Zack crept up the stairs and peeked through the second-floor railing. A wave of his peers streamed into the plaza from the elevators. They charged forward into the gardens of salad, tree-sized breadsticks, and the giant ambulatory pizza, tearing into foodstuffs with aplomb and gorging themselves.

"It's a pizza party, Zack! Who could ask for more?" Pizza-Dravs danced around the plaza, waving ribbons of mozzarella cheese like streamers. "Everybody's coming, fill your stomach and ask for more!"

Cheers erupted from students gathered in the plaza. Zack found himself caught up in the atmosphere and descended the steps, his stomach growling as the air filled with the spicy aroma of hot pepperoni and sausage pizza.

Pizza-Dravs spun to face Zack, spreading its arms and flinging sauce onto nearby buildings. "Were you waiting for an invitation to arrive? You're going to a party where no one's still alive!"

Roaring, the abomination kicked a nearby student, launching them through the air and crashing them into a storefront. The mozzarella monstrosity stood over the fountain in Ishtar Plaza screeching. It swiped at a festive decoration that dared sway too close to its head. A screaming hoard of students fled the building-sized pie slice and charged toward Zack with abandon.

Try as he might, Zack failed to avoid being swept up in the crowd. No matter how far he ran, however, Pizza-Dravs drew ever closer, swatting at some nearby students. It lobbed them into the foliage, splattering a glob of steaming sauce on the ground near Zack. The aroma of herbs—basil, oregano, and garlic—assaulted him.

His toe caught on the leg of a park bench, and he tumbled forward. A cheese-covered hand reached toward him as he righted himself. The pizza giant scooped him up, covering him in a morass of melted mozzarella. Burning hot tomato sauce soaked through Zack's clothes, and a slice of pepperoni slid over his face, threatening to smother him.

Zack screamed, but no sound emerged as burning sauce and molten cheese filled his mouth.

—— ⟨⟩ — ⟨⟩ — ⟨⟩ — ⟨⟩ — ⟨⟩ — ⟨⟩ ——

Jenny walked through the darkened corridors of Messier Habitat. Stifling silence filled the air, muffling even the ever-present sound of the air handling system. Though the corridor remained lightless, Jenny could see apartment doors.

She stopped in front of Twelve Rue Du Châtelet—the apartment in which she lived with her parents when she wasn't at school. She heard voices from behind the door as she approached. The door slid open, revealing Hiri and her parents. Jenny frowned. *The front door doesn't open into this room.*

The young woman wept while Jenny's mother, seated alongside her, held her hands. Her father stood over them, his face a mask of half-flesh and half-metal. His cybernetic eyes burned red.

"It is unfortunate she is dead." Her father's voice sounded metallic and monotone.

Jenny's mother looked up at him, her eyes bloodshot from tears. "We don't know that, François."

"The ship was shot while translating from inside an atmosphere. There is no other possibility, Amélie." Jenny's father clasped his hands behind his back.

Hiri looked up at him, tears running down her cheeks. "How can you be so cold?"

François cocked his head, like a confused dog. "I am broken."

He turned toward Jenny, his glowing crimson eyes burning right through her. "I am broken. I am broken."

Jenny backed away from his outstretched arms. "Jenny. I am broken."

She screamed and fled, the corridors falling away as she ran. Jenny plummeted. Plunging through the bulkheads, redundant walls, and finally the outer skin of the habitat, she continued her descent. Speeding toward the Red Planet, she outstretched her arms. She soared toward Olympus Mons on the horizon to her right. Though she knew she could not breathe where there was no air, she felt calm.

Jenny banked left as she dove through the thin Martian atmosphere. She turned until the great mountain lay before her. Flying unhindered by an environmental suit and strapped into a cloud glider thrilled Jenny, and the thought that she should be struggling for breath as her death rapidly approached tickled the back of her mind.

She didn't care. Flight was freedom.

As she approached Olympus Mons, the Olympian Space Elevator cable came into view. Cars traveled up and down the twin cables, delivering supplies and workers to maintenance stations in geosynchronous orbit. She felt sorry for the workers who had to ride the space elevator. Traveling up the cable consumed the better part of a day, compared to the twenty-minute trips of orbital shuttles.

Jenny dove to buzz the elevator cars before ascending in a spiral around the cables. She climbed higher and higher until the planet fell away beneath her. Her breath caught in her throat.

No air.

Jenny clutched at her throat, struggling to draw breath where there was no oxygen. She tumbled, twisting as she plunged again toward the surface of Mars.

She awoke with a start, coughing and gagging. Her stomach twisted into a knot. Jenny curled up, squeezing her eyes shut.

When the pain subsided, Jenny uncurled her body and opened her eyes. Thousands of distant stars twinkled overhead, and the great whirlpool of the Milky Way hung amidst them above the western horizon. She stared at the vast galaxy, unable to make out individual stars, or determine Sol's location relative to the rest of the galaxy.

She wiped away tears pooling in her eyes. *I hope this isn't my night sky for the rest of my life. Nothing in the sky is familiar.*

Jenny curled up on her side as her stomach twitched again and tucked her arms under her head. She forced herself to think of other things, like puppies and flowers. The flowers that followed their movements that afternoon came immediately to mind, and she drifted off to sleep again. She dreamed of the flowers.

Watching her and waiting.

Chapter 8

"Zack! Zack, wake up!" With a start, Zack sat bolt upright. Light from Athos's sun burned his eyes and he squinted against the glare as he looked around.

Liz knelt beside him. She offered him a cup of water. "The major said we should let you sleep it off, but you started screaming about pepperoni."

Zack sipped the water, then wiped his eyes and mouth with his sleeve. "That was a really weird nightmare."

"I miss pizza too." Liz chuckled. "I haven't dreamt about it yet, though. How are you feeling?"

He finished the water and stretched. "Okay, I guess." The knots in his stomach indicated he was not, in fact, okay. "Hungry. And I have a headache." He pressed his palms against his forehead.

"That'll be the dehydration." She offered him a hand and helped him to his feet. "You haven't eaten for days."

"Days?" Zack rubbed his stomach as Liz led him toward the cooking station. "I kept yesterday's breakfast down."

"That was the day before yesterday, Zack. You were out cold all day yesterday. Jenny, too."

Zack's mind reeled at having lost a whole day. He faltered stepping over a rock, clutching Liz's outstretched arm to steady himself. As they reached the cooking station, he saw Major Jericho over by the entrance to the Athosian ship, speaking with Alpha Primus and Coulson. He watched them for a moment while Liz prepared a plate for him.

"Where's Jenny and Ix?" Zack scanned the camp for his friends.

"They're down by the purifier, refilling our water receptacles." Liz handed Zack a plate with a brown disk and some grey gloop on it. "At least, Ix is. I think Jenny went with him just to do something. She's still pretty weak."

"It." Zack bit into the brown disk. Obviously, a protein patty created by the food dispenser, it tasted slightly of grilled beef and mushrooms with the texture of soggy cardboard.

"Wait? What did you say?" Liz squinted over her nose at him.

Zack swallowed. "You called Ix a 'him.' Ix is a drone. It's not a boy or a girl."

"We don't call people 'it,' Zack." She cleaned the nozzle on the food dispenser. "For a minute, I thought you were swearing about the food. It's not the greatest, but it's what we have."

He swished the patty in the gloop and bit into it. He couldn't identify the flavor in the grey stuff, but it went well enough with the protein patty. "It's probably the worst food I've ever had, but I don't hate it." He chuckled. "I don't like it, either."

Zack spotted Jenny coming up the hill. She approached the cooking station, smiling and waving. "Feeling better, Zack?"

He nodded and grunted in reply since his mouth was full. Jenny lifted the jug of water she carried and poured it into a port on the food dispenser. "Ix is having trouble with the purifier. It wanted to know if you could help out, Lieutenant Herd?"

Liz wiped her hands on her pants. "On my way."

"I'll come with. I want to see Ix." Zack shoved the rest of the protein patty into his mouth before setting the plate down and jogging after Liz. Despite its nondescript flavor and unsettling texture, the food sat well in his stomach, and he felt more energized. He noticed Jenny watching him. As he followed behind Liz, the sense that he forgot something overtook him. He pushed the feeling aside when he saw his friend standing on its back legs tinkering with the top of the purifier.

"Ix! I'm better!" Zack waved at his friend.

Ix peered around the top of the purifier, then clambered down and met them. "I am pleased to see you recovered, Zack." Ix touched Zack's arm. "I was worried."

"I don't really remember much of it, just this really weird dream about a giant pizza stomping all over Ishtar Plaza."

Ix cocked its head and chittered as it regarded Zack.

"What's the issue, Ix?" Liz smacked her hand against the side of the purifier as she walked around it.

"I believe I may have stripped one of the bolts holding the cover on the side of the housing. Do we have extras?"

Liz looked at the area Ix indicated. She shook her head. "Let's see what's going on under this plate. Come here a minute."

After Ix joined her by the purifier, Liz took the wrench it offered her and loosened the bolts holding the plate in place. She examined the guts of the machine after removing the plate and withdrew another bolt from the cavity. Upon comparing the bolt Ix indicated was stripped to the one she withdrew, she met Ix's gaze.

"See, the problem is the interior was designed by a different team than the outer shell, so the bolts are different sizes. There are way more bolts for the interior than are actually needed." After screwing the bolt Ix had indicated was stripped into one of the interior mechanisms, Liz gestured for Ix to hand her the plate. "So, one of the bolts for this cover fell into the inside and you must have used one of the smaller extraneous bolts instead to secure the cover. Don't feel bad. It's happened to me. It's happened to Coulson. It happens to everyone. Here, give me a hand"—she glanced at Ix—"or three or four."

Ix held the plate against the side of the purifier as Liz reinserted the bolts, one by one. She took the wrench from Zack and tightened them while Ix kept the unit steady. She looked around the unit at the Valtraxian. "Hey, let me ask you about something Zack and I spoke about earlier. Doesn't it bother you when people call you 'it'?"

Ix cocked its head. "Why should it? I have no gender."

"'It' refers to an object, not a person, Ix. We use 'they' for other non-binary people."

More than once Zack corrected one of his other friends when they referred to Ix as "he." His face grew red at the realization that he might have been insulting his friend all along.

"The pronoun I use in Valtraxian does not refer to objects." Ix chittered. "As you can hear, it does not translate. 'He' refers to males. 'She' refers to females. 'They' refers to incubators. I do not have a solution that will be readily accepted in Valtraxian society and across the Confederation. However, I can tell you, I am not offended by the use of 'it' as a personal pronoun for myself."

After she finished tightening the bolts, Liz handed the wrench to Zack. She stared at him a moment. "Are you all right, Zack? You look upset. Or are you going to be sick again?"

"Oh"—Zack shook his head—"no, I'm fine. I was worried for a moment that I'd been insulting Ix for years."

"I would have corrected you, Zack, if you had misgendered me."

"It just doesn't feel right to me." Liz crouched at the intake hose of the purifier, running her hands along its length to search for leaks.

"My preferred pronouns are my choice, are they not?" Ix lowered itself down to six legs and followed behind Liz.

"I guess that makes it right."

"How are we supposed to remember everything about stuff like that?" Zack tossed the wrench from hand to hand. "The more I learn about it, the more complicated it gets."

Liz shrugged. "That sums up life. You just do the best you can, apologize when you get it wrong, and try not to make the same mistake twice. Like any subject, you'll learn what's correct through repetition." She looked over her shoulder at Zack. "You seem to do all right, though.

Zack's thoughts turned to their current predicament. "Yeah, well, we wouldn't be stuck here if it wasn't for me."

"Don't be so hard on yourself." Liz regarded Zack. "I don't remember hearing you ordering the Devorans to fire on us or commanding the Athosians to flee to some far-flung corner of the universe instead of just leaving the system."

Ix chittered in agreement. "Yes, you know that is not accurate, Zack."

"All right, we're finished here. I learned something today, thank you, Ix." Liz put her hand on the Valtraxian's shoulder. "I'll try not to mess it up. I assume you'll keep correcting me if I get it wrong, won't you Zack?"

Nodding, Zack smiled. "I promise."

—— 《 》 — 《 》 — 《 》 — 《 》 — 《 》 — 《 》 ——

Jenny contemplated Zack's unfinished breakfast as he left with Liz to go help Ix. She considered finishing his grey gloop before ultimately tossing it into the recycler. Despite her distaste for highly processed emergency rations, Jenny's stomach still grumbled for more food after having gone without for more than a day.

Would they even notice if I took extra? She shrugged. *Probably not.*

Zack's disinterest in the ship they saw overhead while out exploring surprised her. She wondered if he felt all right or if he was putting on a brave face. Jenny returned to her tent and crawled inside. The tent provided protection from the sun's radiation but not the heat, so she left the flap open to allow what little breeze blew across the island to cool the inside somewhat.

She pulled up an image of Hiri on her implants. The young woman's emerald eyes blinked as she smiled. Jenny closed her eyes and indulged for a moment in the looping image only she could see. *I'd give anything to be with you right now, Hiri.*

Major Jericho's voice broke through her reverie. "I'd like everyone to convene in the mess area, please. I have an update from the Athosians."

Jenny's eyes snapped open, and, for a moment her heart leapt as she dared hope that the ship was repaired. Such quick repairs seemed too good to be true however, and she realized the update more likely pertained to the ship they'd seen a few days ago. She crawled out of her tent, meeting up with Zack, Ix, and Liz as they made their way to the cooking station.

"All right, gather 'round." Major Jericho gestured to the ground in front of him. "Glad to see you two up and about." He nodded to Zack and Jenny.

"Is the ship fixed?" Jenny wasted no time.

"The ship!" Zack clicked his fingers. "We saw an alien ship fly overhead when we were out with Lizard the other day."

Major Jericho held up his hands to silence Zack and Jenny. "The Athosians have contacted the ship and its crew. Alpha Primus identified them as Species 7405. Uh, they call themselves the Trilliax Assembly now, apparently. According to the Athosian's database, when they were last encountered, they were in an age similar to our Renaissance: no mechanized travel, just beginning to explore and understand natural science. They were deemed insignificant. A lot can change in a thousand years."

"They're not hostile, then, sir?" Liz stood with her hands clasped behind her back.

Major Jericho rubbed his forehead. "They're neither hostile nor friendly. They're concerned that we're squatting on their salvage rights."

"Salvage? What, that sunken city we saw?" Zack glanced at Jenny and Ix before returning his attention to the major.

"The planet. They've been scavenging on Athos for decades now. Until we showed up, plants were the most sophisticated lifeform remaining.

Jenny's thoughts turned to the creepy flowers that seemed to follow their movements. *What if they're intelligent? Are there worlds where plants take over and evolve sapience when the people are gone? Not in a thousand years, surely.* She raised her hand. "But what about the ship? How... when are we going to go home?"

Major Jericho chewed on his lip, then looked at the ground. "They're working around the clock on it. We may have to trade with the Trilliax Assembly to get the parts and raw materials we need. Then, they'll have to adapt Trilliax parts to this ship."

"So, you don't know? Just say so." Jenny crossed her arms and glared at him.

"Hey!" Liz snapped her head around, scowling at the young woman.

"It's all right." Major Jericho nodded at Liz. "We can't expect the kids to have our discipline. They haven't trained for this." He chuckled and returned his gaze to the ground. "Can any of us say that we've trained for this? This? Being marooned on a planet in a different galaxy... They don't train us for this."

He approached Jenny and put his hand on her shoulder, looking her in the eyes. "We must be patient. Fixing a ship damaged in combat without access to a shipyard is a monumental challenge. We're going to get home."

Chapter 9

Zack scraped the nutrient paste off his plate, clearing every bit before tossing his waste in the recycler. "I want to come with you."

"It's too dangerous." Major Jericho paced, holding his cup of reconstituted coffee close. "We don't know what these Trilliax are going to do, what they want. My main concern is getting you, Jenny, and Ix home safely. This is not a Junior Ranger outing."

"I won't get to go on any of those anymore." Zack kicked a rock.

"I know it's difficult. You're in a new place, you want to explore. I get it." He stopped in front of Zack. "This planet has been ravaged by biological weapons that wiped out all advanced forms of life. That we can even walk around without getting sick is a testament to the resilience of the ecosystem. But we don't know what is lingering out there. You experienced firsthand how toxic the water is. Please, just stay here with Coulson. We should only be gone a couple of days. Hopefully, we'll have everything we need from the Trilliax, the Athosians can finish fixing the ship, and we can get the hell off this planet."

Zack chewed his lip. "Maybe if the Athosians can't get their ship fixed, the Trilliax can give us a ride home?"

"I don't—" Major Jericho furrowed his brow, then shook his head. "I'll look into every possibility that shortens our time here."

Liz trotted over and saluted. Major Jericho returned the gesture.

"We're ready to go, sir."

"Very well." Major Jericho tossed his cup into the recycler. "Listen to Coulson, Zack. Stay safe."

Zack sighed and nodded. "Yes, sir." He watched Liz and the major leave. After a moment, he wandered off to find Jenny. He saw Coulson talking to Ix at the far side of the camp but didn't see his other friend, so he headed toward the tents. He found Jenny sitting at the edge of camp, staring out across the ocean, hugging her knees. Zack called out to her, but her only response was a glance in his direction. After a moment, she gestured for him to sit next to her.

They sat in silence for what seemed like forever to Zack. Finally, she turned and looked at Zack, her lips a thin line across her face. "Do you think they're lying to us?"

Zack frowned and shook his head. "No. What about?"

"Getting home."

"They're working on it, Jenny." Zack tossed a rock into the water. He shifted his seat as a blade of grass dug into his skin. "Major Jericho and Liz just went with one of the Athosians to meet with Trillax... Trilliaxicans... those other aliens to get parts. They'll be back in a day or so, and then the Athosians can finish fixing the ship and we can go home."

They sat for a little while longer, watching the waves roll ashore. Zack tossed another rock into the ocean. "It'll be weird going back to school. All our friends will be in higher classes than us, huh?"

"They may have all graduated by the time we get home." Whispering, Jenny touched her forehead to her knees. "They'll all be adults. Probably married with kids. Ten years..."

"Oh. Yeah." Zack kept hoping Ix's math was wrong about the elapsed time on Cytherea, but Ix was never wrong.

—— 《》 — 《》 — 《》 — 《》 — 《》 — 《》 ——

Jenny reminded herself to be patient with Zack. Though her heart wanted solitude to wallow in misery alone, intellectually, she knew they had to support each other right now. She listened to him talk, nodding and shrugging when he seemed to be asking questions, while she watched the water. The waves lapping against the sandy shore reminded her a bit of the beach at her grandparent's home in Marseille, but oily and toxic.

The breeze blowing ashore from across the ocean smelled nothing like that on Earth or even the breeze that came across Messier Habitat's artificial lakes, however. Athos's breeze carried a pungency with it. After her experience with the water, Jenny hoped the air wasn't subtly toxic. She took a deep breath and extended her legs as she exhaled. When Zack stopped talking, she reveled in the wind being the only sound. Then she heard Ix approach.

"May I join you?" Ix's telltale skittering caught Zack's attention, and the boy looked away.

"I guess. Jenny?"

She shrugged. "We're just sitting here, Ix."

Ix positioned itself on the other side of Zack. It clicked its mandibles before settling in to watch the waves with Zack and Jenny. Ix's presence seemed to soothe Zack's nervous energy. The three friends watched the waves go in and out together until the sun moved past its zenith. *If Mungus were here, it'd almost be like Bestic again. Except without hungry animals trying to eat us.*

"The weather is nicer here." Jenny hugged her knees.

"Hmm?" Only when Ix and Zack glanced at Jenny, did she realize she'd given voice to her thoughts.

"Oh, I was just thinking if Mungus were here, it'd be like Bestic. It's not as cold, though."

"If I had known my life would be imperiled so often with you two," Ix chittered, "I still would have left the hive. My life is richer for these experiences with you, my friends."

Jenny pulled Zack into a hug, reaching past him toward Ix. The Valtraxian rose up and embraced its friends with two pairs of arms. "I did not mean to upset you."

Jenny released her friends. "It's hard being pulled away from everyone you love, especially when it's probably going to be ten years or more before you see them again." She paused for a moment. "This is the part where someone says, 'we'll look back on this when we're old and laugh.'"

Clutching his stomach, Zack shook his head. "I was so sick I forgot a whole day. I don't think I'll ever want to laugh about that."

"Hey!" Coulson shouted as he approached the three. "I'm not sure you should spend any more time crisping in the sun. Maybe move under the tent or go in the ship?"

Zack stood, brushing off his pants. "We can still go in the ship?"

Coulson gestured toward the lumpy craft floating on the other side of the island. "Of course. I set up lunch in there. Maybe we can eat properly at a table. Nothing makes nutrient paste and protein patties taste better than formal place settings!"

Jenny chuckled. She lingered as Zack and Ix headed toward the ship.

Coulson noticed her hesitance and returned to her side. "Something wrong? Besides being stuck on a poisoned planet a million light years from home?"

Laughing, Jenny shook her head. "Isn't that enough?"

"Boy, it sure is." Coulson stared out over the waves as he stood next to her. "It's okay to feel... whatever you're feeling, you know? None of us are thrilled to be here. But the major, he'll figure it out. I've been serving with him my whole career. First deployment was with him to Callisto when that whole thing blew up. The Callisto-Ganymede Conflict?"

Jenny studied that incident briefly in EAC history class. A dispute between laborers and administrators had threatened to cut off water supplies to all the outer system habitats. Her history professor told the class it was resolved with a minimum of bloodshed and minimal disruption to the supply chain; a footnote in EAC history.

"They taught us about that in school."

"I'll bet they didn't tell you the whole story." Coulson picked up a rock and tossed it from hand to hand. "They probably downplayed it, said it was a minor thing, right?"

Jenny nodded.

Coulson flung the rock into the ocean. "That's always how they do it. Simplify, gloss over. Miss the point."

Tugging at his sleeve, Jenny pointed toward the ship. "Maybe you can tell us about it during lunch?"

"Good idea." He followed her across the island to the ship. On the horizon, she saw dark clouds gathering. They seemed to hang there, lingering. She watched them as she approached the Athosian ship but could not determine if they were moving closer.

Zack and Ix waited for them inside in the conference room. Coulson's spread was little more than pucks of protein and nutrient paste arranged on plates. He gestured toward the table. "All right, kids, let's sit and eat."

Ix moved a chair next to Zack out of the way and sidled up to the table. "What is the flavoring?"

Coulson grinned. "Mystery meat and brown veggies. Yum yum."

The Valtraxian chittered and glanced at Zack. "Your mother's waffles are far superior. And her spaghetti."

Zack snickered. "I could go for some waffles right now. Or a cheeseburger." He poked at the protein patty with his spork. "With enough junk on it, you could almost think this was a burger."

"Please, stop talking about better food." Jenny closed her eyes and ignored the slightly metallic flavor of the paste.

Coulson sopped up some of the nutrient paste with a piece of the protein patty. "It could be worse, but you're right. It could be a lot better. They make us eat these emergency rations during training, you know, so we know what to expect."

He grimaced as he swallowed. "I never expected to have to live on this stuff for this long."

Jenny let the others talk while she focused on ignoring the unpalatable taste and texture of her food. As much as she disliked it, it ranked higher than what they'd been forced to eat on Bestic. *Three trips to alien worlds and the only food she found even halfway palatable was what they found on Valtra.*

Before Zack could continue interrogating Coulson regarding the aliens to which Major Jericho, Liz, and Alpha Primus journeyed to meet, Coulson asked a question of them: "What do you know about the Callisto-Ganymede Conflict?"

"Ummm... I've heard of it?" Zack glanced at Ix.

"Zack has not yet reached that level of EAC history in school." Ix related the same information Jenny told Coulson before they came in for lunch.

"Well, I'll tell you what really happened," Coulson sat forward, "and you'll understand why I have no doubt that Major Jericho is going to get us home."

Chapter 10

Coulson looked at each of the Junior Rangers in turn. "Picture it, Galilei City, 4198. Looking out over the rocky ice plains with that spectacular view of Jupiter. From the governor's office, you can see Ganymede just starting to transit those white and orange bands of clouds. It's really something to see."

Zack nibbled his faux food. If he concentrated, he detected the barest hint of beef flavor.

"There's always been competition between the companies that set up on Callisto and the ones that set up on Ganymede. Water is... water and half of what they extract from those moons is broken down into hydrogen and oxygen anyway." Coulson shook his head and sipped his water. "But you know, the Callistans thought their water was better than the water the Ganymedeans extracted and vice versa."

Ix cocked its head and clicked its mandibles. "The problem was a labor dispute of some sort, was it not? Unfair or dangerous working conditions and too little attention paid to the problems by the administration?"

Coulson raised a finger. "That was one problem, but not *the* problem. See, what a lot of people don't know, is that the two companies in charge, their chief administrators were brothers. Brothers who just could not let the other one win. Very competitive." He shrugged. "It's a bad combination when pretty much everyone working in the outer system depends on your water. So, they got into a pissing match over supply shipments and allotments and all sorts of other things."

Zack snickered. His parents tried to watch their language around him, and although he heard worse things at school all the time, it never failed to amuse him when adults forgot.

"Oh"—Coulson seemed to catch on to the source of Zack's mirth—"I mean, they were very competitive."

Jenny nudged Zack. "We understand."

The whir of the air handling system broke through the silence as Coulson pondered where next to take his tale. Zack felt a twinge in his stomach, but he pushed through and continued eating. He imagined his lunch was made from real meat instead of whatever the protein patty and nutrient paste were made of.

"When some sabotage occurred and one of the ships crashed into Callisto, Major Jericho and his squad were sent to deal with the problem. We figured it would just be a matter of getting the two bosses to sit down and babysit them while they hashed out their problems." Coulson pinched the bridge of his nose as he shook his head. "If only it had been that simple."

"They didn't tell us any details in history class, just that the military stepped in and stopped the conflict before it got out of hand." Jenny frowned and shoved her empty plate away from her.

"And out of hand it got. Quickly." Coulson grimaced. "Very few people in either company knew the bosses were brothers. So, some upper management types got the idea that maybe an accident could befall one of the brothers."

Ix cocked its head. "A planned accident? Is that not an assassination?"

Coulson tapped the side of his nose and nodded. "It worked, too. Both of them were killed by the employees of each other's companies while they were on their way to a neutral site for negotiations Major Jericho had arranged." He shook his head and chuckled. "The major knew something was up when both of their shuttles had accidents on the same day within minutes of each other. The ice miners, though? They were all fired up. It almost turned into a shooting war by the time the major got control of it."

Zack thought he heard rumbling outside but looking around the room he noticed no one else seemed to have heard it.

Coulson arranged a bunch of discarded utensils on the table. "A bunch of miners from Ganymede came to Callisto loaded for bear. I mean, I've never seen civilians packing so many weapons. I don't know where they got them from." He threw up his hands. "There ain't nothing to hunt on those moons, and shooting space dust is about as exciting as it sounds. Anyway, they're out there on a plain, lined up like old style soldiers, ready to start shooting at each other, and the major has us land smack dab between their lines."

Ix cocked its head. "That sounds dangerous."

"Yeah, well, you know, loaded guns pointed at us from both sides." Smiling, Coulson rubbed the back of his head. "The major figured they wanted to shoot each other, but they might be a little more cautious about firing on EAC military."

Jenny furrowed her brow. "Were they?"

"We were just one shuttle, maybe a dozen troops, but the major, he called it right." Coulson chewed his bottom lip, nodding. "They could have gunned us down easy, but then, their little spat becomes a major military problem. The EAC probably would have annexed all the water production facilities on both moons, which, I guess they did anyway since both brothers were dead, but at least all the miners got to keep their jobs." He laughed. "They're all better off now, too, since they don't have those two brothers fighting over who had better water."

Zack frowned and scratched his head. "I don't get it. It's water. Water's water, right? What's the big deal?"

Coulson laughed. "You don't have any siblings, do you, kid?"

Zack shook his head.

Another rumble reverberated through the hull. Jenny sat up straight, widening her eyes. "Did you feel that?"

"Heard it, too." Zack's heart skipped a beat as his mind immediately started to spin up worst-case scenarios.

—— 《 》— 《 》— 《 》— 《 》— 《 》— 《 》——

"I'll bet that's thunder. Did anyone else notice those storm clouds on the horizon?" Jenny peered down the corridor toward the outdoors. The sky still looked clear, and the clouds she saw were quite far away.

"I saw them." Ix dragged a finger through the nutrient paste on its plate. "I was unable to determine if they were coming this way."

Jenny cleaned off the last of the nutrient paste with the final morsel of protein patty. "Maybe we should move our stuff in here if it comes closer. We don't know what storms are like on this planet."

She fought against a pang of homesickness. Life in a habitat meant a perfectly controlled environment every hour of every day of every year. Sure, any given area might be a little too warm or too cool for a person's preferences, but one never had to cope with sudden, torrential downpours or dangerous lightning storms. Weather variances remained the worst part of visiting her grandparents in France.

"That's not a bad idea, Jenny." Coulson stacked her now-empty plate with his. "We should keep an eye on those clouds this afternoon. If it looks dicey, we'll bring what we can into the ship." Coulson headed toward the hatch. "In fact, I'm going to start prepping the food dispenser and recycling station to be moved. Once you kids are done eating, you can help me; we'll set it all up in here tonight."

Zack pushed his food around his plate. "What if the storm misses us?"

"Then we'll put it all back out in the morning after breakfast." Coulson looked over his shoulder at the three Junior Rangers as he left the conference room. "It'll be good practice."

Though Zack grumbled, Jenny felt pleased that Coulson took her concerns about the potential for a storm seriously. If this were a proper Junior Ranger outing, their troop leader would help them secure the camp from an incoming storm. And considering no living human or Valtraxian knew what to expect of Athosian weather, she considered it even more important to take precautions.

"Stupid storms." Zack shoveled the last bit of his food into his mouth.

"You do not really believe there is an intelligence behind the weather here, do you, Zack?" Ix cocked its head as it regarded its friend.

Jenny chuckled. "It's just an expression, Ix." She caught herself about to mention how much she missed Cytherea and Messier Habitat, and instead just sighed. "Let's take these plates to the recycler and help Coulson. It's got to be better than just sitting around here."

"Jenny is correct, Zack." Ix gathered up the plates, carrying them easily in his arms.

"Too bad we earned our Wilderness Survival badges on Bestic." Zack followed behind Jenny and Ix. "Do you think we can get an extra ribbon or something?"

"It's not an official Junior Ranger outing." Jenny frowned. She took plates from Ix and fed them into the recycler. "We'll be lucky if the school excuses our absence."

Zack slapped his head. "School? Oh no. They wouldn't suspend us for this, would they? It's not like we're cutting class. We would have stayed on Cytherea if that Devoran ship hadn't started shooting at us."

Ix chittered. "It would be unjust if we were penalized for circumstances beyond our control."

Jenny agreed with Ix's conclusion. She glanced out over the sea and noticed the dark clouds had picked up speed and were moving closer. She pointed to the horizon. "Looks like we'll be sleeping inside tonight."

Chapter 11

After moving the equipment inside the ship and setting up the food dispenser and recycler, Coulson assigned tasks: Zack and Jenny were to break down and bring in the tents and bedrolls while Ix collected the fishing traps and ferried as much water from the purifier as they had containers to hold it. Meanwhile, Coulson would collapse and secure the portable pavilion tent that had been erected over the cooking station.

The work kept the four of them busy throughout the afternoon, incited to urgency by the ever-closing cloud cover and uptick in wind speed with every passing hour. By the time they finished, the sun had slipped behind the clouds, casting a dark pall over the island. The wind whipped Jenny's hair into her face, but she didn't take time to stop and tie it back. After she and Zack hauled the last of the gear inside, Coulson closed the outer hatch against the howling wind outside.

Zack wiped his brow, glancing around the conference room. "Where's Ix?"

Jenny's eyes widened and she darted toward the door.

"Here." A spindly arm shot up from behind the stack of gear that was their tents. "I set up my bedroll here in seclusion, so my nocturnal activities do not disturb anyone's sleep in these tight quarters."

Coulson chuckled as he peered over the top of the pile. "What sort of nocturnal activities does a Valtraxian get up to?"

Snugged in its nest of blankets, Ix looked up at the soldier. "I require less sleep than you humans, so I have been chronicling our adventures here. For posterity."

"It's not a bad idea," Coulson tossed his bedroll to the far corner of the room, "I'd be surprised if they let us talk about this when we get back. Not for a while, anyway."

Zack dragged his bedroll near the area Ix had set up. "We're kind of used to not being able to talk about stuff that happens on these trips."

The howling outside intensified as the wind picked up. The Athosian ship's mass proved impervious to the storm raging around it, but the airlock provided little barrier to the noise of the storm. Coulson assured them a storm would not breech the ship's hull or damage the airlock doors. Once they had finished securing items from camp, they worked on installing harnesses in the seats and hardpoints to strap down their gear for when they finally got back into space.

The storm raged through the night, and the constant roar of the wind eventually receded into the background. Finally, the three humans slept through the night. The next morning, in the absence of a status update from the Athosians, Coulson risked opening the ship so they could answer nature's call.

Dark clouds hung overhead as far as they could see, but no rain fell. The ground, saturated with water from the previous night's rainfall, squished beneath their feet. After taking care of business, they walked the perimeter of the island until they reached the rocky shoreline where the water purifier had been erected.

It was gone.

"It's like it was never here." Coulson rubbed the back of his neck and swore.

Wrinkling his nose, Zack peered into the murky water. "Can we build another one?"

"It took days for the Athosians to fabricate the parts for that one." Jenny hugged herself and bit her lip.

Coulson took a deep breath, then spun on his heel. He patted Jenny on the shoulder as he passed her. "Ix collected enough water before the storm to last a couple of days, and we still have the portable purifiers. I have some tablets we can toss into water we've boiled, too. It'll be all right."

They followed him back to the ship. As they climbed the hill, a craft similar to the one Jenny, Zack, and Ix saw on their last hike with Liz streaked overhead, then banked and circled the island. It came in for a landing across the tide pools that led to the mainland.

Zack pointed at the ship. "Hey, maybe they brought Major Jericho and Liz back!" He took off running toward the ship.

"Wait, Zack!" Coulson shouted after him.

Heedless of the mud splashing up on his pants, Zack ran toward the far shore of the island. Opaque, white gas vented from the underside of the angular ship as it set down across the tide pools. A hatch on the underside of the ship's nose slid open and a ramp unrolled with a metallic clacking sound.

Zack stopped short, unwilling to traverse the slippery rocks littering the channel, even though the tide was out. Sea spray, propelled by the wind, splashed upon him as he watched three squat creatures waddle on elephantine legs out of the craft. Arms jutted from the junctions of each of their three legs. Zack noticed a pair of eyes above each arm, and a mass of fleshy tendrils topping their cone-shaped bodies.

The aliens jabbered to themselves before leaping across the stones. Zack backpedaled, bumping into Coulson.

"It's not safe. We need to get back to the ship, Zack." Coulson pulled Zack back, placing himself between the young man and the aliens. While one hand gripped Zack's arm, he noticed Coulson's other hand gripped his still-holstered pistol.

"Where's Liz?" Zack tugged against the soldier's grip to no avail as he peered toward the alien craft. "And Major Jericho?"

The aliens waddled toward them. Zack noticed they each held spike-covered devices in one of their three-fingered hands. Coulson walked backward, pushing Zack along.

"Now, we don't want any trouble. My commander is talking with some of you folks right now. You're Trilliax, right? We just want to fix our ship and go home."

Glancing over his shoulder, Zack saw Jenny and Ix approaching. The aliens raised their devices at the sight of the two additional castaways.

"Whoa, whoa, whoa. They're just kids. We need to stay calm. We need..."

A green light flashed from the device held by the lead alien, and Coulson jerked backward. He fell to the ground, smacking his head against a rock. Zack wrenched his arm out of Coulson's now-slackened grip and saw a jagged hole in Coulson's chest. Blood welled in the wound and seeped out, staining the ground red.

—— 《 》 — 《 》 — 《 》 — 《 》 — 《 》 — 《 》 ——

The world seemed to move in slow motion as Coulson fell. Jenny screamed for Zack, but her own voice seemed muffled to her ears. The young man turned and ran toward her and as he reached her side, time caught up with them.

"Ix!" Jenny called for the Valtraxian as she grabbed Zack's hand and ran with him. The three ran across the muddy ground toward the ship. Zack slipped in the mud, bringing Jenny down with him. Ix stopped to help them regain their footing. Without glancing back at the aliens who were almost certainly pursuing them, they leapt through the outer hatch and sealed the airlock behind them.

"They... they..." Zack's breaths were quick and ragged. "Is he... Coulson..."

"I believe he is dead." The Valtraxian rubbed his arms, chittering.

Collapsing into a chair, Jenny pulled her legs up and hugged her knees to conceal her trembling. The viewscreen shimmered and an Athosian appeared on the screen, bobbing in the fluid environment the rest of the ship contained.

Each of their ten eyes blinked in sequence as they spun in place. "Did we just monitor weapons fire outside?"

"Those aliens... the ones that just landed," Jenny pointed toward the airlock. "They killed Coulson. Are they Trilliax? Did they kill Major Jericho, too?"

Try as she might, she could not control the quaver in her voice. She squeezed her eyes shut and forced herself to take slow, controlled breaths.

"This is a less than optimal situation. Stand by." The viewscreen went mute as the Athosian communicated with others.

After a few moments, the quiet slosh returned. "I have just been in contact with Alpha Primus. All is well."

"What? All is well?" Jenny's eyes snapped open. "We saw them shoot Coulson!"

Ten eyes blinked in sequence. "Apologies. I meant Alpha Primus is alive as are the humans accompanying him. I have no information on the dispositions of the aggressive tripodal sapients on the adjacent island. Stand by."

Jenny swiveled in her chair to face Zack. Muddy handprints marred the chair where he held onto it to climb in. He slumped over the table, his shoulders shaking as Ix stood next to him, stroking the young man's arm. The Valtraxian's antennae drooped. A message pinged in Jenny's implants.

From Ix.

I believe we are in great danger right now. Zack is more upset than I have observed in the past. I do not know how to comfort him.

The Athosian on the viewscreen spoke before Jenny could respond to Ix. "The Trilliax which attacked you are part of a rival faction to the ones with whom Alpha Primus is meeting. They have now been informed of our situation and are ending the meeting immediately. Alpha Primus expects to return by nightfall."

The screen went blank. Jenny stared across the table at Ix. "We're not opening that airlock until Major Jericho returns. Yes?"

"Agreed."

Closing her eyes, Jenny leaned her head on her knees. The image of Coulson's blank face and the gaping wound in his chest seared into her mind, and no matter what she tried to think of, it always came to the forefront. She thought of school, but Coulson was there. Her parents... in her mind their faces transformed into Coulson's. Puppies played around his body. Only Hiri remained Hiri. She pulled up Hiri's image in her implants and kept that in her focus. She stayed that way until the gentle whoosh of the air circulation system lulled her to sleep.

Chapter 12

After Zack silently sobbed away the terror of witnessing the Trilliax scavenger kill Coulson, he curled up on his bedroll and stared at the foot of the conference table. Ix hovered for about an hour and eventually returned to its nest after checking on Zack. Hearing soft snores from Jenny combined with the sound of the air circulation system, Zack found his own eyelids growing heavy.

He didn't sleep, though. A knotted, twisting feeling in his stomach kept him from relaxing completely; although he was thirsty, Zack dared not risk drinking for fear of needing to relieve himself before Major Jericho returned. Instead, he focused on the strange whirling pattern on the curved legs of the table.

I wonder how they made this? I wish I could talk to them. Maybe after we get home...

While he contemplated the furniture, the gentle bobbing of the ship in the ocean made his eyelids droop. His stomach pangs proved no match for the adrenaline crash, and his eyes closed. Soon after, he drifted off to sleep, his nightmare replaying over and over in slow motion. First, the aliens raised their weapons and fired. Then he screamed in silence and watched Coulson die.

When the airlock door opened, he awakened feeling as though he'd just fallen asleep. Jenny occupied one of the chairs at the table, dark circles accentuating her bloodshot eyes. Major Jericho stood in the passageway and regarded the children with a grim countenance.

"Are you injured?" He looked at each of them in turn.

Jenny shook her head, as did Zack, unable to meet his gaze.

"None of us, save for Sergeant Coulson, were injured by the Trilliax, Major Jericho." Ix skittered around the table and approached the adult.

The major's shoulders slumped. "Thank goodness for that. We were apprised of the situation before we headed back here. Lieutenant Herd is dealing with Coulson's body now. You did the right thing locking yourselves inside the ship."

He joined Jenny at the table and gestured for Zack and Ix to sit. "But, what happened to the camp?" He looked around the cluttered conference room. "Why is all of our gear in here?"

"A storm came through last night." Jenny sniffed and wiped her nose on her sleeve.

"Jenny and Coulson thought we should bring stuff in, in case it was bad." Zack sat next to Jenny. "We couldn't get the purifier in. It's gone now. The storm washed it away."

Major Jericho rubbed his forehead. "We saw a storm on the horizon but didn't realize it was quite that strong. It was the

51

right decision to pull everything inside." He looked around the conference room and raised his eyebrows. "We may as well just start recycling tents and the other gear we don't need. The Trilliax had some compatible technology that's going to greatly speed up repairs. It turns out much of their space flight technology is reverse engineered from derelict Athosian ships they scavenged. Alpha Primus thinks we can get off planet tonight, spend a day, no more than two more days in orbit testing systems before we can leave."

Raising her head, Jenny stared at the major. "Truly? Only two more days?"

"That's what they tell me." Major Jericho leaned back in his chair and laced his fingers behind his head. "I have no reason to believe otherwise. In fact..."

He shifted his gaze away from Jenny. Zack furrowed his brow. "Is everything all right?"

The Major let out a breath. "Lieutenant Herd is finished. We should go see Coulson now."

—— 《》 — 《》 — 《》 — 《》 — 《》 — 《》 ——

Jenny, Zack, and Ix followed Major Jericho across the island to Coulson's body. The sun, setting now, had dried most of the wettest areas over the course of the day and had burned off what clouds lingered after the storm. As they approached the channel, Jenny saw Liz had dragged Coulson's body farther from the shore as the tide came in and covered it with a dark gray blanket.

Liz knelt at her comrade's side, her hair fluttering in the breeze. She looked up as the group approached. When she saw Zack, she leapt to her feet. "This is your fault! Coulson is dead because of you, I know it. Don't deny it!"

Zack stepped back, gasping. Tears welled in his eyes as his gaze alternated between Liz and Coulson. Major Jericho stepped up beside him and placed his hand on the boy's shoulder. Jenny took Zack's hand and squeezed it. "That's enough, Lieutenant."

"He should be thankful we're here to protect his ass whenever he wants to go running around." Liz stood, her hands clenching into fists. "Now Coulson's dead because of him."

Major Jericho clenched his jaw. "I said, 'that's enough.' You are out of line, Lieutenant." He pointed toward the beach. "Go walk it off."

Liz glared at them both for a minute before storming off. As Zack stammered, Major Jericho knelt in front of him and placed both hands on the boy's shoulders.

"Don't listen to her, Zack. It was not your fault. They served together for a long time; she's upset."

Shaking his head, Zack continued to stare at Coulson's shrouded body.

"Hey. Hey, look at me."

Lifting his head, Zack sniffed and wiped his eyes.

"This is not your fault, Zack. Okay?"

"But, if I hadn't—"

"No, don't do that. You weren't doing anything wrong. I ordered Coulson to keep an eye on you, and he did. You were supposed to be safe here in camp. No one could have foreseen this. As a soldier under my command, his death is my responsibility, not yours."

"It's not your fault those aliens shot him." Jenny squeezed Zack's hand again. Ix chittered and stood on the other side of Zack, stroking his friend's arm.

The major glanced over his shoulder at Coulson before returning his attention to Zack. "Now, I know the three of you have been cooped up in the ship all day. Go relieve yourselves, stretch your legs"—he looked over his shoulder—"don't go the way Lieutenant Herd went. When you're finished, go back to the ship, and wait there for me. Do you understand?"

Zack sniffled, nodding. "Yes, sir."

Major Jericho glanced at Ix, then Jenny. "I expect all three of you to tidy up the conference room a bit. Give us some room to walk around the table at least. Not to mention, the lieutenant and I will need to sleep in there, too. We'll stow most of our gear in the entry room just inside the airlock. We're going to need space in there for Coulson, too. The lieutenant and I will make sure he's covered and secured, but we're not leaving him here."

"We'll get to work on it right away." Jenny tugged on Zack's hand. "Let's leave the major to his work, Zack."

The three Junior Rangers walked together for a bit, then split up to afford each other a measure of privacy. Jenny found herself wandering toward the rocky area where the water purifier once was and wondered whatever became of the food trap they put out. After relieving herself, she looked out across the rocks at the waves breaking against the shore. No sign of the traps remained. She picked up a stone and chucked it into the water. *It's not like they caught anything edible anyway. Everything on this rock is dead, just like Coulson, and that's how we'll all end up.*

"Careful there."

Jenny started at the sound of Liz's voice before sighing and pulling her hair away from her face, although she had no means of securing it. Liz meandered toward her; hands thrust in her pockets.

"With our luck, some sea monster will get riled up and jump out and eat you."

"That wouldn't surprise me."

"Hey, I'm sorry I yelled at Zack." Through tear-brimmed eyes, Liz regarded Jenny. "It was uncalled for. I just... Coulson was my friend, you know?"

"You should be telling Zack this."

"I will. But you were all there, so I owe all of you an apology for my outburst."

"I'll let Zack know to expect you." Jenny left Liz at the rocky shore and met up with Zack and Ix at the ship's airlock. After entering the ship, the three rearranged the gear in a more organized manner, leaving space for Coulson's body behind the pile of rolled up tents. Jenny moved her bedroll closer to Ix's and Zack's. By the time they were finished, Major Jericho and Liz returned, carrying Coulson's body.

The major and lieutenant placed him in the spot prepared by Zack, Ix, and Jenny, then arranged some of the gear so he was hidden from casual view. Major Jericho and Liz made dinner for everyone, and together they ate at the conference table. Jenny made a point of sitting with her back to the door to mitigate their less-than-ideal dining situation in the cramped, cluttered setting that featured a dead body in the adjacent room. Understandably, no one seemed to be in the mood for conversation. Once they finished eating, Liz gathered up the dishes and ran them through the recycler.

A crackle over the comm system presaged an announcement from Alpha Primus. "Secure yourselves, please. We are going to attempt to take off."

Jenny glanced over to see Zack safely seated and she had barely seated herself before the ship rumbled. After a moment of intense vibration, she felt the familiar sensation of being pressed down into her seat. A few minutes later, even that feeling subsided. The time they spent securing the cabin paid off; few loose objects floated as they achieved orbit.

Liz unbuckled herself and floated across the cabin to secure the tumbling trinkets and gear. While she did that, Major Jericho pulled a black cube out of his pocket. "The Trilliax have been pretty thorough about scouring this planet for tech. I traded them my sidearm and ammunition for this."

The object reminded Jenny of one of the components connected to her cloud glider's control computer. Zack leaned forward. "What is it?"

"It's the MDC, the Master Data Core, of an Athosian star cruiser that the Devorans captured during the war. Apparently, it crashed here. The Trilliax stripped it a few weeks ago. These things contain all the flight data, ship's logs, everything you need to determine why a ship was where it was found. They're designed to survive ships crashing from orbit."

He pulled a small portable projector from another pocket. "And with this, we can see what's on it."

Chapter 13

Major Jericho set the MDC on the table. Zack shifted impatiently in his seat between Ix and Jenny as the major connected the portable projector to the Devoran device.

"Should the kids be here for this? Maybe we should wait until we get home." Liz regarded the three Junior Rangers.

Zack glanced at Jenny and Ix. Major Jericho connected his power source to the MDC and projector. "This is all ancient history to us."

"To us, yes." Liz gestured at the data storage unit. "But there are Devorans still alive whose parents fought in that war."

Zack heard the pulsing drone of the ship's engine settle to a dull thrum as they reached orbital altitude. His stomach lurched as a force pulled down on him toward the deck plates.

Major Coulson tumbled to the floor. "Whoa. What is that?"

Alpha Primus's voice crackled over the comm system again. "We have achieved orbit. Are you feeling the effects of the gravitational well generators?"

"The what?" Major Coulson peered around the room to see if Alpha Primus appeared on a view screen. He settled for looking up at the ceiling while he spoke.

"They simulate the effects of a gravity well to provide terrestrial lifeforms such as yourselves a more comfortable environment during spaceflight. If everything you need is working for now, we will begin testing some of our other systems."

"Yes, we're all fine here right now." Major Coulson opened his mouth to continue speaking, but the background hiss of the comm system fell silent, indicating anything he said would go unheard. "Well, this is kind of impossible."

Ix cocked its head. "Indeed. If they have figured out how to create artificial gravity without a mechanical solution and shared it with the Confederation, it would cause a paradigm shift in spacecraft design."

Zack shook his head. "I don't understand what you're talking about."

Ix turned to him. "Our current technology requires us to—"

Major Jericho held up his hand. "We can have a physics lesson later. Let's look at this log while we have time."

"Are you sure, sir?" Liz glanced at each of the young passengers in turn.

"I'm certain the Devorans will try to suppress as much of the truth as they can, especially once they find out we have this." Major Jericho took his seat opposite Liz and picked up the control box. "But it appears they committed a war crime of unprecedented scale here, and I will not let them silence us. The more who know the better. Besides, after all this time, who knows if this thing will even work?"

"And you don't think this will endanger the kids?" Liz crossed her arms and frowned. "With all due respect, sir."

A knot formed in the pit of Zack's stomach. Jenny reached over to squeeze Zack's hand. She chewed on her lip, and her eyes flicked back and forth between the major and his subordinate.

"It won't if we make this public as soon as we get back. There would be too many questions. You know how Devorans don't like those difficult questions." Major Jericho fiddled with the controls, then pressed the <Play> button.

A holographic image of a Devoran wearing a sapphire and gold military uniform flickered into view above the MDC. He operated controls in front of him, out of sight from the holoimager, then sat back and cleared his throat, speaking in Devoran. Zack turned on his C7's translator function.

"Captain's Log: I'm... not sure of the date. The payload was successfully delivered. The results were... unexpected, though I believe that command knew exactly what they ordered us to drop on Athos. A major extinction event is occurring. Even from orbit we can tell that the ecological devastation will render this planet unsuitable for higher lifeforms for generations. The Athosian homeworld is, for all intents and purposes, destroyed..."

He clicked his teeth together, before continuing. "This... genocide is not what my officers and I signed up for. Our infiltrators returned from their missions with reports of civilian Athosians, families, living lives not dissimilar to our own. Unfamiliar species, too, living and working alongside them. Not slaves, but peers. An advanced, peaceful society living under the yoke of an oppressive military regime. But my crew and I did as we were ordered."

Zack scarcely noticed the pain from Jenny squeezing his hand. Next to him, Ix chittered and cocked its head.

"We will, no doubt, return home to many accolades. We'll be hailed as heroes. My officers and I have decided that such accolades are inappropriate and unacceptable. We will not be returning home. I have given the order, upon the advice and consent of my officers, to de-orbit this ship. We will die with Athos. I will state for the record that my crew's performance, without exception, has been exemplary."

Only the gentle whoosh of air from the ventilation system broke the silence in the room.

"The war is a lie. Yes, there is a faction of Athosians bent on establishing dominance over life in our galaxy, but they are not a monoculture, no matter what our government would have us believe, nor are they a majority. We have discovered evidence there is a sizable counter-faction of Athosians working from within their government to depose our enemies, a fifth column. I have included what we've found in this log. Perhaps a future expedition to Athos will find this and make use of it before the Devoran people become what they claim to fight against. This is Captain Drellex Fon signing off. May our children forgive us."

After a 3D directory listing the various files included with the log replaced the captain's image, Major Jericho shut down the projector. "Drellex Fon... history records indicate he and his crew were lost on one of the final missions of the war."

"So, they used a captured ship to infiltrate Athosian space and place biological and chemical weapons on their homeworld..." Liz slumped in her chair. "No wonder that's all they say about him. No ship name, no details of the mission, just that he and his ship were lost with all hands."

Jenny finally released Zack's hand. "They didn't tell us about any of this in our history classes."

Flexing his hand, Zack shook his head. "They didn't say much about the war at all in mine. Just that the Devorans won and Athosians should never be spoken of. Ever."

Liz snorted. "Yeah, because they know what they did. I've always suspected some massive generational guilt there."

"Denial seems more appropriate." Major Jericho disconnected the projector and returned it to his pocket.

Ix shifted in its seat and chittered. "This is confusing to me."

"War never changes." Major Jericho sighed. "The longer it drags on, the more monsters it creates. When a people are deceived into supporting an unjust war, it's very easy for them to become that which they claim they're fighting against."

"Lies beget lies." Jenny's voice, a mere whisper, caught the major's attention.

"That's right. Governments repeat the lies over and over and have to keep lying to cover up the other lies until the truth gets lost. Every lie told incurs a debt to the truth. Eventually, the debt must be paid. Often in blood."

Major Jericho rubbed his temples. "I'm going to get dragged over the coals for showing that to you, but history has shown time and time again that young people like you are the debt collectors to the liars of previous generations. Valianna is deeply disappointed in what her people became during the war, what her father became. I won't let this be buried."

Zack's encounter on Cytherea with Valianna Hallox, daughter of Emperor Hallox V, seemed like a lifetime in the past. But, in reality, he met with the Devoran noblewoman less than a month ago.

"They're just going to tell us we can't talk about this again. This whole trip." Zack scowled and rested his head on his hand.

"It happens every time we go somewhere and find Athosian stuff."

"As an EAC citizen, in EAC space, you're not under Devoran jurisdiction. They can tell you that, but you're under no obligation to comply." Major Jericho looked at each Junior Ranger in turn. "So, tell people what you know. What you've seen. Tell them the truth of Drellex Fon's final mission."

—— 〈〉 — 〈〉 — 〈〉 — 〈〉 — 〈〉 — 〈〉 ——

Watching the Devoran captain's confession only served to increase Jenny's anxiety. She'd hoped, perhaps foolishly, that once they all got home, she could concentrate on her studies and spend time with her parents and Hiri and have nothing more to do with Athosians, militant Devorans, and possibly even the Junior Rangers.

She stewed on the revelation that the Devorans deliberately destroyed Athos and then lied about it for longer than humans knew about other intelligent life in the galaxy. *Why now? Why us? Why couldn't the Ersidians discover this five hundred years ago? Sometimes I wish I'd never met Zack.*

Jenny felt a tightness in her stomach as she looked at her friend conversing with Ix. She shook her head in regret for her harsh feelings toward him. *It's not his fault. He has good intentions.* She noticed Liz engage in a brief discussion with Major Jericho before she approached Zack and Ix. Meanwhile, Major Jericho came Jenny's way.

"Can I have a moment of your time?" He gestured for Jenny to follow him into the entry room near where they'd concealed Coulson's body from view. She positioned herself so the corpse did not lie within her field of vision as the major poked around in their gear.

"The Athosians seem to have failed to take into account we'll have certain biological needs for the next couple of days. Since privacy is a luxury in emergency field situations, we'll set up a private area inside the airlock apart from Coulson's body for changing clothes and whatnot." He gestured toward the door next to where they stood. "Hopefully, the Athosians can lock out the outer door controls so we can't have a fatal accident."

"Zack will appreciate that. He's already been spaced once." Jenny glanced at the airlock door.

"What? Seriously?" Major Jericho stopped in his tracks.

"During a Junior Ranger excursion to an abandoned research station in orbit over Venus. This older student seemed to really hate Zack and thought it was a good idea to space him." Jenny furrowed her brow as she tried to remember the name of the station they visited, but it wouldn't come to her. She had no trouble remembering Barry, though. *At least if we're trapped in this galaxy, I will never have to hear about him or his friends again.*

"Wow, that... that goes beyond a prank. That's attempted murder." Major Jericho gathered up the rest of the gear and opened the airlock.

"Barry really didn't like Zack." Jenny followed the major.

"How did a kid so messed up make it into Cytherean Academy?" Major Jericho set the latrine components down, then took the tank from Jenny and set it aside.

"I think his father was on the board of governors or something."

"Oh. One of those." Major Jericho's flat tone told Jenny all she needed to know about his opinion on that subject. He squatted to assemble their makeshift wash station. Jenny stood by and handed him parts as he asked for them. He instructed her to hold pieces in place while he tightened them with one of the parts that served as both a handle and a wrench.

"You don't say much." He glanced up at her as he tightened a nut. "Are you doing all right?"

Jenny thought about what she could say. She was scared. She was tired. She was angry that she kept getting pulled into dire situations that always seemed to be Zack's fault. Intellectually, she knew he didn't try to cause trouble deliberately; he was a magnet for misfortune. "I just want to go home. I just want to get back to my life."

Major Jericho finished tightening the nuts. "We would all like that, but I'm afraid even if we have no more hiccups, it'll be a while before things are back to the way they were."

"Or never."

He stood and put a hand on her shoulder. "I'll be honest with you. I think you're more right than you know. This ship and its technology, the Athosians, hell, even the Devorans firing upon us before we left. We don't even know how long we've really been gone. I just hope that when we do get back to our lives, we'll at least be able to recognize them."

Jenny stomach tightened into a knot, and her mouth went dry. "What do you mean?"

He grunted and rubbed the back of his neck. "Yeah, I probably shouldn't have said that. Look, we train for the worst-case scenario. The worst-case scenario in this case is pretty bad. But things have a way of working out. It's not just the Devorans versus Cytherea. The Ersidians are part of the Confederation government, the Valtraxians, and others, too. They're not going to let the Devorans run roughshod over the EAC just because Zack stopped them from killing an Athosian baby."

"I guess I'm mostly worried people in our lives will have given us up for dead and moved on." Jenny thought about Hiri.

She'd just started getting to know her when they were ripped apart. For the first time in years, her parents seemed to be focused on the family, rather than their careers too.

"I understand what you mean." He patted her on the shoulder. "I have family waiting for me, too. If we've been gone years, well, that's rough on everyone."

Jenny sniffed. *That's an understatement.*

Chapter 14

After Liz apologized, Zack turned to Ix. "Since we're basically on our way home and my C7 has plenty of power left, do you want to play a game? You can connect with your implants, right?" He pulled out his device and held it out to Ix.

The Valtraxian cocked its head and regarded Zack's handheld communications device. "I was not aware you had any suitable multiplayer games on your C7."

Zack activated his C7 and scrolled through the menus. "Well, I don't. Don't you have anything downloaded I can play with you?"

Ix clicked its mandible and stroked Zack's arm. "Not without a VR implant, I am sorry."

"Oh." Zack put his C7 away. He noticed he could no longer see Jenny or Major Jericho. Liz sat on her bedroll, reading something on her implants. "Did you see where Jenny and Major Jericho went?"

"Into the airlock, I believe."

Zack's eyes widened. "Why? We're in space, right?"

"Apparently. Perhaps they wanted to have a private conversation." Ix skittered away from the table to its sleeping area, then gestured for Zack to sit beside it.

With a sidelong glance toward the airlock, Zack unbuckled himself and joined Ix. The Valtraxian tapped its fingers together and chittered for a moment. "I have been contemplating my earlier calculations."

"Which ones?" Zack figured Ix referred to the elapsed time they'd been gone but asked anyway on the chance that Ix had been working on other math problems and he'd just forgotten about them.

"Our travel time."

"Yeah. We'll get home, all our friends will be old and we'll still be in school with a bunch of new kids." Zack leaned back, supporting himself with his arms.

"The Athosians are in possession of technology which seems to violate the laws of physics as we know them. Taking those variables into account is impossible, therefore my initial calculations are most likely grossly inaccurate."

Zack scratched his head. "So, it's not been five years? Or ten years or whatever?"

Ix's mandibles clicked. "I do not know. This artificial gravity we are experiencing is unattainable by our understanding of science. This ship performed a superluminal translation within the gravity well of a planet deep within the well of a star. Our jump drives won't engage that close to a massive object, even with all the safety features disabled. Since the Athosians have demonstrated propulsion technology beyond that of which we are capable, it only stands to reason we cannot apply our understanding of physics to any aspect of their ship's travel."

"Well, why don't we just ask the Athosians how long we've been gone?" Zack glanced toward the airlock as Jenny and Major Jericho emerged.

Jenny slumped toward her bedroll, but then seemed to change her mind at the last moment and instead joined Zack and Ix, sitting on the floor to face them. "What are you two talking about? Not planning on getting into trouble, are you?"

Ix cocked its head. "I never plan on that."

"I don't either, it just seems to happen."

Jenny chuckled. "You do seem to have bad luck. I hope the next time, I'm not around you when it happens."

"I was telling Zack, the Athosians seem to be a very advanced species. It is possible they are higher on the Kardashev Scale than any other known civilization in our galaxy."

Jenny furrowed her brow and glanced at Zack, before looking again to Ix. "I don't know what that means."

Inwardly, Zack let out a sigh of relief. "Yeah, I don't understand what you're talking about, Ix."

"The Kardashev Scale is a method of measuring a civilization's level of technological advancement based on their energy usage. Most of the civilizations in our galaxy are close to Type One civilizations. That is, they can harness all of the energy that falls on their homeworld from their star. I believe the Athosians may be closer to Type Two. Possibly beyond."

Jenny pinched the bridge of her nose. "So, what does that mean?"

"What, they can do two stars?" Zack noticed Major Jericho was now talking to Liz. He wondered what they were talking about. Hopefully, coming up with something for them all to do while they were cooped up for the next couple of days.

"Type Two civilizations can harness all the energy radiated by their home stars—"

"No, no, no." Jenny held up her hands. "I mean, what does that have to do with our situation?"

"It means, it is possible they are capable of things we believe to be impossible. Therefore, you should not assume our travel time estimates are correct, as they are based on our technology, not Athosian technology."

"So... maybe we haven't been gone forever?" Before Ix could answer Jenny held up her hands again. "I didn't mean that literally."

"Wow." It finally occurred to Zack what Ix had implied. "Maybe we've only been gone a couple of weeks? Or however long we've been stuck on Athos." The thought brought a smile to his face. The trip to Bestic took a week of elapsed time, one way. If this trip took no longer than that, he'd come home, and it'd be just like any other Junior Ranger excursion. It was the best news he'd heard since they fled Cytherea.

—— 《 》— 《 》— 《 》— 《 》— 《 》— 《 》——

"I don't think we should get too excited, Zack." Jenny wanted to believe in Zack's newfound hope that their travel to and from Athos was instantaneous, but it really seemed too good to be true. Despite her pessimism, Ix's admission that it lacked confidence in its earlier calculations lightened Jenny's mood. The thought of having been gone ten years was almost too much to bear. The possibility that it could now be much less time than that gave her one more reason to look forward to their upcoming translation jump.

"Jenny is correct." Ix settled down onto its bedroll. "We really know nothing more than we did when we first arrived on Athos."

"But we can guess that it's way better than ten years total, right?" Zack looked from Jenny to Ix and back to Jenny.

Ix chittered. "I think it is safe to assume that is correct. I cannot believe the Athosians would be capable of creating artificial gravity like we are experiencing without having more advanced propulsion technology than the Confederation."

Jenny decided to head off a technical discussion about technology. "Assuming it's not been years and we get back, what's the first thing you're going to do? Zack? Ix?"

Ix cocked its head. "I suppose I will have to contact my professors and inquire about an extension on several projects in which I was involved. Otherwise, I will fail."

"You'd think they'd take it easy on us. It's not like we meant to get flung into a different galaxy." Zack's brow furrowed. Jenny could feel he was now worried about all the schoolwork he was in danger of failing for repeated absences.

Jenny patted Zack's knee. "Don't worry about that. Some kids are weeks late back from break because a transport has an engine failure; they don't get failed. Apart from school stuff, what are you going to do, Zack?"

"I gotta talk to my parents, they'll be worried sick. But—" He rubbed the back of his neck as his face turned red.—"I guess I need to visit Rio if she's still healing and see if she still wants to go to the Yule Ball, assuming we haven't missed it. And if we have, I guess apologize."

"I'm sure she'll understand." Jenny hoped she could count on Hiri to be as sympathetic.

"What about you, Jenny?" Zack looked up at her, though he didn't have to lift his head quite as much as he had when they first met.

Jenny sighed. "Talk to my parents, Hiri... I guess I'm just worried she gave up on me and moved on. I wouldn't expect her to put her life on hold for years, besides, that'll make her much older than me, maybe even out of school. It's hard to make plans when you don't even know what you're going back to."

"Well, I have good news on that front." Jenny jumped at the sound of Major Jericho's voice behind her. She turned to face him and noticed he had taken off his boots.

Grimacing, he sat on the floor between Jenny and Ix. Liz sauntered over, smiling from ear to ear. She sat on the edge of the conference table. "Did you tell them yet?"

"I was just getting to that." Major Jericho grinned. "Alpha Primus has finally broken his silence and let me ask some very direct questions about their technology. Breathe easy, when we get back, we won't have been gone ten years."

Jenny shut her eyes and bit her lip. She tried to focus on the unspoken "but" to keep her hopes from soaring to unrealistic heights.

"They admit the jump out here was rocky, so they're not certain of their elapsed time calculations on the trip out here. Worst case"—Major Jericho held up his finger—"and keep in mind they believe this is highly unlikely, five years elapsed time to get out here. That's not the good news."

Five, ten, both are long enough that anything good won't really matter.

"The good news is, when their drive is repaired, the trip home will take a couple of hours, elapsed time."

Ix's mandibles snapped. "That is impossible."

Major Jericho chuckled. "That's what I said. Their best estimates indicate the trip out here probably took somewhere between a couple of weeks and a couple of months. Six at the most. Which—" he shrugged—"is also impossible according to our understanding of relativity and physics."

"*Excusez-moi.*" Jenny felt herself teeter, and she was glad she was sitting. "You mean we may have only been gone six months?"

Liz nudged her from behind. "Pretty cool, huh?"

Jenny's breath quickened and she couldn't stop the tears from falling. She felt Major Jericho's hand on her shoulder. "I don't know about you, but I'm going to be very glad to get home to my spouses and have them not be suddenly ten years older than I am."

Jenny snickered. She pulled Zack over and hugged him, laughing. "We don't have to start over!"

Once everyone had laughed or cried out their joy at the news Major Jericho brought, he stood and looked down at the Junior Rangers. "Every time we pack our gear for a mission, whether we're going planet-side on a First Contact, to a habitat for a demonstration, or whatever, we get issued a few... special items. They're intended to raise morale in dire situations or—and I think this case definitely qualifies—they can be used for a celebration. Lieutenant Herd?"

She jumped off the table and clapped her hands together. "Now we're talking. I hope you kids like ice cream. We've got vanilla, chocolate, rum raisin, butter pecan, and um," she chuckled, "Coulson liked some exotic flavors, like Ersidian sweet root and piney grub and that other, disgusting one. Major?"

"Kerrolian bleeding fungus."

While Coulson's choices sounded unappealing to Jenny, the thought of butter pecan ice cream made her stomach rumble in anticipation. "How do you have ice cream?

Major Jericho's mouth dropped open and he put a hand on his chest. "Hey, not all of our really cool tech is used for pushing spaceships or blowing shit up."

Chapter 15

Zack bounced from his seated position so hard he fell over. He laughed as Ix helped him up. "Ice cream! You actually have ice cream? Ix! They have ICE CREAM!"

Major Jericho and Liz laughed as they unsealed the black pack that Major Jericho always kept near him in camp. Inside it lay a hard-sided crate. Major Jericho pressed his thumb to the lock and it popped open. White mist spewed from the unsealed container when he lifted the lid. He set the cover aside. Liz rummaged through a pack and procured five stainless steel sporks.

"All right, who wants what?" Major Jericho looked over his shoulder. "Some of us may have to share, because I'm telling you right now, I didn't get stuck in a faraway galaxy to eat grubby roots and bloody fungus."

"Chocolate!" Zack bounded toward the major but stopped short when Jenny stepped in front of him.

"I would like some rum raisin, please."

Major Jericho tossed a 500-milliliter container to Zack, then handed one to Jenny. He looked at the Valtraxian. "Ix?"

Skittering forward, Ix tapped its fingers together. "I am incapable of tasting subtle nuances in flavor, so if it is all sweetened dairy product, the Ersidian sweet root and piney grub or Kerrolian bloody fungus will be fine."

"Thanks for taking one for the team, Ix." Major Jericho handed Ix a container labeled with neon blue letters on an olive green-and-magenta checkerboard. He held out one for Liz. "Butter pecan, right?"

"You remembered!" Beaming, she took the ice cream.

"Well, good old vanilla for me." He sealed the pack and shoved it aside, then sat at the table. "I could go for some dark chocolate syrup and a cherry right now."

Liz rolled her eyes back in her head as she sucked on the spork. "Oh, toppings. To have such luxuries, I'd think we weren't in the service anymore. Or at least, I'd think we were back at headquarters."

Zack tugged at the lid. It came loose without warning and flew across the cabin. "Oops."

"We'll get it later." Major Jericho waved his spork at the pack on the floor. "Don't feel obligated to eat it all at once. We can put them back in the cooler for later. Even though it's open now, it'll still keep cold for two or three days. By then, we can have all the ice cream, burgers, and other junk food we can cram into our mouths or mandibles."

As he plunged the spork into the cold, chocolate delight, Zack contemplated if he wanted to eat it all at once, or not. He felt like it'd been years since he'd had any real food. He promised himself he would try to save some for the next day and brought the spork to his mouth. The ice cream felt silky and creamy as it melted on his tongue, the chocolate rich and deeply satisfying.

After savoring a couple of sporkfuls, Zack glanced over at Ix. The Valtraxian stabbed at the ice cream it held and brought the spork to its mandibles. Ix hesitated before tasting it.

"Well, how is it?" Zack spoke around the spork in his mouth, determined to prevent curiosity from interrupting his dessert.

"It is very cold." Ix clicked its mandibles on the spork. "I detect sweetness, but the piney grub is not as grub-like as I expected. I am surprised I can actually taste it."

Zack shrugged. "I guess you really like piney grub? I've never even seen one."

"They're fat, yellow worm-things about the same length as the distance between the heel of your hand to the tip of your middle finger." Liz crunched on a candied pecan from her ice cream. "They have four bulbous green eyes and they're covered in hairy spines. Ersidians love them, of course."

"Ew. Sounds like a gross caterpillar." Zack tried not to think about eating them for fear it would put him off his ice cream.

"It is nothing like a caterpillar." Ix clattered its mandibles across its spork, slurping up ice cream. "It does not metamorphosize into an insect. It simply burrows and aerates the ground, eating algae and fungi, similar to Terran earthworms. The Ersidians raise them for food."

Zack stomach lurched. He stood and retrieved the lid to his ice cream container. "I think I'll save the rest for tomorrow."

His stomach lurched again and he noticed Jenny frowning. She placed a hand over her stomach.

"Did the grub talk get to you, too, Jenny?" Zack sat at the table across from her.

"No." She shook her head. "Something's wrong."

Major Jericho sat bolt upright. "If you're going to be sick," he pointed toward the airlock. "Use the latrine while it's still clean."

Jenny bolted for the airlock. Zack's breath quickened and he doubled over as his stomach knotted itself. "Uh-oh."

"I got this, Major." Liz thrust a gunny sack at Zack.

Zack fingered the rough synthetic weave of the sack as he fought to keep the ice cream and dinner inside his stomach. He retched. When his insides were finished turning themselves inside out, he drew the bag shut and leaned back. "Nuts. That was really good ice cream."

Liz took the sack from him. "I'll check on Jenny." She headed toward the airlock.

Major Jericho moved to sit next to Zack. He put his hand on the back of the young man's neck. "How do you feel? Feverish? Does your stomach hurt? Headache?"

Zack thought about it for a moment and shook his head. "I feel like I just puked, but other than that, you know, pretty normal. I wasn't feeling bad before the ice cream."

Liz and Jenny returned from the airlock. Jenny reported feeling similarly. Major Jericho inspected their containers of ice cream. "I can't believe we got a bad batch. Lieutenant Herd, run samples through the analyzer. See if the milk went rancid or something. It wouldn't be the strangest thing to happen on this trip."

She took the containers and placed them at the end of the conference table while she searched through the gear for the portable analyzer. After a few moments, she returned with it and place a spoonful of the rum raisin in the device, then the chocolate.

"They're both fine, Major. Whatever made them sick wasn't the ice cream." Liz stowed the containers in the cooler then collected hers, Ix's, and Major Jericho's.

"We'll have to have you checked out when we get home." The major tapped the handle of his spork against the table. "I'm guessing it's something related to what made you sick on the planet."

Zack rubbed his sides and shifted a bit to allow cool air from the air circulation system blew on him. "I've been eating the other food just fine."

"So have I." Jenny slumped in her chair and stared up at the ceiling.

"Our rations are pretty bland. That was full-fat dairy ice cream. Neither one of you have had anything that rich since we left Cytherea."

"At least we didn't eat it all." Jenny sighed and glanced at Zack. "Hopefully we'll get home before the cooler fails and it melts.

"Yeah, hopefully." For a brief moment, Zack wondered if they were stuck eating boring, bland food for the rest of their lives. No pizza, no fried cheese, no burgers. Just flavored nutrient paste. The thought dampened his excitement for returning home.

—— 《》 — 《》 — 《》 — 《》 — 《》 — 《》 ——

They ate rations for the next couple of days. Since they couldn't help the Athosians test systems, there was little to do except chat, straighten gear they'd already secured and straightened, and sleep. Jenny chose to spend part of that time composing messages to her parents and Hiri to send as soon as they connected to the hypernet again. She counseled Zack to do the same and heard him recording messages to his parents, Rio, and Dravs during his various trips to the latrine.

On the second day of orbit, just before they were about to eat their midday meal, Alpha Primus's voice crackled over the intercom. "We have completed our testing. All systems are operational. We will be leaving orbit in the next five minutes, then translating once we're out of the planet's gravity well."

Major Jericho raised an eyebrow. "Is it safe to translate this deep in a solar gravity well?"

"It is safe for this ship, yes. There may be slight fluctuations in the ship's gravitational field and lighting systems when we translate. These should not persist for more than a few seconds. Do you require anything before we depart?"

Major Jericho looked to each traveler in turn. Their collective silence indicated no one wanted to cause a delay.

"No, we're all fine and ready to go home."

"Acknowledged."

"We probably should hang on to something." Liz braced herself against the table. "We don't exactly have proper seats and restraints if the gravity cuts out."

Jenny reached for Zack's hand and offered him a smile. He grinned and bounced in his seat, then braced his knees and free hand on the table. Unlike every other ship Jenny had ever traveled on, the Athosians did not offer a countdown to translation. Fortunately, the ship's second translation did not resemble in any way the one that brought them to Athos. Jenny normally found the stretching sensation unpleasant, but with the Athosians' repaired drive, she barely felt any effects from the jump. "Is that it? Are we home?"

The rapid-fire pings from notifications assaulting Zack's C7, as well as the cringing around the room as Major Jericho and Liz' received notifications via their implants answered Jenny's question. Zack scrambled to silence his C7's notification alert. Having long ago shut off tactile indicators from her communication implants, Jenny checked to make sure her messages sent before loading the notification screen. The number steadily counted upward into the hundreds. A rock settled in the pit of her stomach, and despite common sense warning her not to, she checked the date.

Three months. "That's it? Three months?" She looked around the room. "We were only gone three months!"

Still a long time to be without contact, a quarter of a year felt far less traumatic than the worst-case decade they all expected.

"Alpha Primus did say our jump drive technology was primitive compared to theirs." The lines of worry and dread

Major Jericho's face carried for the duration of their ordeal vanished as a smile spread across his face.

As if on cue, an Athosian voice crackled over the ship-wide communication system. "We've arrived in the Sol system. However, there appear to be sizable fleets of Devoran and human ships in orbit around the second and third planets of the system. We are calculating a new jump to a safer destination."

"No wait—" Before Major Jericho finished voicing his concern, the ship lurched slightly and Jenny felt an ever-so-slight sensation of being stretched. When the sensation ended, she watched as her communications implant updated again. Only a few minutes elapsed.

"Where are we now?" Zack activated his C7 and scrolled through the notifications.

Jenny checked her settings to see which network her implants connected to for updates. *Please be in our galaxy.*

She found her answer just as a gruff voice intruded over the comm system. "Unidentified ship: your arrival to the Ersidian Sovereignty is unscheduled. Please identify yourselves."

"Ersid?" Zack's eyes lit up. "We went to Ersid?"

Liz and Major Jericho swore in unison. They then looked at Zack, Jenny, and Ix. Major Jericho cleared his throat. "Sorry about that. Involving the Ersidians massively complicates things."

Ix cocked its head. "The Ersidians are among the founding members of the Confederation. Will they not be willing to render assistance?"

"Yeah, they're founders of the Confederation, but they've been spoiling for a fight with the Devorans for centuries." Liz shut her eyes and pressed two fingers to her temple; a common gesture for one concentrating on the information fed to them by their implants.

"What do you kids know about Ersid? Any of you ever been here?" Major Jericho pushed himself up from his seat and opened the door to the entry room to check on Coulson's body.

"No." Zack and Jenny answered as one.

"I have not." Ix's reply overlapped his friends'.

"Our friend Mungus is here. He goes to the Royal Citadel." Zack bounced in his chair, then noticed Major Jericho near Coulson's body and shrank into his seat.

Ix clicked its fingers together. "Ersid is the largest satellite of the second planet in this system. Measured against Terra, Ersid is slightly larger with a correspondingly higher gravity—"

"I meant Ersidians as a society, not literal facts about the planetary system." Major Jericho clasped his hands behind his back as he stood in front of the blank walls the Athosians provided them as a viewscreen.

"Ersidians talk about honor a lot." Zack furrowed his brow as he thought. "A lot of people think they're all talk."

Jenny sniffed. "They're certainly not all talk about their hair."

"If we disembark here, please, please"—Major Jericho leaned forward—"please let me do the talking. No comments. No interjections. They can be very particular about protocol. The Ersidians you've encountered so far are laid back and relaxed because they're not on their homeworld."

Ix chittered and glanced at Zack. "Mungus is laid back?"

Major Jericho banged on the wall. "Hey, can you hear us? If we're at Ersid, you're going to want me to do the talking here. Or at least include me."

The screen snapped on, split into two halves. On the left, the amorphous shape of Alpha Primus floated outside their environment suit in the fluid medium Athosians called home. On the right, a black-furred Ersidian scowled. A high-colored white military uniform contrasted against his dark fur.

"This is Major Thomas Jericho of the Earth-Alpha Centauri Alliance. I have three civilians with me, as well as one of my aids—"

The Ersidian reached forward and tapped his screen. "I have audio, but no video."

"Apologies." Alpha Primus bobbed. "We did not have time to install cameras in the environment we created to sustain their life, though they do have access to a viewscreen."

Major Jericho took a breath and started again. "We have been fired upon by Devoran ships, and I hereby request asylum for myself, Lieutenant Elizabeth Herd, Zack Jackson, Jenny DuBois, and Ix"—the major looked over his shoulder at the Valtraxian—"in accordance with the Treaty of—"

The Ersidian waved his hand. "I do not need the whole recitation. I have standing orders to assist any EAC vessel during this... conflict, and since the Athosians are no longer recognized as a sovereign government, we will assume it applies to you as well. I am transmitting coordinates for your ship to dock."

Alpha Primus spun slowly as the coordinates arrived. "This vessel requires a body of water in which to land."

"Water? What about a hover dock with clamps?" The Ersidian stared into the screen and blinked before shifting his gaze downward. Each time Major Jericho tried to interject, the Ersidian held up a single finger.

"That is acceptable."

Finally, the Ersidian returned his attention to the screen. "I have obtained authorization for you to dock at The Valiant Citadel Space Dock. Be advised, as this is connected to the grounds of the royal palace, any deviation from the assigned flight path will result in your immediate destruction. Any sign of weapons powering up, the same. Is that understood?"

Zack's heart seized, and his stomach knotted.

"Your instructions are clear. This vessel is unarmed. We will comply." The screen blanked out.

Major Jericho threw up his hands and returned to his seat. "I don't know why I'm surprised."

"We are just passengers, sir." Liz brushed a lock of hair behind her ear.

"And we're going to Ersid." Zack grinned at Jenny. The young woman did not return his smile.

Chapter 16

The Athosians did their passengers the courtesy of keeping the viewscreen on in the conference room as they made their approach to The Valiant Citadel in Taella City. The ship flew over forested foothills toward a city constructed on and within the sides of mountains. Although the emerald foliage reminded Zack of home, the vibrant verdant hues resembled a painting more than any forest he had seen on Earth. From their current position, the city glittered like shards of ice jutting from the mountainsides.

As they came about, light from the setting sun reflected off metal structures in the city and bathed the mountains with a golden glow. The silver spires of the royal palace caught the sunlight and glowed pink and red as the ship swooped around on its approach to the cliff-side lake. The ship skimmed over Lake Xarth's surface before banking toward a gap between the two tallest peaks. Following lights that appeared ahead and to the left, they could soon see the docking facility.

The curved glass panel façade of the space dock facility was built into the carved-out mountainside, spanning a kilometer or more, and reflected the ships coming and going. Individual dock-like piers jutted from the outer walkways, with masses of conduit and cables dangling from them like jungle vines.

Through the viewscreen, they saw a contingent of guards marching in lockstep out onto the docks, their sharp white uniforms a crisp contrast to their dark fur and the grey and black stone work of the facility.

After the ship swooped around and approached the dock, the screen switched off. Major Jericho crossed his arms and sighed. "Don't get too excited. We may have to stay on the ship a bit."

"Not too long, I hope." Zack bounced in his seat. "I have to go."

"I hear you." Major Jericho chuckled. "I almost gave up hope of ever using a regular lavatory again."

"Or a proper shower." Jenny brushed her hair out of her face.

"Or a bath." Liz nodded at Jenny.

The sound of docking clamps attaching themselves to the ship reverberated through the hull.

"Do they have pizza and cheeseburgers on Ersid?" Zack looked at the major through wide eyes. He hoped whatever made him vomit up the ice cream was gone, or there existed a pill, or shot, that could fix it.

The major laughed. "I'm sure they'll be able to rustle up something close. Don't get too excited though, they have to examine you and Jenny first, and we're probably going to have to have some proper Ersidian meals first."

"You should like that, Zack." Jenny smirked. "I hear it's all fatty meat and salt."

Ix cocked its head and chittered. "I assume you are not speaking literally."

The airlock door whooshed open, flooding the conference room with natural light. The armored form of Alpha Primus eclipsed the blinding glare. "Please exit. The Ersidian Commander has assured us you will be treated as honored guests."

At first, no one moved, then one by one, they followed Major Jericho's lead and exited the ship. A faint fruity aroma wafted by on the breeze. Ersidian shuttles whizzed by. At a nearby dock, Zack saw another ship that resembled a metal slab with domed buildings on it. Near the horizon, gossamer clouds painted a pink-and-orange sky. When Major Jericho stepped off the gangplank, dozens of white-uniformed Ersidians soldiers snapped to attention as the travelers set foot on sovereign Ersid soil. The group turned and proceeded toward the building.

A brown-furred Ersidian, his chest laden with medals resembling armor plating, held up his hand as the group neared the end of the dock. The Ersidian officer saluted Major Jericho once they stopped.

The major returned the salute. "Major Thomas Henry Jericho, EAC Fleet Command Diplomatic Corps. Not exactly protocol, is it?"

The Ersidian grinned, accentuating a scar that ran from the bottom of his eye down to his throat. "Under normal circumstances, no. But you are the first travelers to ever return from another galaxy, isn't that right? Torgusmanfarrinan, son of Korvannistik, Honored Smith of Clan Grizzlemaw, Commander of the Silver Guard of His Superior Ferocity King Gruncikammer, son of Mandikarrinus the Impatient, Seventh Sovereign of the Kingdom of Ersid and Ruler of the Ersidian Sovereignty."

Zack attempted to recite the name to himself but lost his place somewhere around the third syllable.

"Torg is acceptable since you humans seem to have trouble with our names." The commander looked past Major Jericho at the rest of the group. "That goes for the Valtraxian, too, even though I know you're able to remember it, right?"

Ix tilted its head. "Yes, Commander Torgusmanfarrinan."

"I am your liaison. Anything you need, I'll see to. I've been instructed to bring you anything you need to make you comfortable for the night. Unfortunately, you have to be quarantined until we determine whether you've brought any contagions back with you, so I hope you have comfy bunks in that ship."

"Not really, no." Major Jericho's shoulders slumped. "The ship wasn't configured for us to be passengers, so we're using bedrolls on the floor of a conference room. Aren't you breaking quarantine by standing here talking to us?"

Commander Torg glanced at the sky. "Eh, even with this breeze out here, you're far enough away that I'm not worried. So, you're roughing it, eh?" The Ersidian chuckled. "I'll see about getting you some tents and cots set up out here. The weather should cooperate for the next couple of days, long enough for us to get you quarantined indoors, anyway. It can get windy, so don't set up too close to the edge."

"We appreciate that. We have tents, and the bedrolls I mentioned, but I imagine yours are better."

"Absolutely." Commander Torg pointed to the junction where the dock met the stone of the port's sidewalk. "Stay on the dock. We need to erect some barriers. It's only temporary, and you'll each have to submit to a full medical examination before you're permitted to leave. Understood?"

"Yes, standard quarantine protocols. No problem." Major Jericho looked over his shoulder, fixing his gaze on Zack, then turned back to Commander Torg. "One of my soldiers was killed in action. Would it be possible to have his body stored in an appropriate facility until we can get him home? Right now, he's with our gear. Not ideal, you understand?"

"Completely." Commander Torg turned and barked some orders in Ersidian to one of his troops. The soldier saluted and jogged toward the building. "I've sent for a team to double-time it with appropriate protective gear to have him removed. We'll keep him in our morgue for now. Is there anything else?"

"Zack and Jenny became ill while on Athos and have been having trouble consuming anything more complicated than our emergency field rations. They need medical examinations ASAP, and would it be acceptable to stretch our legs here on the dock, or would you prefer for us to stay in the ship until our quarantine area is set up?"

"It's your choice. Just uhh, don't fall off the dock, right? It's a long way down." Commander Torg looked past Major Jericho at the three Junior Rangers. "We'll get a doctor suited up and get them checked out."

Zack peered over the edge. Below the space dock, gnarled trees grew among jagged crags. While there was a guard rail, nothing prevented someone from climbing over it. The bottom looked to be at least several hundred meters away.

"I wonder what's down there?" Zack glanced at Ix.

Before the Valtraxian answered, Commander Torg responded, "Rocks, trees, glommy birds, and creeping crystals.

It's a royal nature preserve, so don't get any funny ideas about exploring."

"We're not going anywhere until you say so, Commander." Major Jericho looked over his shoulder at Zack. "Right?"

"Right." Zack nodded.

"Fine." Commander Torg waved a paw the size of Zack's head. "Unpack what you need for the night. I'll have some food brought out for those of you who can eat it, and we'll deal with everything else in the morning."

"Thank you, Commander." Major Jericho turned to Liz. "Once they've taken Coulson, I want you to help me set up my tent out here. Anyone else who wants to sleep out here on the dock is welcome, but only unpack what you need for tonight. I have a feeling they'll have temporary quarters for us by tomorrow and we can unpack more fully. Until then,"—Major Jericho spread his arms—"stretch your legs, and welcome to Ersid."

—— 《》— 《》— 《》— 《》— 《》— 《》——

Despite her disappointment at not actually being home and not being able to eat real food, Jenny felt relieved to be somewhere safe. Zack and Ix weren't terrible roommates—certainly they were less obnoxious than her dorm mates back on Cytherea—so she elected to stay with them in the conference room while Major Jericho and Lieutenant Herd set up tents outside on the dock.

Leaving Zack and Ix to entertain themselves, she leaned back in her chair to place her feet on the conference table and sorted through three months' worth of messages. The first were messages from her girlfriend asking if she was all right just after the Athosian ship fled Cytherea, then came the increasingly frantic messages from Hiri, her parents, and her friends when it seemed like she had disappeared. She stopped reading after the third message of that type and scrolled through the rest. Jenny noticed after about a month elapsed, she received messages from only Hiri and her parents. Despite her misgivings, she opened the first of these later messages from Hiri.

The young woman's face appeared in Jenny's view. Hiri's puffy eyes indicated she'd been crying. Her hair hung limp, framing her face, and she started and stopped a couple of times before finally finishing her message. "Jenny, some people think there's no point in even sending this, but I disagree. A couple of days ago, you and Zack and umm... Ix? You were declared dead."

What? What? Jenny stopped the message and played it again to make sure she did not misunderstand Hiri. She let it continue past the declaration of death.

"The Devorans say they have confirmed the ship you were on was destroyed when it made a translation jump just after leaving Venus's atmosphere. But no one has seen this evidence. Certainly, nothing came down on Venus, and if the ship had broken up that close to the planet, something would have been noticed. The EAC is saying they have no evidence that confirms the Devorans' claim, but they don't have any evidence that contradicts it, either."

Hiri paused to wipe her eyes. "I can't believe you're gone. I won't believe it. I know that you must have had a really good reason for not sending me a message these last several weeks. The Devorans won't even say what ship you were on, but everyone here says it was Athosian. There have been a lot of fights every time a Devoran is around and someone says something like that. I think Verrak has spent more time in detention for fighting than he has in the dorm.

"It's getting scary around here. We can't see them from the city, but people are saying more and more ships are arriving every day, EAC and Devoran. Once Devoran ships arrived, Princess Valianna made a big show of leaving. School administration has locked out the news channels in our dorm rooms, so everyone knows something big is about to happen. I'm worried. I miss you. I hope you're safe."

After Hiri's message ended, Jenny closed her comm interface. She didn't think she could stand to listen to the panicked voices of her parents at the moment. To her relief, the airlock door whooshed open. A hulking Ersidian wearing a positive pressure personnel suit and carrying a bag slung over his shoulder entered. His bulky, muscular form crammed into the bright red-and-black suit made him resemble some sort of demon. An assistant followed him, carrying a large case. She erected a privacy screen in the corner, then unpacked.

"Two humans and... a Valtraxian? I was only told to examine the humans. Valtraxian: out!"

Ix chittered and rubbed four pairs of hands together. "I... well... that is..."

Jenny sat up. "It's all right, Ix. You know how gruff Ersidians can be."

"Gruff?" The Ersidian shook his head as Ix passed him on its way out. "No, I'm Dr. Zedokorian Kinkorrian, son of the Honorable Jessikmandagus the Lesser, Advisor to Mandikarrinus the Impatient, Seventh Sovereign of the Kingdom of Ersid."

"Um"—Zack stood and straightened his shirt—"can we just call you Dr. Kinko?"

A rumble arose from the doctor's throat, magnified by the speaker built into his suit. "Dr. Zedokorian would be more appropriate if you insist on shortening my name."

"We mean no offense, Doctor." Jenny gestured for Zack to sit in the chair opposite her.

The physician approached Zack, towering over him. "Now then, both of you behind the screen and strip down."

Jenny felt her face grow hot, and she noticed Zack turn beet red. "What? Together?"

Another rumble from the doctor. "Ugh. Humans. I'd assumed your rumored hang-ups were exaggerations. It's more efficient to examine you together since I have to do both of you and this suit is as uncomfortable as sticking a piney grub up your nose, but whatever." He pointed at Jenny. "You. Girl. Go wait in the outer room there while I examine this cub. When I'm finished, I'll send him out to send you in."

He turned to Zack as his assistant left. "Is that acceptable?"

"Fine with me." Jenny jumped up from the chair. "Tell him everything, Zack. He's here to help." She whispered, "I hope," under her breath as she entered the outer room, still cluttered with all their gear, and shut the door behind her.

Chapter 17

Once Jenny closed the door, Dr. Zedokorian directed Zack behind the privacy panel. "Take off your clothes and stand in the scanner. Try not to move until I tell you the scan is complete."

Zack did as instructed and waited in the scanner, a two meter tall semicircle of metal embedded with shiny circular discs. After a minute or two, the doctor told him to get dressed and take a seat. "Leave your jacket off, I need to draw blood."

When he emerged from the private scanning area, Zack watched as Dr. Zedokorian opened a pouch at his side and laid several instruments on the table, none of which looked familiar to Zack. Although he recognized a syringe lying next to several vials.

"This is going to hurt, isn't it Dr. Zevorkian?"

"Zedokorian." The Ersidian peered through his faceplate at Zack. "Ancestors take me, you humans are scrawny and hairless." He poked Zack in the chest. "Does anything hurt?"

Zack rubbed his sternum. "Other than where you just poked me, not really. I feel fine."

Dr. Zedokorian grabbed Zack's arm and leaned over to have a closer look. "Hm. Fine hairs... what are these brown spots?"

"Um, freckles?"

He turned Zack's arm over, so the elbow faced down, and flicked the inside of his elbow with a finger. "They usually take blood from here, right?"

Zack felt sweat roll down his back, despite the chilly air blowing down on him from the air handling system. "You've done this before haven't you?"

"Of course, I have. But I've never gotten up close and personal with a human before." He grabbed the syringe and fitted a needle to it, then swabbed Zack's arm with an alcohol patch. "This won't hurt nearly as much as a ziki sting."

"Well, that's good." Zack shivered. He had no idea what a ziki sting was, but if an Ersidian thought it hurt, he didn't want to know.

Dr. Zedokorian knelt to meet Zack's eyes. "You don't pass out for needles, do you? You okay with blood draws and shots and things like that?"

Zack nodded and frowned. "Yeah, I guess. They don't really use needles when they give us shots anymore."

"Yeah, well, it's still the best way to get blood out." He set down a vial full of dark red blood and squeezed Zack's arm. "Done."

"What?" Zack looked down at his arm to find the physician's giant gloved hand clamped around his elbow. "Wow... I didn't feel that at all."

The doctor chuckled and set the syringe on the table while he bandaged the draw site. He picked up a long, wand-like instrument from the table. After he flicked a switch on it, the forward half of the shaft glowed blue. "You'd almost think I was a professional."

Dr. Zedokorian leaned against the conference table and put the blood vial in his pouch before withdrawing a small tablet. He gestured for Zack to move his chair adjacent to him. "I'll have to send your blood to the lab for analysis. I don't suppose you saved any of the vomitus?"

"Ew, no." Zack grimaced at the thought.

"Of course not," The doctor grumbled. "That would have helped my analysis." He studied the screen of his tablet. "What did you eat and drink on... Athos, was it?"

"Yeah..."

Dr. Zedokorian looked over the edge of his tablet at Zack. "Really? It's true? You guys actually went to Athos? I heard rumors it was in a different galaxy."

"It is, the one we call the Large Magellanic Cloud."

"Huh. I don't know which of ours that corresponds to, but wow." He returned his attention to the tablet. "So, food? Water?"

"We couldn't find any food to eat and all the plants seemed toxic, so we just ate EAC emergency rations. We used a military purifier to filter all our water. That's all I had until the ice cream I puked up."

"Hm. Really?"

"Oh, umm, I swallowed some water when Jenny and I got stuck and the tides came in really fast. We had to swim and there were pretty high waves."

Dr. Zedokorian lowered the tablet. "You drank unfiltered water from an alien planet?"

Zack recoiled from the Ersidian. "Not on purpose! We almost drowned."

"Why are there traces of zykornium-gamma in your system?"

"What?" Zack had never heard of the compound.

"It's a Devoran chemical agent. It was declared illegal a couple of centuries ago." He flipped the tablet around and pointed toward green glowing spots clustered in Zack's abdomen. "Why is it in your gastrointestinal system?"

Zack's breath quickened. He gripped the arms of his chair. "I don't know."

"Hey, hey, calm down." The physician put his hand on Zack's shoulder. "It may not mean anything. I don't have a baseline for comparison because I don't have access to your medical records. For all I know all humans have trace amounts of zykornium-gamma in their systems."

"Maybe it was in that water we drank." He wondered if the filtration units really cleaned the water everyone consumed, but no one else except he and Jenny got sick. "The unfiltered water."

"That would actually make sense." Dr. Zedokorian tapped his finger against the top of the tablet. "But how would a Devoran chemical agent get to Athos in another galaxy?"

For a moment, Zack considered claiming ignorance, then he remembered what Major Jericho said about making sure as many people knew as possible and not keeping quiet no matter what. "There was a crashed Devoran ship there from the war. Actually, it was an Athosian ship the Devorans captured and used to sneak to Athos. Their log said they dropped a bunch of chemical and biological weapons on the planet."

"Oh, krunk." The doctor tried to bury his face in his hands, but his helmet stymied him. "Krunk and krunk. And you saw it?"

"The last log entry of Captain Drellex Fon, captain of that ship, but not the crashed ship itself." Zack nodded. "He said it would make the planet uninhabitable for higher lifeforms for generations, or something like that."

Dr. Zedokorian held up his hands. "This is way beyond my pay grade. Just go send the girl in, and I'll examine her, then get these samples to the lab."

"All right." Zack grabbed his backpack on his way out. He opened the outer door to find Jenny leaning against a bulkhead, tears in her eyes. "He's ready for you."

"Yes, all right." Jenny wiped her eyes. "Sorry, just listening to the messages from my parents. Bad idea."

"Are they okay?" Zack hoped no further calamities had befallen her parents.

"*Oui, oui*. Fine." She hugged him. "It's just hard. Hopefully they'll hear our good news soon."

Zack supposed he should listen to his messages at some point. He had some from his parents, Dravs. Even his grandparents sent messages, and usually they didn't contact him even for his birthdays. Once Jenny joined Dr. Zedokorian, Zack left the ship and joined Ix on the dock.

—— 《》 — 《》 — 《》 — 《》 — 《》 — 《》 ——

Before Jenny shut the door, Dr. Zedokorian directed her to step behind the privacy panel, disrobe, then stand in the scanner. The portable scanner they had set up wasn't terribly different than ones she'd seen on Messier Habitat or on Cytherea, albeit sized for an Ersidian. Once she undressed, she stood in the scanner, clenching her jaw as cool air from the circulators blew on her. After Dr. Zedokorian indicated her full-body scan had completed, she dressed while he uploaded the data and prepared syringes to take blood.

"Have a seat and hold out your arm." His commanding no-nonsense approach reminded Jenny of her father before his accident. She did as instructed and looked away as he prepared to insert the needle.

"Feeling all right? No unusual aches, pains, growths, bruises, spots?"

Jenny shook her head. "No."

"Good. Did you happen to save any of the vomitus from either episode of GI distress?"

She grimaced. "No, but maybe in the latrine." She gestured toward the airlock.

"No good. It would have been broken down within hours." He furrowed his brow as he looked at her face. "What's wrong with your eyes? They look very irritated."

"I was listening to messages from my parents and girlfriend while waiting. They were told we were dead."

The doctor grunted. "Hm. You're young for the tech you have implanted." He sat at the conference table and glanced at his tablet. "Oculus B3s, Hyperdyne Systems 20A2s, and Omnicor Hypernet X?"

Jenny sat next to him. "People from Messier get them with their ocular and comm implants, even if they choose not to use them. Saves future surgeries. I haven't set up the AI digital assistant."

"Ugh, cyborgs. You humans and your implants." Dr. Zedokorian snorted. "Whatever, it's your body."

Jenny bit her lip to keep from retorting. During her brief flirtation with Mungus, he held similar views regarding her implants. Ersidians used them only as a life saving measure, rather than a life enhancement.

"You have the same trace amounts of zykornium-gamma in your gastrointestinal system as the boy cub. Is that normal for humans?"

"What is that?" Jenny never heard of such a thing and wouldn't know if it was normal in any case.

"It's a Devoran chemical agent. It's been illegal for centuries."

The water! "It's probably not normal, but both Zack and I got sick from swallowing water when we had to swim across an inlet."

"Krunk." Dr. Zedokorian thumped the table. "If I only had a baseline for comparison. It'll be weeks before I get your medical records, assuming your guardians allow me access. By then, you probably won't even be here."

I do not want to eat these stupid rations for weeks. "I have my medical records. I should be able to connect to your tablet and transfer them, assuming it uses standard hypernet protocols."

He glanced up at her. "Really? That would be tremendously helpful." He tapped the screen a few times. "Okay, go."

Jenny searched for the tablet among available connection points. Fortunately, between her implants and the hypernet portals, they translated the Ersidian script into a language she could read. A few moments later, she connected and transferred her records, then severed the link.

"Got it. Thank you, Jenny is it?" After he gathered up his gear, he stood. "I'll get these samples back to the lab. I'll check back this afternoon with an update."

Jenny followed him out. A warm breeze blew across the docks. Zack and Ix stood at the far end, looking down into the forest floor while Major Jericho and Lieutenant Herd conversed with Commander Torg, who kept a safe distance at the other end of the dock. She joined her friends.

"How was your examination, Jenny?" Ix adjusted his stance, clinging to the rails surrounding the corner of the dock.

"It was a medical exam. Like an Ersidian, he couldn't help but be judgy about my implants."

Ix cocked its head. "Was the doctor not an Ersidian?"

"He was, Ix." Zack turned around to face his friends.

"I do not understand."

Jenny waved. "Never mind. Hopefully, they'll figure out what's wrong. I'm tired of EAC emergency rations."

"Me too." Zack nodded in agreement. "Hey, they got our ice cream into a proper freezer, though, so once we can eat real food again, we'll have that waiting for us."

Jenny chuckled. "I'm sure we can get more ice cream. We can get pretty much anything like at home here." She looked out toward the cloud-streaked blue sky. "Well, maybe not exactly like home. But close enough."

"Hey, Major Jericho's coming." Zack pointed down the dock.

The major jogged over to join them. "I have some updates for you." He stood with his hands clasped behind his back and legs slightly spread. "Do you want the bad news first, or the good news?"

All three answered in unison. "Bad news."

"I don't blame you." He cleared his throat. "The Devorans and the EAC are having a stand-off above Venus. There have been shots fired, some deaths. Things are tense and, well, there's a lot of talk about war."

Jenny sank back against the railing.

Zack gasped. "War? Between us and the Devorans?"

"Cytherean administration has been taking the side of the Devorans, which, surprises no one since Devorus bankrolled

Cytherea to begin with. But the EAC council and chancellor take a dim view of Devoran ships invading their sovereignty and firing upon an EAC settlement. The EAC never recognized the Athosians as a hostile government, since that war was over way before our time on the galactic stage. I'm sure you all know by now the Devorans claim the ship was destroyed when it left Venus and us with it. We were declared dead by the Confederation approximately two weeks after we left. The EAC just had us officially listed as missing."

Jenny nodded. The messages she received from Hiri and her parents confirmed that. "But now they all have messages from us, the ones we sent when we translated back from Athos?"

"Yes, they should." Major Jericho chuckled. "Our reappearance is going to put a serious hitch in the Devoran narrative. News hasn't caught up out here yet, though that should happen today, depending on relay traffic. At any rate, ready for the good news?"

All three Junior Rangers nodded their affirmation.

"The Ersidians have not only notified the EAC and the Confederation that we're alive and well, including our families, but also they have issued a statement that we've been granted political asylum from the Devorans and are under their protection. The Devorans are willing to bully the EAC while we're petitioning entry into the Confederation, but they won't be eager to butt heads with a founding member. So, we're safe here."

Jenny relaxed a bit. Zack looked up at the major. "So, when can we leave the dock?"

"That's another bit of good news. We still have to stay quarantined until the medical staff has run complete examinations on Ix, Lieutenant Herd, and me, and until they figure out if what is affecting the two of you is contagious. However, they've arranged for quarters for us here at the space dock. We'll each have our own rooms, a common area, a rec room, and access to a fabricator. It'll be like a vacation where you just stay in your suite."

Jenny didn't think that sounded so bad. At least, it would be no different than staying in her dorm for a couple of weeks, except without obnoxious roommates, so possibly even better.

"Plus, the Ersidian government invited all of our families here, should they want a reunion before tensions die down enough for us to safely return to Cytherea. It'll be a few days before we hear back about that, of course."

Jenny's heart soared for a moment before she remembered the invitation probably would not include Hiri. "Just our families?"

"It's funny." Zack glanced at her and Ix. "My parents didn't want me to come to Ersid with the Junior Rangers, but now I'm here and they're probably going to come out here to see me. Mom hates space travel."

"I don't even know if my parents are well enough to travel." Jenny glanced at Ix who had no family to speak of. As usual, the Valtraxian's emotions remained impossible to glean from a glance.

Zack nudged her. "Don't worry, my mom is mom enough for all three of us."

Chapter 18

Zack grabbed his pack from the pile and passed Ix its gear. A team of Ersidians in protective suits had helped cart all the gear to the common area of their new, temporary home. Everyone immediately started sorting personal belongings from field equipment. Since each Junior Ranger had one bag or less, they finished within minutes.

The common area of the suite they'd been assigned resembled the common room of Zack's dorm. There were six doors leading to the other bedrooms and the kitchen and dining area, plus the entry door. A sunken space in the center of the room contained chairs to serve as a conversation area. They surrounded a low circular table with a built in comm system. A fabricator was installed into the wall between one of the bedrooms and the kitchen door. From outside the bedrooms, Zack could see each one had access to a private lavatory, as well as its own holoviewer.

"I guess we live there for now, Ix." Zack pointed toward one of the rooms off the common area.

"We each get our own room, Zack." Major Jericho moved some of the gear against the walls of the common area to free up the central conversation space.

Ix cocked its head. "Zack and I have always stayed together. If there is room, I do not see a reason to change that."

Liz looked at the pile of gear. "Well, if Ix isn't going to take that room, we could store all this extra gear in there."

"Good plan." Major Jericho carried one of the crates toward the unused bedroom. "If you kids help, we'll be done in no time."

With the five of them moving gear together, they finished in less than ten minutes. Once done, Major Jericho plopped into one of the armchairs.

He sighed as the doorbell chimed. "That figures."

"I got it." Jenny activated the door panel. Attired in a protective suit, Dr. Zedokorian greeted her on the viewscreen. She opened the door for him.

"All right, your blood is analyzed, and thanks to Jenny providing her medical records, I have an answer." He gestured for everyone to sit in the conversation pit as he pulled up information on his tablet.

"While it would be ideal to have access to Zack's medical records, I'm fairly confident about these results. The trace amounts of zykornium-gamma I found in the lining of Zack and Jenny's gastrointestinal tracts is most likely the result of accidental ingestion of contaminated water. Your military filtration systems did their job and removed all contaminants, so the rest of you don't have to worry, though I'm still going to examine all of you." He eyed both Major Jericho and Liz, then Ix.

"The cubs' blood work came back normal for humans, as far as I could tell. I've shared the analysis, anonymously, with a human colleague over in Grantiz. Of course, it's all over the news that you're here, so it doesn't take a genius to figure out whose blood samples I would have sent, but he's trustworthy."

"Okay, so the blood was normal, but what do we do about the chemical weapon exposure?" Major Jericho sat forward, furrowing his brow.

"Here's the problem with that." Dr. Zedokorian sighed. "Zykornium-gamma was outlawed before we or the Devorans even knew about humans, so no one knows what it does to your systems."

"I guess that's why our equipment couldn't detect it in the water." Liz glanced at Major Jericho.

The major nodded. "There were a lot of unidentifiable compounds in the water."

"That's not surprising. There is good news, however. We know what it's supposed to do."

Zack swallowed and glanced at Jenny. "How is that good news?"

The doctor turned to look at Zack. "Well, you didn't die horribly upon ingesting it. If you'd been Athosian it would have broken down all your cell membranes. Unfortunately, it seems to have caused damage to the mucosal lining of your stomach and intestines."

Jenny placed her hands on her stomach and frowned. "What kind of damage? Will it heal?"

"I can't say. It will, or it won't. Maybe you'll heal in a few months and you'll never have trouble again. Maybe you'll have chronic ulcers, cancers, maybe you can't eat regular food again."

"I don't like the sound of that." Zack looked down at his stomach. The thought of living the rest of his life on military-grade nutrient paste brought tears to his eyes.

Dr. Zedokorian shoved the tablet into his pouch. "If you were Ersidians, I'd tell you to look at it as a challenge of strength and will. Of course, if you'd been Ersidian, zykornium-gamma probably would've killed you already. I do not agree with many choices you humans make, about your lifestyles, about your medical practices, but regardless, I cannot solve this problem for you."

"So we're stuck with this." Jenny slapped her gut. "Whatever this is."

"I can't solve it for you, but I can give you some"—he sighed—"advice. Get scanned every week or so. While you're here, I'll be happy to do it. If it improves, great. Start eating regular food with caution. If it doesn't improve, or it starts getting worse? I'll refer you to Doctor Sterling over in Grantiz; he can consult on a GI replacement."

Zack sat up. "What's that?" He wondered if it was the type of enhancement Ix had that enabled the Valtraxian to eat pretty much anything.

"They'll replace your stomach and intestines with either cloned replacements or a cybernetic nutrient extraction system."

"That is what I have, Zack." Ix reached over and stroked its friend's arm.

"So, all food will taste the same if I have that?" Zack glanced over at Ix.

"No, they'll just replace your stomach and intestines, not your taste buds. Unless you replace your mouth with a Valtraxian's, you'll still taste food the way you used to. In the meantime, I'll have better supplements delivered. EAC emergency rations are perfectly edible and nutritious but they're not satisfying. We make a range of supplements for our asteroid miners that actually have flavor and varied textures, but they are gentle on sensitive digestive systems. They should be fine for you. Now, back to the exams." Dr. Zedokorian pointed to Major Jericho. "You first, Major. I can examine you in your room."

"Sure, Doctor." After pushing himself out of his chair, he approached the bedroom he'd chosen. The Ersidian doctor followed.

Jenny sat slumped in her chair, staring into space. Zack sighed. "I guess we're not going to be finishing that ice cream any time soon."

—— 《》 — 《》 — 《》 — 《》 — 《》 — 《》 ——

With access to the hypernet, Jenny wasted no time researching nutrient extraction implants. While a few more weeks of eating nutrient paste wouldn't kill her, she already decided she was not willing to face a lifetime of it. She expected Zack to make a similar decision if he hadn't already.

As she suspected, and Ix confirmed in his conversation with Zack, a cybernetic nutrient extraction system would replace her stomach and intestines with a more robust, efficient system capable of extracting nutrients from almost any organic matter and would filter out many known toxins, provided they weren't absorbed through the mucus membranes in the mouth.

Through the information covering her vision displayed by her implants, Jenny watched Major Jericho and Dr. Zedokorian emerge. The doctor then convened with Liz in her room. Major Jericho chatted briefly with Ix and Zack, then he went into the kitchen.

Upon opening her messages, she confirmed no new communications had arrived. Even with hypernet relays, there had been just barely enough time for messages to come back from the Sol system. She matched the current time against a chart she found with average hypernet transit times. Jenny frowned. According to the chart, transmissions should reach their destination within eighteen hours. Since she sent the messages in the brief time they were near Venus before jumping to Ersid, she noted some response, any response should have come in already.

"Zack?" Jenny shifted her focus from her implants to her environment. "Have you gotten any responses to the messages you sent to your parents yet?"

Zack pulled out his C7 and checked it. "No. Has it been long enough?"

"Yes, this morning." She tried to think of reasons why neither of them had received responses yet. "Even if they were taking their time, they should have sent something back by now."

"That is odd." Ix rose from the chair in which it had been curled up. "Even variations in orbital position would not cause this large of a variance in time delay."

"Do you"—Zack looked at his friends—"do you think the Devorans are doing something to keep our families from responding?"

"They wouldn't do that. Would they?" Jenny locked eyes with Zack. After a moment, she leaned back and searched the news for any information regarding the EAC and Devoran fleets around Venus.

Ix beat her to it. "According to this report by the Galactic Press Corps, the Devorans deactivated the EAC hypernet relays in the inner system. All comm traffic has to first travel to the outer relays at light speed, adding an additional seventeen hours before any comm traffic reaches the hypernet."

"Why would they do that?" Jenny closed her hypernet windows. "That doesn't seem like something they should be able to do. We're not even part of the Confederation."

"I do not know, Jenny."

"Know what?" Major Jericho sauntered out of the kitchen swigging from a bottle of beer.

Jenny looked over her shoulder at him. "The Devorans shut down the inner system hypernet relays back home. That's why we haven't heard back from our families yet."

Major Jericho scoffed. "That's... they wouldn't... that would be an act of war more egregious than firing on a ship docked to Cytherea."

"GPC is reporting it, Major." Ix cocked its head and chittered. "I can send the story to you if you like. Several other news agencies have recirculated the story. All news and communication coming from the Sol system is encountering an additional seventeen-hour delay."

The major set his beer down on the conversation pit table and swore. He activated the built-in comm system. A holoviewer rose from the center of the table.

"How may I help you?" the monotone voice of an Ersidian AI answered.

"Connect me to Commander Torg of the Silver Guard, please."

"Acknowledged. Stand by."

"What can I do for you, Major?"

Major Jericho stared at the scarred, brown-furred face of Commander Torg that appeared on the holoviewer. "Did you know about the Sol inner system comm relays being down?"

Furrowing his brow, Commander Torg scratched his chin. "Yes. My apologies. I assumed since you had been to the Sol system before coming here, you knew about the relays. The Devorans were censured in parliament over that move, but a censure and a bucket of spit will just get you wet."

"Is there anything else you are assuming we know about the situation in the Sol system? Keep in mind, we were there less than a minute before we had to jump again. Assume we know nothing about the current situation." Major Jericho stood with his hands on his hips as he stared down at the holoviewer.

With the comm relays down, Jenny worried things on Venus were worse than anyone knew, but she was grateful her parents, at least, were recovering from their injuries on Vilicus. Hiri, on the other hand, was stuck on Cytherea in the middle of the storm.

"I swear by my ancestors I wasn't withholding information from you." Commander Torg rubbed his brow. "The comm relays are down, and that's the reason there's such a large EAC and Devoran fleet presence in the system. A few shots were exchanged in the early days, but now it seems they're just locked in a staring contest. Marshall Voss insists the EAC is holding Princess Valianna hostage, while the EAC claims she's been granted asylum."

"She's not a hostage." Major Jericho clenched his fists. "She was on Cytherea temporarily en route to Vilicus."

"People know Voss is just posturing and he doesn't really care what's going on with the last daughter of a deposed royal family. He's just using her as an excuse."

"Plays well for the homeworld, eh, but the military knows he's full of"—Major Jericho glanced at Zack, Jenny, and Ix—"hot... air?"

Jenny chuckled at his odd hesitance to swear around them now. He didn't seem to hold back much on Athos, and it wasn't like they didn't hear language like that a dozen times a day from fellow students or even on holoprograms and in games.

"That's putting it mildly."

Major Jericho glanced at the trio again. "This isn't exactly a secure channel, if you know what I mean."

"Yes, I'm aware the holoviewer there is in the common area, and I can see the kids. What are your names again? Jack Zackson? Jenny Dubbaw?"

"Zack Jackson, Jenny DuBois, and Ixilchitil." Zack shifted in his seat, then leaned forward to get a better view of Commander Torg.

"Marshall Voss was all over the news the first few days after your disappearance, scapegoating the human kids. Says they gave aid and comfort to a hostile alien species, causing a direct threat to Princess Valianna, every Devoran citizen working on Cytherea, and to the Confederation itself. He talked up some sort of assault on Devoran troops, too."

Jenny's face grew hot, and she glanced at Zack from behind the holoviewer. He slumped back in his chair, his eyes wide.

"Look"—Commander Torg held up his hands—"I know it's frustrating being stuck there, and with news being slow, doubly so. But I cannot break quarantine. I'm told there's evidence some or all of you have been exposed to chemical and biological weapons, not to mention potential pathogens and microbes. Your desire to get back into the thick of things does not outweigh my responsibility for public safety. As soon as you all are cleared, His Superior Ferocity King Gruncikammer, son of Mandikarrinus the Impatient, Seventh Sovereign of the Kingdom of Ersid and Ruler of the Ersidian Sovereignty wants an audience. Frankly, we like the EAC better than we like the Devorans, so don't think you have to go it alone. Just don't be like King Mandikarrinus, all right? There's a reason he died while His Superior Ferocity was still a cub."

"Yes, I get the point." Major Jericho let his hands fall to his sides. "Thanks for your candor."

"I'll be in touch." Commander Torg ended the call.

Jenny understood Commander Torg's point as well, but that didn't ease her anxiety. She almost preferred the total radio silence of Athos to the long communication delay that increased her worry over the safety of her parents and Hiri. After picking up his beer, Major Jericho stalked off, pausing a moment to pat Zack on the shoulder. Jenny slid off her chair and moved to the one next to Zack.

"Ignore that liar Voss, Zack." Jenny touched his arm to get his attention. "He can't do anything to you, and I don't think the Ersidians will let him anyway."

"But what happens when I go back to Cytherean Academy? And now my parents have been hearing that I threatened the entire Confederacy?" He buried his head in his hands.

At least you're not the one who slapped a soldier. Jenny had no answer for Zack. All she and Ix could do was hold his hands and offer comfort as he came to grips with being declared a public enemy.

Chapter 19

Zack brushed off his friends' attempts to cheer him up. He shuffled into his room, shutting the door behind him. When he flopped on the bed, the ultra-plush bedding swallowed him like a fluffy monster. He twisted and flailed until he righted himself, then grabbed his pack and used it to pull himself upright.

"This is nuts. I didn't do anything wrong." He stared at the wall, hoping for something, anything to happen. Part of Zack wanted to succumb to despair, but instead, he found himself growing more and more angry. "I didn't do anything wrong!"

An overwhelming desire to see and hug his parents overcame him. He fumbled for his C7, lying back in the plush morass once he freed it from his pocket. He found the first message from his parents and played it.

They appeared on his screen, sitting together. His mother's red-rimmed eyes indicated she had been crying, and the deep lines of his father's frown creased his face. "Zack, please reply as soon as you get this message. The news reports are saying you were involved in some sort of terrorist plot on Cytherea. We heard that you managed to get on some mysterious ship that fled the city, they're saying it was Athosian? I don't even know how that's possible."

His mother put her hand on his father's arm. "Honey, we love you. Wherever you're hiding, please let us know you're all right."

The next several messages became increasingly frantic. Zack didn't have the heart to listen much past the first few seconds of each, so he switched to the first message from Dravs.

The blue-scaled Devoran's head spines bobbed as he adjusted his seat. "Hey Zack, um, first of all, thanks for all the various injuries you gave me lately, because I am really glad not to be involved in that plozik nest you poked."

Zack made a mental note to look up ploziks as Dravs continued. "People are saying you managed to get on that Athosian ship that jumped away, but that's"—he chuckled and looked off-camera—"I mean, you wouldn't get on an Athosian ship, right?"

Dravs's eyes glistened. "They... they say it blew up. When it jumped. That can't be, we would have seen the explosion from here and if it blew up, you'd be... you'd be dead. I hope you're not dead, Zack. I know you find me pushy and annoying sometimes, but you're my friend."

Zack paused the message. "Skip?"

He frowned at the long pause before remembering he'd turned off his C7's AI to conserve battery power on Athos. He reactivated it. "Yes, Zack?"

"What's a plozik?"

"A plozik is a lifeform native to Devorus. It resembles a Terran wasp, particularly in its aggressiveness. It possesses a painful sting and has been reported to chase quarry several kilometers in defense of its nest. Despite their superficial resemblance to insects, ploziks are closer, physiologically-speaking, to Terran reptiles."

"Got it."

The door creaked open. Ix stuck its head through the crack. "Are you all right, Zack?"

"Not really. I was listening to my messages to get my mind off the Devorans thinking I'm some sort of terrorist and I think it just made things worse."

Ix entered the room fully and pushed the door shut, then skittered up onto the bed. The ultra-plush mounds stymied the Valtraxian and Ix fell to the ground, clawing at the comforter.

Zack rolled to his side and looked down at Ix. "Are you all right?"

"Ersidian beds are very soft. I was not expecting that."

"It's like being swallowed by a cloud." Zack pushed down as much of the mattress as he could before extending a hand to Ix.

The Valtraxian leveraged itself onto the bed with Zack's aid. "I believe I will be using the blankets for a bed like we had on Cytherea. This is too soft, even for me. I would get lost."

"You know, maybe we should try to see Mungus while we're here." Zack rolled over to look at the ceiling. "Do you think they'll let us go places once we're done with quarantine?"

"I do not see why not, but we may be required to resume our academic studies here if we're unable to return to Cytherea soon. We've already missed three months of classes."

They chatted about school for a bit, then surfed the holoviewer channels until Liz came to check on them at dinnertime. Zack didn't relish the thought of weeks and weeks more of eating wet cardboard-flavored emergency rations, but it beat starving as the alternative. After dinner, he retreated to his bedroom again and checked his C7. The new message indicator showed three new messages, one each from his parents, Dravs, and Mungus.

He listened to the one from his parents first. His father appeared on the screen. "Damn, it's good to hear your voice, son. Your mom and I can hardly believe it. The EAC never went so far as to declare you dead, but the Devorans sure wanted everyone to believe it. I don't know that I really trust what we're being told about what's going on; there's so many conflicting reports, and with the relays down, we seem to be behind several days. Where are you now? Not back on Cytherea, I hope, not with those fleets facing off over Venus."

Zack realized his parents responded to his message before they received the one from the Ersidian government. He opened a reply message. "Mom, Dad, it's crazy. We had to jump to Ersid almost as soon as we got back home because of the fleets over Venus. We didn't know the relays were down, so I don't know how much you heard. Hopefully, you've gotten the message by now that the Ersidians have invited you here. We're in quarantine because we... we went to Athos. The Devorans wasted the planet, and they're worried we brought a disease or something contagious back with us. So far, we all seem to be okay. Well, except me and Jenny. We got stuck having to swim once and swallowed some of the ocean water and got really sick because of all the toxins in it. The emergency rations stay down, but we can't eat any real food without throwing up. The doctors are going to keep checking us to see if it's going to get better on its own, but maybe bring my medical records when you come, it might help. Um... I love you guys and hope you come here. I don't know how long they're going to want us to stay with all the trouble back home. Ix and Jenny are here, too, in case you didn't know. They're doing just fine." He looked up to see Jenny standing at the door. "Um, I should go. You should come here. Bye."

He sent the message then put his C7 down. "What's up?"

"You got a reply from your parents?" Jenny entered the room and leaned against the wall, looking at the puffy surface of Zack's bed with suspicion.

"Yeah. I don't think they got the message from the Ersidians yet. What did yours have to say?" Zack assumed Jenny came to see him because she received a reply from her parents.

"About what you would expect. They asked more questions than anything. They'd heard we'd been killed and they were very confused." She shook her head. "I have the sense their recovery from the accident didn't go well after we disappeared, so I don't know if they're going to be able to come here."

Zack thought for a moment about the communication delay. "By the time we find out whether or not our parents are coming here, we'll probably be out of quarantine."

Jenny smiled and nodded, then thrust her hands in her pockets. "I've already decided, if this doesn't get better, I'm getting that cyberstomach. I'm not eating that paste the rest of my life."

He'd been giving it some thought, as well, with every bite of the nutrient paste. "I kind of wish we could just get it done now. Maybe we can ask to eat separate from Major Jericho and Liz? I don't know what they were eating tonight, but it looked so good."

"Good idea, Zack." Jenny flashed a smile. "I'll go ask them right now."

—— 《》— 《》— 《》— 《》— 《》— 《》 ——

To Jenny's relief, Major Jericho and Liz understood her and Zack's request and seemed mortified they hadn't considered it. Both he and Liz promised not to have any regular food around Zack or Jenny. The next day, a team of Ersidian laborers suited up and converted the spare bedroom they'd been using for storage into a remote learning center for the three students. They removed the bed to make room for three terminals, and Major Jericho and Liz rearranged the stored gear to give each of the kids their own private study space.

At first, they weren't enthused about resuming school remotely on Ersid, but the boredom they faced stuck in the suite under quarantine proved worse than school. After a few days, Zack and Jenny realized the quarantine enabled them to proceed at a faster pace than they'd have been able to in classrooms full of other students.

After a week of quarantine, frustrating communications delays with their friends and parents, and an increasing disgust with nutrient paste, Jenny and Zack felt a sense of elation when Dr. Zedokorian returned for their follow-up scans.

They all gathered in the common area as he set up his equipment. "So far, none of you are showing any signs of any diseases or other contagious conditions, which is good. There is still the potential for viruses with long incubation periods for which you're asymptomatic, but I'm going to take blood from all of you again, and if nothing shows up in it or on your scans, I'm confident it'll be safe to let you out, as it were."

Under the doctor's supervision, nurses wearing protective gear set up a portable analysis lab, and erected the portable scanner behind a privacy screen as they had on the Athosian ship. As they finished up, he turned to the assembled visitors. "The Athosians have been surprisingly forthcoming sharing medical information from Athos before the Devorans wrecked it. There's no evidence that any Athosian diseases that were known at the time were cross-species transmittable, and it's highly unlikely any novel viruses evolved in that time that pose a risk to anyone in this galaxy."

He adjusted his protective suit. "I'll start with the blood draws. They can be analyzed while I'm doing the individual examinations."

Dr. Zedokorian started with Ix. "Any changes? Feeling all right?"

The Valtraxian chittered and bobbed up and down. "I am fine, though I am finding the hypernet access speed to be substantially slower than I am used to."

Jenny chuckled. *I'm not surprised Ix's main complaint is about the hypernet speed.*

The doctor grunted. "I can't do anything about that, but you're not wrong. It's glommy gut-slow here."

He handed the vial of Ix's blood to one of the nurses and moved on to Zack. "You? How's your eating?"

Zack looked away from his forearm when the doctor inserted the needle. "I'm sick of nutrient paste, but I've been afraid of eating anything else."

"That's understandable. We'll know after your scan today if you can risk trying some real food again." He finished up with Zack, handed off the vial and moved to Jenny.

She reported the same concerns to Dr. Zedokorian that Zack did. Jenny had been tempted to try eating a regular meal, but like Zack, she didn't relish the thought of vomiting again. She missed the textures and flavors of real food. At this point, she longed for it almost more than her parents or Hiri.

Once the doctor took all the blood samples he needed, he started with the full body scans. Jenny waited for her turn in her room, taking the chance to review some school assignments. When the physician entered, he instructed her to go behind the screen, disrobe, and stand in the scanner. Once he completed the scan, she dressed while he reviewed the data.

"Do you want the good news or the bad news?"

Jenny grimaced and pulled her shirt over her head. "Why does everyone keep asking that? Just tell me. The good news never buffers the bad."

"Well, the bad news is, there's no improvement in the condition of your stomach lining or intestines. In fact, there's actual deterioration."

"I'm not surprised. Can you just refer me for the surgery already?"

Dr. Zedokorian growled. "I don't really see that I'm going to have a choice. We'll need your parents' consent, however, since you're still considered a minor by EAC laws."

"I'm sure they'll consent. What's the good news?"

"There are no traces of anything in your system that would keep me from releasing you from quarantine at this point. Assuming nothing turns up in your blood or those two military people out there, I'm going to recommend lifting the quarantine." He opened the door and returned to the common area. Jenny followed him and took a seat next to Zack as the doctor informed Major Jericho it was his turn.

Jenny glanced at Zack. "Did he tell you any good news?"

The young man nodded. "He said he might let us out of quarantine, but he said my stomach got worse.

"We have to get our parents' consent to get the cybernetic nutrient extraction implants, so you might want to send your parents a message about that."

Zack pulled out his C7. "That's a good idea. Do you know if your parents are coming yet?"

Jenny received word this morning while she, Zack, and Ix worked on schoolwork. "My mother is. Papa still can't travel. Yours?"

"Both of my parents." He laughed. "I don't know what Dad said to Mom to get her to come. She hates space travel."

"Perhaps she still fears for your safety." Ix cocked its head as it regarded Zack. "After coming so close to losing her offspring, perhaps she feels she must be by your side, no matter the personal risk."

"She loves you, Zack"—Jenny smiled—"more than she hates space travel."

"I guess."

The emergence of Major Jericho from his exam interrupted Zack's ruminations. Dr. Zedokorian moved immediately into Liz's room. The major took a seat near the trio. He leaned back and laced his hands behind his head. "It's looking pretty good."

"Our stomachs are getting worse." Jenny sighed and looked up at the ceiling. If she could, she'd undergo the surgery today.

He leaned forward. "I'm sorry to hear that. I know it's uncomfortable and discouraging, but it can be fixed. At the very worst, you'll end up with cyberstomachs, then you'll be able to eat pretty much anything. You'll never gain weight from eating too much, you won't have stomach aches or anything like that."

Zack clicked his fingers. "Hey, remember on Bestic, Jenny? When the ship blew up, it overloaded your implants? Can that happen with cyberstomachs?"

Jenny rubbed her temple. The electromagnetic pulse from the Baden-Powell's engines detonating high in the atmosphere damaged the first set of implants she had, but they'd since been replaced with more modern, EMP-hardened models. "Those were old, cheap implants. I don't think newer ones will do that?" She glanced at Major Jericho for confirmation.

"She's right. You can get older implants that are susceptible to EMP and other disruptions, but even middle-grade implants will be hardened against that. Don't cheap out and you'll be fine." Major sat back in his chair. "If they release us from quarantine, will you kids be all right here during the day? I'll have to return to my duties, and I expect there's a lot to catch up on."

Jenny stared at Zack a moment. "We should have enough schoolwork to keep us busy most of the time, and our parents will be showing up soon, so I imagine they'll have us move wherever our parents will be staying."

Zack held up his hands. "Hey, don't look at me, I'm not going anywhere."

The young woman chuckled. "I don't think any of us are any time soon."

Chapter 20

Once he finished examining Liz, Dr. Zedokorian packed his gear while his nurse finished analyzing the blood samples. After reading the analyses over her shoulder, he addressed the travelers, "As I suspected, there is no evidence of any foreign pathogens in your blood. Except for the GI damage to Zack and Jenny, your scans are clear. I feel confident recommending lifting your quarantine. Once that is approved, Commander Torgusmanfarrinan will stop in to brief you on what's next."

Zack grinned at Jenny.

Dr. Zedokorian clasped his hands behind his back. "Please do not try to leave this suite until you hear from Commander Torgusmanfarrinan."

"Well, I guess it doesn't really change anything for us, Ix. Not yet, anyway." Zack turned to Ix.

"That's correct." The doctor pointed at Zack. "You're still under quarantine until Commander Torgusmanfarrinan releases you. Any questions?"

Major Jericho stood. "No, Doctor. Thank you, you've been very helpful."

Dr. Zedokorian and his nurse packed up and said goodbye as they carted away their gear. Once they left, Major Jericho addressed the group. "I don't know what the Ersidians have planned for us once quarantine is lifted. But I do trust that no matter what demands the Devorans make, they're not going to acquiesce. We've been granted asylum here and you should be prepared to stay for quite some time if your parents don't waive Ersidian protection and take you home. I expect we're going to have to answer a lot of questions, from the Ersidians, from whomever the EAC sends, and possibly representatives from the Confederation."

Major Jericho sighed, regarding them all. "We all know things the Devorans would rather us never speak of. Just remember, you're EAC citizens and not obligated to keep what you've seen secret. As far as the EAC is concerned, and I've not been told any different, it's ancient history. Talk about it. Be honest about what you saw, what you experienced. I firmly believe this truth needs to be told."

Thus far, Zack had refrained from describing in detail their experiences in messages to his parents or his friends. He spent so much time responding to Mungus's inquiries about when he was getting out of quarantine, he felt as if he didn't have time to say anything else and do his schoolwork, too. But now, now he finally had an answer for Mungus. Or, at least, he would once Commander Torg came to release them from quarantine.

Commander Torg's visit came just a few hours after Dr. Zedokorian left. For the first time, he made a personal appearance at their suite. "Since I'm here, I'm sure you can guess what news I bring."

Major Jericho let the Ersidian in. He looked tall from a distance at the dock, but up close, he resembled a small building next to Zack. The commander gazed around the suite, nodding in appreciation. "They must like you, Major. This is a pretty sweet set-up."

Major Jericho offered Commander Torg a beer. The commander declined with a wave of his hand. "I'm still on duty. It's official, your quarantine is lifted. His Superior Ferocity King Gruncikammer, son of Mandikarrinus the Impatient, Seventh Sovereign of the Kingdom of Ersid and Ruler of the Ersidian Sovereignty requests your presence tomorrow first thing. All of you."

Jenny's eyes widened, and she averted her gaze as she stared at her feet. Commander Torg noticed her discomfort. "I recommend you avail yourself of the fabricator we've provided for you and wear something suitable for meeting a king."

Zack glanced over at Major Jericho. The major paled. "We're more than happy to answer any questions the king has, but from a diplomatic standpoint—"

Commander Torg held up a paw the size of Major Jericho's head. "You're worried about the youngsters committing unforgivable insults? See that braid all three of them are wearing? Ersidian Honor Braid. With the three of them wearing those, you'll be lucky if His Superior Ferocity even addresses you, Major."

Zack felt a flutter in his stomach, and his hand dropped to the braid he wore at his waist. He wondered how much Ersidian etiquette he could learn before breakfast.

—— 《 》 — 《 》 — 《 》 — 《 》 — 《 》 — 《 》 ——

Jenny knew exactly what she wanted to wear for their upcoming meeting with the king. Unfortunately, the fabricator the Ersidians provided them with did not have those patterns loaded and she never bothered downloading them from the fabricator at home. Back on Cytherea, if she needed a pattern from home, she only had to wait a few hours at the most. Here on Ersid, with the communication delays, she figured she'd be waiting a week, or she could purchase those patterns again. Naturally, her parents had paid for them before; they were much too expensive for the basic allowance she received as a student, and there was no way she could justify dipping that deeply into her savings.

The limited selections in the Ersidian-provided fabricator included a few utilitarian Terran fashions, many offerings tailored for Ersidians, and a smattering of selections for other species commonly found working on Ersid. A few of the Ersidian choices appealed to her, but she took one look at the customization interface and decided she did not know enough about altering garments to risk it.

Jenny spent most of the night browsing clothing patterns on the hypernet looking for something that she liked, was fashionable, and didn't exhaust her weekly student stipend. Such restrictions weeded out most of the designers' collections she normally browsed. She settled on an ensemble from DeForest's winter collection, a strapless sapphire blue dress with silver trim, a silver belt, and matching silver shoes. Once she sent the order to the fabricator, she sent Zack a message asking if he needed help finding something to wear.

His reply didn't inspire much confidence. "I can dress myself!"

She went into the common area to check the fabricator. Major Jericho stood at the panel, inspecting its output. She approached him. "Aren't you wearing your uniform?"

"My dress uniform is still on Cytherea." He held up a pair of mirror-finish shoes. "Even still, this is much easier than polishing shoes that have been in the field for weeks."

"Ix is lucky. It doesn't have to wear clothes at all." Jenny liked appearing fashionable and put-together, but she would rather have spent her afternoon doing anything other than clothes shopping.

"Ix is going to at least polish its carapace, right?" Major Jericho's slanted smile told Jenny he was joking.

"I would not be surprised." Jenny left the major to his clothes. Since hers could not begin fabricating until his finished, she wandered into the kitchen. Zack and Ix sat at the table poring over their tablets. While Jenny dispensed a glass of water, she peeked over Zack's shoulder. He appeared engrossed in a game of some sort.

"I know what you're thinking." Zack kept his attention on his screen. "I've already sent my clothes to the fabricator. I'm behind Major Jericho in the queue."

"Oh." Jenny was, in fact, intending to inquire about his clothing. "Sorry, I'm not trying to be bossy."

He shrugged. "I don't want to blow it tomorrow. Mungus would never let me hear the end of it."

Jenny pulled a chair over to the table. "That's true. Will he be there?"

"I don't think so. He's still attending the Royal Citadel."

Jenny remembered Mungus's tantrum when he received the message from his father that he'd be attending as soon as he returned home from their Valtra trip. He shattered a tablet and almost attacked a fellow Junior Ranger over it. "Has his mood about it improved?"

Zack paused his game. "I think so. He seemed happy that he finally got to punch stuff without getting in trouble for it."

Jenny laughed. "Maybe he'll be more relaxed now."

"He is Ersidian." Ix chittered. "Is that possible?"

Chapter 21

Zack tugged at his collar as he waited with Jenny, Ix, Liz, and Major Jericho in the throne room's antechamber. The major had gotten them up early so everyone had a chance to get cleaned up and looking their best before their audience with His Superior Ferocity, King Gruncikammer.

He glanced over at Jenny. The young woman sat with a hand pressing into her belly, a sign, perhaps, that her breakfast of the bland paste they were forced to eat sat about as well with her as it did with Zack this morning. A bead of cold sweat rolled down his back.

"It's perfectly normal to be nervous." Major Jericho slouched on a bench and rubbed his hands together. "You're about to stand before the sovereign of one of the oldest and most powerful governments in the galaxy."

"Have you ever met him, sir?" Lieutenant Herd looked up from her tablet.

"No, I usually deal with assistant ambassadors and the like. I don't hang out with rulers."

Zack scratched his neck as he regarded the major. "You hang out with Princess Valianna."

"Vali... the Princess is a special case." Major Jericho clenched his jaw. "We go way back."

Lieutenant Herd grinned, but the door opened, interrupting her reply.

A grey-furred Ersidian wearing a high-collared formal suit pushed the door wide and beckoned them in. "His Superior Ferocity will see you now.

Major Jericho hopped to his feet. "Remember: stay calm, bow when I do, and don't speak unless he addresses you directly."

The group of travelers followed the older Ersidian into the hall. A plush green carpet stretched the length of the hall, from the door to the throne's dais. Zack's eyes were drawn to the gleaming vaulted ceiling. Embedded lights cast a warm glow from hidden fixtures and illuminated painted reliefs of Ersidian history on the ceiling.

Black curtains obscured the walls at the far end of the room. Atop the dais sat a single stone chair, and on it sat an Ersidian with silky fur the color of cinnamon. Garbed in emerald and black and wearing a gold-and-silver crown with spikes that looked like they were designed to impale people, His Superior Ferocity, King Gruncikammer regarded their approach. Two hulking Ersidians wearing body armor and wielding axes with blades the size of Zack's torso stood guard at the base of the dais. To the sides, various onlookers, members of the court, whispered amongst themselves.

The old Ersidian stopped several paces from the base of the dais and bowed. "Your Majesty, may I present Major Thomas Jericho of the Earth-Alpha Centauri Alliance, Lieutenant Elizabeth Herd, also of the EAC, and Geneviève DuBois of Messier Habitat, Zack Jackson of Terra, and Ixilchitil of Terra."

Major Jericho bowed and gestured for the rest of them to follow suit. Zack did so, watching the major for a cue to rise. The major held the bow for a moment, then straightened.

"I am told you have quite a tale to tell, Terrans." The king's voice rumbled, a deep, sonorous thrum. "And apparently, a Valtraxian of Terra."

"Yes"—Major Jericho spread his hands—"unfortunately—"

The king cleared his throat and frowned. "I had not finished."

Major Jericho flushed and bowed in apology.

The king regarded the children, his eyes fixed on their honor braids. "I will decide on the final status of your request for asylum after I hear your fantastic tale and judge its merits. But first, unless I am mistaken, the three cubs wear the braids of Ersidians. Where did you get them?"

Zack's back stiffened as he looked for Jenny to answer first. She glanced at him, then at Ix. The Valtraxian chittered. Lieutenant Herd nudged Zack.

Zack stepped forward and bowed. He practiced Mungus's name half the night just in case someone asked. "There were given to us by our friend, Mungaborrarius Tonnarvassas. We were all crashed on Bestic together during a Junior Ranger trip a couple of years ago."

One of the guards at the base of the dais started at the mention of Mungus's name but regained his composure quickly.

"One of your sons, Goreborrarius?" King Gruncikammer turned his attention to the guard who reacted.

The guard turned to look at his king. "My youngest, Your Majesty."

That's Mungus's dad? Now that he took a good look at him, Zack saw the resemblance in their green eyes and the warm sepia shades of their fur.

"I have heard this tale." The regal Ersidian nodded. "I release the three cubs into your charge, Goreborrarius, while I speak to Major Jericho.

Goreborrarius bowed and gestured to Zack, Jenny, and Ix. "Follow me, if you please."

Ix proceeded behind Goreborrarius, but Zack and Jenny looked to Major Jericho instead. After a moment, he nodded. "We'll catch up at the suite after."

The three Junior Rangers followed Goreborrarius out of the royal audience chamber, past murmuring members of the court to a corridor leading away from the throne room. From there, he led them into a sitting room appointed with plush seating in a central sunken area. Once they were all inside he closed the door, then faced them and sunk to his knees, pulling off his helmet and allowing his massive mane of braids to spill down around his shoulders as he prostrated himself before them.

"You saved my son, and I owe you a debt greater than I can ever repay.

Except for Ix's chittering, the room fell silent. Zack and Jenny looked to each other, unsure what they should say or do. Zack shuffled his feet, then cleared his throat.

Jenny bit her bottom lip. "We all saved each other on Bestic. He did as much as we did."

Goreborrarius stood and shook his head. "Not just pulling him back from the precipice on that planet. You don't know what he was like. Your friendship means more to him than you know." The Ersidian look at each of them in turn. "All of you."

"Where is Mungus?" Zack looked around the room as if expecting to find his friend hiding somewhere. "I was hoping we'd get to see him, since we're on Ersid for a while, it seems."

"Soon. He's obligated to complete his duties, then will be able to join you here."

Zack grinned at Jenny. "This will be just like one of our Junior Ranger trips with Mungus here."

The young woman's mouth formed a thin line, "Hopefully with less danger."

—— 《》 — 《》 — 《》 — 《》 — 《》 — 《》 ——

After spending much of the morning with Goreborrarius and disappointing Mungus's father with their medically necessary dietary restrictions when he invited them to lunch, Jenny and Zack returned to their shared suite to continue schoolwork. Ix, having worked ahead while the others slept, took advantage of its newfound freedom and chose to visit Taella City's Museum of Engineering and Invention.

Jenny found the remote learning modules for many of her classes easier to deal with than listening to Cytherean Academy's instructors drone on and on. Classes with lab work, however, were a different matter. Even if the communication relays in the Sol system weren't down, there was no practical way for her to participate in labs or group projects. Alternate coursework had been provided instead, and she noticed it came from the Confederation Ministry of Education and Learning.

Jenny paused for a moment and opened up a mathematics module she'd completed earlier. Supposedly, classes without labs were coming to them direct from Cytherean Academy, yet she saw clearly on the credits page, ownership attributed to the Confederation Ministry of Education and Learning.

She shrugged. *It doesn't seem any different. As long as I don't have to repeat classes, who cares?*

As she finished up the last of her daily assignments, a message pinged in her comm implant. She intended to ignore it for the moment, but saw it came from Cytherean Academy Student Administration. Jenny opened the message and scanned it without paying attention until a single word caught her eye. She then reread it from the top.

> Ms. DuBois,
>
> It has come to our attention that reports from the Galactic Confederation of your death were inaccurate. As a result, we have updated your status accordingly. Unfortunately, your slot in the student population has been reassigned and you will need to sit out the rest of the term until a slot reopens. Due to your extended absence, you will be required to repeat the current term upon your return.
>
> Please complete the attached application forms and return them with the signatures of your parent(s)/guardian(s) at your earliest convenience.
>
> Sincerely,
> Calvin Hoover, Assistant Registrar

Jenny sneered and closed the message. She composed a quick message to Hiri asking her girlfriend if she'd heard anything official from the school about herself, Zack, and Ix now that the school updated their status to alive, then sent another one to her parents. As she sent the message, part of her wished they could come to Ersid, but she figured their recovery wasn't far enough along for them to safely travel all that way.

She shut down her terminal and headed toward the kitchen of the suite. She reached for the food preservation unit's handle before stopping to remind herself it contained nothing she could eat or drink at the moment. She resigned herself to just having a glass of water.

Were the relays not off-line, I could have had that consent from my parents for the surgery by now. She finished her drink and approached Zack's and Ix's room. *I wonder if he got the same letter I did?*

Chapter 22

Zack yawned and stretched; his eyes were bleary from forcing himself to concentrate on the viewscreen. Learning the Ersidian language from the remote learning materials and an AI didn't seem nearly as fun to him as taking the class with his friends. After he finished the module, he closed down the terminal, leaned back, and rubbed his eyes.

After a moment, he checked messages on his C7. Apart from a few mundane updates from his parents and Dravs, he saw nothing noteworthy. The absence of any messages from Rio bothered him, though. He composed a quick reply to the most recent message from Dravs and asked his friend if he'd seen or heard from the young woman lately. Zack didn't believe she would just ghost him.

As he sent the message to Dravs, his C7 pinged with the notification of an incoming message. He pulled up his inbox, expecting a message from Mungus; however, he discovered correspondence from Cytherean Academy instead.

Zack's eyes widened as he read the message.

Mr. Jackson,

It has come to our attention that reports from the Galactic Confederation of your death were inaccurate. As a result, we have updated your status accordingly. Upon review of your records, your repeated disruption of activities and the student body gives the administration cause for concern. As a result of your actions, Cytherea sustained damage and several injuries were reported. It is only through the lobbying efforts of several academy instructors that criminal charges against you have been waived.

It is the decision of the Board of Governors that you are not Cytherean Academy material. As such, you are immediately expelled from Cytherean Academy. Your class records have been released for access to the next institute of learning you attend; however you will not be welcomed back to Cytherean Academy nor to Cytherea itself. Your personal effects have been collected and transported to your home of record.

You may appeal the ban from Cytherea in writing once you have completed your education and are legally an adult. Your expulsion from Cytherean Academy is not subject to appeal.

Good luck in your future endeavors.

Sincerely,
Calvin Hoover, Assistant Registrar

Zack's face burned as he rocked back in his chair. *Expelled?* "What the f...."

The door slid open, and Jenny rushed in. "Zack, I just got a letter from Cytherean Academy." She stopped when he spun in his chair to face her, his brow furrowed and mouth agape.

He licked his lips. "They sent me one, too."

Jenny plopped down on his bed. "I have to repeat the year. Can you believe it?"

"I got expelled."

Jenny stared. "What?"

Zack leaned back in his chair and stared at the ceiling, fighting back tears. "What am I going to do now? How am I going to tell my parents?"

Jenny leaned forward. "What did they say? The school, I mean? Why are they expelling you?"

Zack read from his C7, still open to the letter. "It says I'm not Cytherean Academy material because of the damage it sustained and the disruptions I've caused. I'm banned from Cytherea, too. They sent my stuff home."

She held out her hand. He passed his C7 to her. She scanned it briefly and handed it back to him. "It's not right."

Zack's mind reeled. Without Cytherean Academy, he'd have to go back to school in Wyoming. It wasn't a bad school, but it didn't offer the advanced science classes he'd been planning on taking and most of the students were local humans. *No, I can't go back there. We're leaving Wyoming to go to Vilicus. Do they have schools there? They must.*

All of his hopes and dreams evaporated. *I can't join the Galaxy Rangers without going to one of the Academies, and the EAC doesn't have any others. Cytherean Academy was the only one. But the EAC is joining the Confederation, so we'll get more schools, right? But I can't wait until they open, can I?*

Jenny shook his knee. "Zack!"

He blinked and looked up at her. He realized she'd been trying to get his attention for a while.

"Major Jericho is back. He's calling for us."

Zack sighed and nodded. "Maybe he has good news."

Jenny and Zack joined Major Jericho in the common area of their suite. By its absence, Jenny assumed Ix was still touring the museum. She noticed Lieutenant Herd was also absent. The major gestured for Zack and Jenny to take a seat as he sat on one of the plush benches.

"Well, that went very well." The major regarded them for a moment. "But I see by your faces that you've both gotten bad news?"

"We heard from Cytherean Academy." Jenny glanced at Zack, who stared ahead with a blank expression on his face. "I'm going to be held back a year because they gave away my slot when the Confederation declared us dead."

"Oh." Major Jericho sat back. "That's unfortunate, but I suppose under the circumstance it's understandable."

"I got expelled." Zack's voice cracked.

Major Jericho's brow knitted and his eyes narrowed. "What? Why?"

"They said"—Zack choked on the words, then he swallowed—"They said..."

Zack stopped trying to speak and handed his C7 to Major Jericho.

The major took a moment to read the letter, then swore. He handed the device back to Zack. "They caved to Devoran pressure. I guarantee it. Unfortunately, I can't do anything to help with this, Zack, but if I think of something, I'll let you know."

He pinched the bridge of his nose and pressed himself back into his seat. The cushion squeaked under his weight. "Well, my news is probably not going to make you feel better in light of your news."

Jenny shrugged. "You said it went well, so I don't see how it could make things worse."

The major watched Zack for a moment. "Are you all right?"

Zack shrugged, then nodded.

"Well, after all the formal garbage was out of the way, the king had all the various regional and planetary governors conference in, as well as the heads of the military ministries. I told them everything. Now, maybe you're not aware, but Ersidians and Devorans might get along now, but the Ersidians have always been wary of the Devorans, and they were livid when they saw those log entries. Half of them wanted to send the Sovereignty First Fleet to Sol right then and there to kick the Devorans out."

Jenny learned about some contentious history between the Devorans and Ersidians in school, but she didn't think tensions were high enough for such a quick response.

"I cautioned them that might not be the wisest course of action just now. The admiral of the First Fleet agreed, fortunately."

"But what does it all mean?" Jenny had not kept up with intragalactic politics, and now that she seemed to be involved, willing or not, she felt out of her depth.

"We're safe here. The Ersidians are going to provide everything we need; they would just prefer we don't go off world. They're sending engineers to help get the Sol communication relays up and running again and they're going to make sure your families know they're welcome to join you here, if they wish."

Zack shrunk deeper into his seat. "How long before they show up?"

Jenny looked at her friend. "Probably weeks, Zack." She returned her attention to Major Jericho. "So, what do we do until then? Is there any point to doing any of this schoolwork now?"

Major Jericho crossed his arms and sighed. "Well, look, I'm not your guardian. I'm not going to be around to keep an eye on you all day. You should work on the modules the Ersidians are providing you. They should be accepted for credit anywhere you end up going to school." He kept his eyes fixed on Zack. "There's plenty to do here in the city. Shopping, parks, museums, shows. They'll send an escort with you since you're, well, technically, we're all political refugees right now. I don't want you to get lost. Explaining that to your parents would be fun."

While Major Jericho went to the kitchen for a drink, Jenny checked the unread messages in her comm implant. She saw one each from her parents and Hiri. Before opening them, she glanced over at Zack. He sat still, staring vacantly ahead. "Hey, did you finish all of your modules today? Zack?"

"Um. No. I have one left. I don't really care to finish it today, to be honest."

Jenny moved to sit next to him. "I don't think anyone can blame you for that. Maybe we can help each other remember to do everything? So, we don't fall behind?"

"I guess."

Jenny, of course, would have no trouble with that since the education interface already loaded her comm implant's calendar with a daily schedule and reminders so she wouldn't fall behind.

"I wish we could go get some ice cream, Zack." She put her arm around him and squeezed. "When our stomachs are fixed, we will, all right?"

He offered her a crooked half-smile. "I'll try to save some for you."

"So, you'll be okay? I just got a message from my parents I want to watch."

Zack nodded, and Jenny left him with Major Jericho. She shut the door to her room and queued up the message from Hiri first. Her girlfriend's face popped into Jenny's vision and she noted the young woman's hair was pulled back in a pony tail this time. Her eyes looked bright and fresh, unlike the first message she got when they arrived home from Athos.

"Hi, Jenny!" Hiri waved and smiled. "Obviously, I got your message. I told as many of our friends as I could, but I didn't want to broadcast it."

She shrugged. "It turns out, it didn't matter because a couple of days later, the school retracted the announcement of your death." Hiri's smile faded. "Their correction was worded weird though and made it sound like you weren't coming back to school. What's that about? Do you know? Things are still wild here. I mean, here on Cytherea, we're all safe and school is going on almost like normal. But, you know, everyone knows there's a Devoran fleet up there and all our own ships and everyone is just waiting for the spark to light the fire. It's tense."

Hiri's reports were not far off from what Jenny was hearing from Major Jericho. Jenny hoped her parents were safe on Vilicus. She paused Hiri's message and opened the one from her parents.

Her mother appeared sitting in what looked like a park. *Probably one of the green spaces in the habitat.* Behind her, Jenny saw people walking. Dark circles surrounded her mother's eyes, and her eyelids drooped. "Geneviève, we were so glad to hear from you. It's difficult with this delayed back and forth to really understand what has happened, but we've gotten other messages from a Major Thomas Jericho?" Her eyes narrowed. "Is that right? Hm. Well, we trust that you are safe and that makes us happy. Your father is well. He's having adjustments made to his new cerebral implants. He wanted me to reply while that was being done since"—she chuckled and motioned at her face—"obviously, I haven't been sleeping well. Once he's recovered, I'll be coming there. He hopes he might be able to travel now, but I don't expect him to come along. Not this soon. We love you, Geneviève. We're glad you're safe, and I, at least, will see you soon. Papa will see you then; we'll call him together when I arrive."

Jenny smiled and saved the message. *With the delay, she's probably already on her way.*

Chapter 23

Zack struggled keeping up with schoolwork during the days, despite Jenny's attempts to keep him motivated. Since technically he was not currently enrolled in school anywhere, he just couldn't bring himself to care. If his parents knew, they'd said nothing in any of their messages, and now that they were on their way to Ersid, he decided he wasn't going to say anything until they arrived.

As he tried to focus on a math problem, he heard Ix skitter off the bed and move up behind him. "Zack, you have stared at that same problem for the last hour. Perhaps we could go outside for a bit? It might clear your mind."

Zack stretched. "I guess. It's hard to concentrate, it's hard to care, and I'm hungry for some real food, Ix."

He sent Jenny a quick message letting her know he was going outside with Ix before the two of them left the suite. The winding corridors inside the palace complex confused Zack, so he followed Ix since he assumed the Valtraxian had memorized the quickest and most direct route to their destination.

Colorful tapestries depicting Ersidian history tempered the stark, stone construction of the palace's corridors. From pre-industrial days to the development of transportation and space flight, from endless wars to their current, long-lasting peace, the tapestries covered the gamut. Green carpet ran down the center of every corridor, allowing ample space for admirers to examine the tapestries without obstructing traffic.

Ersidians, Kerrolians, humans, and even the odd Devoran went about their daily routines in Taella City's center of government, paying no mind to the young human and Valtraxian in their midst. Ix led Zack out of the maze of corridors to the palace gardens.

The palace gardens contained several discrete areas showcasing local flora. A path of fine gravel provided a tour of sorts past blooming flowers, colorful shrubs, and trees with low-hanging fruit available at no charge to passersby. Zack marveled at the number of people who wandered the gardens in the middle of the afternoon.

"I didn't expect it to be this busy."

Ix skittered up onto a boulder near the path set amongst a sandy area with other, smaller scattered stones. "It is traditional for visitors to the palace to enter through the gardens, especially first-time visitors."

"Oh. I guess we skipped that showing up in a spaceship." Zack climbed up onto the rock next to his friend.

"Yes, due to the nature of our arrival, we entered through the palace's private space dock." Ix cocked its head and chittered. "I think you would have liked coming through the city and the gardens better."

"I doubt I would have ever been able to visit the palace if we hadn't shown up on an Athosian ship." Zack watched as a portly Ersidian chased his two small cubs through the shrubs, trying to herd them back onto the path.

Zack pressed his hand against his stomach as his guts knotted. "I hope we don't have to stay here for a long time, though. I miss home. And I want to get this stomach thing fixed."

Ix stroked Zack's arm. "They will fix you, but I cannot tell you how long we will have to stay here."

"Hey!"

Zack's eyes widened at the sound of a gruff Ersidian voice.

"Climbing on the Sacred Rock of Canoga Falls? Have you no respect you scrawny human?"

Zack flushed and slid off the rock. He faced the approaching Ersidian, whose crooked grin and familiar countenance made him laugh in spite of his embarrassment.

"Mungus!"

The Ersidian dashed forward and gathered Zack into a tight hug. "Ha ha! Hey, I am so glad to see you."

Mungus set Zack down. The Ersidian stood taller than Zack remembered, more muscular and less flabby, evidence of hard training. He wore the colors of a Citadel cadet, blue and gold.

Ix cocked its head. "Mungus, you are looking well. I am happy to see you."

The Ersidian regarded Ix over Zack's head. "Thanks, you too. You've molted a few times, huh?"

"Indeed."

"Sorry about the rock, Mungus." Zack looked over his shoulder where Ix remained perched on top of the rock. He didn't see any signs identifying it or warning visitors to keep off.

Mungus cuffed Zack on the shoulder. "I was just joking. It's just a rock. Although"—he scratched his head and examined the boulder—"I think this one actually did come from Canoga Falls. You can tell by the striations." Mungus pointed toward light colored lines running circumferentially around the boulder. "Just there, see?"

Zack blinked and stared at Mungus. "You're into geology now? When did that happen?"

The Ersidian laughed, stepping out of the pathway to let a group of palace visitors pass. "I practically grew up here, what with my father being part of the guard and all. I wouldn't know an igneous rock from a metamorphic rock if you took me out into the hills."

Ix chittered and sat up, then settled back down.

Mungus raised an eyebrow. "Were you about to explain the difference to me, Ix?"

"Yes."

He laughed and put his arm around Zack. "You've come a long way since I first met you. Both of you have."

Zack cringed as a pain shot through his intestines. "Yeah, literally."

Mungus didn't seem to notice. He peered at the visitors to the palace grounds. "Where's Jen-Jen... err, Jenny? She's with you, right?"

"She's still working on school stuff, right, Ix?"

Ix scampered off the rock as Mungus walked them back toward the palace. "Yes, I believe she was taking an exam."

"Sounds fun." Mungus's flat tone matched Zack's opinion of tests. "I went to your suite. Very nice, by the way. There was an EAC officer lady there. She said she saw you coming out this way, so I thought I'd see if I could find you rather than waiting around with someone I didn't know."

"Oh, Jenny's there, too. She's just in her room." Zack's back started to ache from the weight of Mungus's meaty arm and he ducked out from under it with an apology.

"If she's doing schoolwork, I wouldn't have wanted to disturb her. Why don't we get something to eat?" Mungus pointed toward the east end of the palace ground where several food kiosks were set up near outdoor tables.

Zack pressed his hand into his stomach again. The pressure relieved the discomfort. "Jenny and I drank some bad water on Athos, and it messed up our stomachs. We're going to have to have them... replaced."

"What? Seriously?" Mungus stopped and put both hands on Zack's shoulders as he looked him in the eyes. "What was in that water?"

Zack looked up to meet Mungus's gaze. The Ersidian's brow furrowed and his mouth hung slightly agape. Zack felt tears well up in his eyes. "The Devorans poisoned the planet. They killed almost everything. It's still toxic. I'm... I..."

Mungus pulled Zack into his stomach, wrapping him in a furry hug. "I want to hear all about this Athosian trip if you are allowed to talk about it. You'll be all right here, Zack. The four of us are together again, and we're going to look out for each other."

Zack felt Ix place a spiny hand on his shoulder. "Yes. Yes, we will all be all right now."

—— 《》— 《》— 《》— 《》— 《》— 《》——

Jenny slumped in her chair as she reviewed the last of her answers. The unfamiliar format of her botany exam had her second guessing some of her answers, and she remained certain the Confederation-supplied course materials deviated from that to which she grew accustomed at Cytherean Academy. Finally, after she decided reviewing the test a third time did not benefit her, she submitted the exam and logged off.

As if he somehow knew when she would finish, Zack called from the common area. "Jenny! Jenny, guess who's here?"

His parents can't have arrived already. She smoothed out her clothes and checked her hair before opening the door. When she saw Mungus standing with Zack and Ix, a smile sprang unbidden to her face. She rushed out into the room and wrapped her arms around him.

"How are you doing, Jenny?"

She let herself enjoy the security of his strong arms for a moment before pulling away and brushing hair out of her face. "I've been better. But I'm glad we're all here right now."

They all descended into the conversation pit and sat on the benches at the far end, nearest Zack's and Jenny's rooms.

Sighing, Mungus rubbed his thighs. "So, can you tell me anything about what happened to you? You got kidnapped by Athosians or something?"

Jenny chuckled. It never ceased to amaze her how twisted facts became in the rumor mill.

"We were not abducted, Mungus." Ix settled into a position half-on and half-off the end of the bench. "We were privileged to be present at first contact between humans and Athosians when Devorans fired without provocation on the Athosian ship where the meeting took place. They fled for safety and we, unfortunately, were on the ship at the time."

Zack, Jenny, and Ix took turns filling in the details for their friend. When Zack hesitated and choked up while describing the encounter with the Trilliax that ended with Coulson's death, Jenny glossed over it.

"The Trilliax were kind of scary, but they gave us the ship logs from the Devorans that told us everything about what they did." She reached over and gave Zack's hand a squeeze. "Major Jericho wants us to tell as many people as we can about how the Devorans destroyed Athos. He says if we spread the truth around enough, it'll be harder for the Devorans to continue covering it up."

Mungus let out a long breath. "You know, I'm not going to say I'm sorry I missed it, but you three get into some serious trouble when I'm not around."

Zack chuckled and wiped his nose on his sleeve. "We seem to get in trouble when you are around, too."

Mungus laughed and put his arms around Zack and Jenny, pulling them to his sides. "Yeah, I um... you know things are better now. I've gotten help."

He swallowed and rubbed the back of his neck. "The doctors at the Citadel basically told my sire that I would never become a guard like him with my untreated condition."

Jenny furrowed her brow. "What condition?"

Mungus shook his head. "I don't remember the proper name, but it's a problem with hormones and brain chemicals and stuff. Made me angrier than I should have been. Poorly controlled emotions, stuff like that. We knew about the chemical imbalances that affected my moods since I was a cub. I was ashamed to talk about it, and my sire didn't... he couldn't accept that a regulator implant was the only solution. You can't just will away something like that, but you know, we Ersidians don't like cybernetics."

"Yeah, that's what the doctor said when he told Jenny and me about our stomachs." Zack cringed and laid his hand over his belly.

"They put the implant in and... well, no more wild mood swings. No more flying off the handle at... petty foolishness. I'm sorry if I ever scared any of you." The Ersidian looked at his friends one by one. "No one has ever stuck around like you three before. Thanks for being my friends."

Chapter 24

Spending the next couple of days hanging out with his friends almost made Zack forget about the increasing discomfort from his stomach. Even the periods in the mornings dedicated to doing schoolwork didn't seem so pointless. Afternoons, the three of them took advantage of Mungus's presence to explore Taella City a bit. He seemed happy to show them around some of his favorite spots, promising to take them back to some of the eateries just as soon as Zack and Jenny got their cybernetic nutrient extractors implanted.

The third morning after Mungus's arrival, Zack and Jenny both received messages shortly after they settled in to work on school assignments: their parents had arrived in Ersid's solar system and would be planet side by the afternoon. Emerging from their rooms at the same time, they found Ix chatting with Lieutenant Herd in the conversation pit and Major Jericho pacing the room as he spoke to someone via his comm implant.

The major gestured for them to wait until he finished his call. Once he did so, he approached them. "Well, kids, your parents arrive today."

"We saw the message." Jenny sat on the bench next to Ix. Zack joined her.

"Lieutenant Herd and I will be packing up and shipping out." Major Jericho nodded at the lieutenant and gestured behind him. "Your parents will take our rooms here."

Zack sat forward, furrowing his brow. "You're leaving? Where are you going?" While he was excited to see his parents again, Zack felt like Major Jericho was the most important factor keeping them safe. Not that he lacked faith in the Ersidians, but Major Jericho was there, in their suite, with them every day.

"Duty calls, Zack." He took a seat to avoid looking down at the three Junior Rangers. "I didn't go to Cytherea to handle a first contact situation. Now that you're safe again and reunited with your parents, I have to meet back up with my team and go on to our next assignment."

"What's more important than this mess with the Athosians and the Devorans?" Jenny leaned back and crossed her arms.

Major Jericho straightened up and sighed. "I'm not at liberty to discuss our assignment. It is important though, vitally important to the EAC and the Confederation. I guarantee you, you'll hear about it before you leave Ersid." He stood. "But not from me." He jerked his thumb toward his room. "I need to finish packing. I won't leave without saying goodbye. You three are extraordinary, and despite everything, it's been my honor and privilege to get to know all of you."

As Major Jericho returned to his room to pack, Ix changed seats to sit closer to Zack and Jenny.

"Wow... it's kind of unreal." Zack shook his head. "My family has never been away from Earth together. My mom hates space travel, and now she's going to be here on Ersid. And your parents will be here, too, and we'll all be living together with Ix."

"Just my mother." Jenny pursed her lips. "My father can't travel yet." She looked around the suite. "She's going to complain about how small this is, especially since they're having us all share."

"It'd be even tighter if Mungus was staying with us, so I guess it's good that he lives around here and doesn't have to." Zack pulled out his C7 to check his messages, but no new ones had come in.

"Even though I have faced few of the challenges the two of you have endured on this trip, I, too, am eager to go home and return to normalcy." Ix settled into the bench next to Zack.

Ix's mention of home reminded Zack that going back to school would be different for him than his friends. "At least the two of you will be able to see each other. I can't go back to Cytherea ever." He clenched his jaw and tried not to think about making all new friends.

"I am sorry, Zack." Ix chittered. "Perhaps when the situation with the Devorans is resolved, the administration will rescind your ban."

They heard a *thunk* followed by a string of expletives from Major Jericho's room, then a shout that everything was all right. Zack crossed his arms and slouched. "I still haven't told my parents I got expelled."

"Do you want us around when you do?" Jenny put her hand on his shoulder.

Zack shrugged. "I don't know. I probably should get it over with as soon as they get here, so maybe, I guess so." Zack didn't believe his parents would overreact the way he saw parents behave in holovid shows, but nevertheless he dreaded the inevitable conversation about his future.

—— 《》 — 《》 — 《》 — 《》 — 《》 — 《》 ——

Jenny patted Zack's shoulder and sighed. "Well, let me know if you want help. I'm going to go take a walk to distract myself from how much I want some real food right now."

She left Zack and Ix and headed toward the palace gardens. Jenny gazed at the fluffy clouds casting shadows on the ground as they crossed in front of the noon-time sun. She appreciated the opportunity to study up close some flowers she'd previously seen only in the gardens at school. Their trumpet-like blooms fluttered in the wind, a visual display they evolved to attract pollinators. Their petals painted a colorful tapestry of rainbow swirls across the garden bed. Jenny enjoyed learning about plants from across the galaxy and their life cycles. Just being in proximity of the blooms while the breeze caught her hair calmed her mind and eased her knotted shoulders. She found a small stone seat and lowered herself onto it. Resting her chin on her hand, she lost herself in the flowers.

What do I do? Do I just go back to school, repeat the year, and pretend nothing happened?

She shared no classes with Zack and each of them moved in their own circles of friends most of the time, yet she recognized the school sought to scapegoat him. She wondered if the school intended to inform the student body they were expelling Zack and why, or if they'd take their cues from the Devorans who helped bankroll the academy.

But what can I do? I'm just a student. They could kick me and all of Zack's friends out of school, and hardly anyone would notice.

"It's just not right." Jenny picked up a pebble and turned it over in her hands, examining it. Tiny green crystals embedded in the smooth, grainy surface flashed in the light from Ersid's sun. Upon concluding the stone held no answers for her, she tossed it into the flower bed.

She resumed her wandering through the gardens, picking a path that avoided visitors as much as possible, eventually pausing under the boughs of a local tree with drooping branches tipped in jagged leaves that resembled saw blades.

According to an information plaque, ancient Uurts made a salve from the crushed up saw-toothed leaves of the tree. Jenny wished her problems could be solved with something as simple as crushed up leaves. *Maybe I should just quit, too. That'll show them.*

Exactly what it would show the Cytherean Academy administrators, Jenny could not say.

A breeze picked up, carrying the smell of roasting meat layered atop the heady floral scent of blooming flowers. Rarely did roasting meat smell so appetizing to Jenny, but after weeks of eating nothing but nutrient paste, even one of Zack's greasy cheeseburgers sounded good to her.

She left the saw-blade tree behind and attempted to find some respite from the delectable aromas wafting past on the breeze. No matter where she walked in the palace gardens, the breeze seemed to follow her. To her dismay, she noticed she'd inadvertently moved closer to the food vendors from which the delicious smells originated.

Jenny did an about-face and smacked into an Ersidian woman following behind her. The woman reached out and steadied Jenny who staggered from the impact.

"My apologies." The Ersidian woman's deep voice bore a slight sibilance. "I did not expect you to change course so quickly, cubling."

Jenny pinched the bridge of her nose. "I'm sorry. I should have been paying attention."

"I am no expert, but you look unwell."

Chuckling at first, Jenny looked up into the big green eyes peeking from under a furrowed furry brow. "You're right." She winced as a pain shot through her intestines, then held up her hand to stop the Ersidian from catching her. "I'm fine, though. Everything is being taken care of. I just wanted some fresh air."

"Strange that you are here and not in hospital." The woman seemed to be searching the various groups of garden visitors for someone, while addressing and casting sidelong glances back at Jenny.

"Everything about me being here is strange. If you want to know more, ask Commander Torg."

The Ersidian woman crossed her arms. "You're a guest of Commander Torg?"

"He's our liaison." Jenny sidestepped around the Ersidian, who, undeterred, followed behind her.

"I will have to speak to him about letting sick humans roam freely in the palace gardens."

Jenny bit back a reply, stopping in her tracks. She took a deep breath and faced the Ersidian woman. "I'm unwell due to an injury, not an illness."

"I see." The Ersidian frowned. "You were attacked? By an honorless *kravot?*"

"It was"—Jenny winced as another pain shot through her gut—"Devoran."

Scowling, the woman smacked her fist into her palm. "Honorless scalebacks, attacking a cubling like you. May all their ancestors be cursed."

Jenny chuckled. *Their descendants probably will be once all this gets out.* "I should go. Thanks for your concern."

Jenny left the Ersidian behind to stew and mutter over Devorans, and she circled back the way she came. Upon encountering a small group of Ersidian students listening to their teacher lecture under the saw-blade tree, Jenny passed them quietly and returned to the flower beds.

Just then a text-only message from Zack popped into view. "They're here."

Chapter 25

Jenny burst through the door of the suite just as Zack took a seat in the conversation pit next to Ix. Breathless, she looked around the room. "Where are they?"

Major Jericho emerged from the kitchen, carrying a cup of coffee. "You have some time yet. Their transport landed at the public spaceport, so Commander Torg will bring them here."

Zack bounced in his seat as he clenched his jaw. Butterflies in his stomach added to the discomfort he now felt on a daily basis from the Devoran toxins. He reviewed in his head again and again what he planned to tell his parents, yet he still couldn't find words that would soften the blow of having been expelled from Cytherean Academy.

Ix stroked Zack's arm. The Valtraxian chittered but kept any thoughts to itself. Jenny sighed and plopped down next to Zack.

"Why do I feel like we're waiting in the principal's office?" She gathered her hair behind her head and secured it with a tie.

"Do you really think your parents are going to be upset to see you?" Major Jericho sipped his coffee. "Nothing that happened was your fault, and I will gladly make that clear. I think you're worrying over nothing. They'll just be happy to see you safe."

Zack huffed. "At least Jenny's mom will be. I still have to tell my parents I was expelled from school."

"I'm sure we'll all lend moral support"—Major Jericho nodded toward Zack—"but that's a conversation you have to have on your own."

Mom, Dad, I'm really happy to see you, but I got expelled from school. Zack sighed and went over it again. *It's good to be home, but I have bad news: I was expelled from Cytherean Academy. I got expelled from school, but at least I'm alive, right? Don't be mad, be glad. I got expelled from school, but I came home alive!*

As he tried out different turns of phrase in his head, he tried to ignore Jenny questioning Ix about the Valtraxian's nutrient extraction implant. Any other day, he would be interested in hearing all about it, but figuring out what to tell his parents consumed his every thought.

Their wait seemed to drag on for hours, and Zack interrupted the stress of obsessing over how to talk to his parents by checking his C7's chronometer repeatedly. Time seemed to move more slowly the more frequently he checked. After the fifth time he checked the time, Jenny snatched his C7 out of his hands.

"That's not helping. You need to relax." She turned off his C7 before handing it back to him.

He looked at it, eyes wide. "But... what if they try to send me a message?"

"They're going to be here any minute now, Zack." Jenny glanced toward the door. "I'm sure it can wait."

As if on cue, the door chimed. Zack sat bolt upright, and his hands trembled. Major Jericho opened the door. Commander Torg greeted him before ushering in a woman who resembled an older Jenny with shorter hair.

Jenny jumped up from the bench and ran to hug her mother. After Jenny's mother, a few soldiers carrying luggage followed, and finally his parents.

His mother's dark hair, pulled back into a ponytail, looked disheveled, and bags under her eyes hinted at how well she tolerated the voyage to Ersid. Beside her, holding her hand, stood Zack's father. Grinning, he scanned the common area of the suite until his eyes fell upon Zack. "There he is!"

Zack rose to meet his parents as they ran to him. They gathered him close into a crushing hug. He couldn't understand a word his mother said to him, but he became aware that his shoulder was wet.

"Mom, you're soaking my shirt." He wiggled in his parents' embrace but was unable to dislodge them.

Finally, his father released him and stepped back, wiping his face. "We're just happy to see you safe, Zack."

His mother nodded and dried her eyes. Sniffing, she ran her hand through his hair. "Your hair got long."

Zack tried not to roll his eyes. He hadn't been able to use the shampoo that suppressed hair growth for several weeks, so while she was technically correct, it wasn't as if his hair had grown as long as Jenny's while they were on Athos.

"You must be Major Jericho?" Zack father extended his hand and approached the officer. "Carlos Jackson. This is my wife, Lucy Pepple. We're eternally grateful for everything you've done."

Major Jericho nodded and smiled. "We all helped each other."

"Amélie Dulac," Jenny's mother nodded toward Major Jericho. "Thank you for returning my Geneviève safely home. Or close to home."

Major Jericho held up his hands. "I'm sure you all have a lot of questions."

"If I may, Major." Commander Torg stepped forward as the soldiers hauling luggage set the bags down and departed. "I just have a few things to go over, then I'll leave you to it."

"Certainly." Major Jericho gestured for the new arrivals to take a seat. "Commander Torg is our liaison with the Ersidian government."

The Ersidian clasped his hands behind his back. "First of all, welcome to Ersid. You are honored guests of His Superior Ferocity King Gruncikammer, son of Mandikarrinus the Impatient, Seventh Sovereign of the Kingdom of Ersid and Ruler of the Ersidian Sovereignty. Your children have been granted political asylum, and because of the current tension in the Sol System, we are happy to host you all until such time that it is safe to return to your lives there. You are free to move about the public areas of the Valiant Citadel, including the palace gardens, and transportation is available to you should you wish to avail yourselves of amenities Taella City has to offer."

Carlos glanced at his wife. "That's very generous of you."

Amélie nodded in agreement. "Thank you very much."

"I recommend you stay close to the Citadel for the next couple of days. Dr. Zedokorian will no doubt want to meet with you, and now that your legal guardians are here"—he gestured at Zack and Jenny—"there's some official documentation we need to finish."

Carlos put his arm around Zack. "Understood."

"For now, rest up and enjoy your evening." Commander Torg slapped Major Jericho on the shoulder. "I'll be in touch tomorrow, probably in the afternoon."

Zack swallowed, wincing as a wave of pain shot through his stomach. Major Jericho stepped out to speak privately to Commander Torg.

Lucy furrowed her brow and lifted her son's head. "Is this what you told us about? The stomach problems?"

"It comes and goes, but it's worse today because..." Zack bit his lip to keep it from trembling.

Ix chittered and reached across Lucy to touch Zack's arm. "Zack, would you like me to tell them?"

Zack shook his head and inhaled.

"Tell us what?" Carlos gazed at Ix and then at his wife before returning his attention to Zack. "Whatever it is, you can tell us, Zack. We'll get through this together."

With trembling hands, Zack turned on his C7 and pulled up the letter from Cytherean Academy. "I can't... I tried... here." He handed his father the device.

Carlos's eyes narrowed as he read the letter. "Those motherf—" He squeezed his eyes shut and sighed. "Please explain to us why you think they're wrong, Zack." He handed the C7 to Lucy. She gasped when she read the letter.

"The Athosian I found was just a baby. They couldn't hurt anyone, and the Devorans would have killed them. I just wanted to help them get back to their family, or whatever Athosians have that are like families."

"It is true, Mr. Jackson, Mrs. Pepple." Ix clacked its mandibles together. "Zack helped that infant Athosian return to their people. That is all."

Lucy clenched her jaw and glared at her husband. "The Devorans are scapegoating our son. I knew someday their financial stake in Cytherean Academy would hurt someone." She handed the C7 back to Zack and wiped tears off his face. "It's disappointing the academy administration would play politics with your education, Zack, but frankly, this is an excellent opportunity."

Zack licked his lips. The butterflies in his stomach subsided, but he felt like his brain was in a fog. "What do you mean?"

"Vilicus has an excellent school, Zack. EAC Department of Education and Confederation Education Ministry accredited." Carlos gave his son a squeeze. "You might miss a few classes during the transition, but your education will be just as good."

"I already have a job teaching there," Lucy kissed the top of her son's head. "Maybe you'll be one of my students."

Zack wriggled out from under his parents as he felt himself flush. "Way to make things awkward, Mom."

As Zack related to his parents the bad news from Cytherea, Jenny's mother took her aside. "Did you get expelled from school, too?"

Jenny shook her head and frowned. "No. They told me I'd missed enough that I'd have to repeat the year. The Ersidians are providing us with Confederation learning materials that are just as good as what we'd be learning in Cytherea, but I get the sense the academy won't care."

She kept her eyes fixed on Zack as the young man's face ran the gamut from dread to terror to relief to embarrassment as his parents fawned over him. Ix seemed unsure how to both be supportive and not get between Zack and his parents. It eventually crawled over the back of the bench to exit the conversation pit.

"The most important thing, Geneviève, is that you are safe now." Amélie gazed around the suite. "Take me to your apartment here and I'll get cleaned up. Then we'll go out to dinner."

Jenny rubbed her forehead. "Mother, this is why I say you don't listen to me. I can't eat anything except that nutrient paste, which restaurants don't serve, so there's no point in me going anywhere else for food. This, here, is where we're all staying. I have my room," Jenny pointed behind her, "Zack and Ix have a room, you have a room, and Zack's parents have a room. We all have our own WCs and the kitchen is over there if you want to cook something."

Amélie narrowed her eyes and looked over Jenny's shoulder toward the kitchen. "We have to cook our own food here?"

Jenny threw up her hands. "We're not on holiday! We're living here because the Devorans will probably try to kill us if we go back home."

Just then, Major Jericho returned, and Lieutenant Herd emerged from her room. The major made quick introductions before asking everyone to gather around. "All right, the lieutenant and I will be leaving now. Mr. Jackson and Mrs. Pepple, Mrs. Dulac, our rooms have been cleaned and are ready for you to occupy. All the bedrooms in this suite are essentially the same, so I leave it to you to determine who goes where. We're not leaving to rejoin our unit for a few days yet, so we'll be around. Is there anything you need from me before we go?"

Amélie crossed her arms and huffed.

Jenny glared at her. "My mother is disappointed we don't have room service. I told her we're not on holiday."

"Indeed not." Major Jericho approached Jenny and her mother. "The kitchen is fully stocked, though you may not be familiar with all the native ingredients. If you find cooking tonight too tiring after such a long voyage, I suggest some of the food kiosks in the palace gardens, or you can take a transport into the city and go to a restaurant. However, we've been trying to avoid rubbing your children's noses in the fact that they can't enjoy proper food right now. But it's up to you."

Zack's father cleared his throat. "Maybe Lucy and I could treat you, the lieutenant, and Amélie, was it? To dinner. To thank you for taking such good care of the kids under extreme circumstances. I'm sure they can handle a dinner of nutrient paste on their own, and we're going to have plenty of time to catch up, it seems."

Jenny leaned close to her mother. "We're going to be here a while. Zack, Ix, and I will be fine on our own tonight."

Amélie pursed her lips, then lowered her gaze. "Yes, of course. Perhaps a short rest, and then I'll freshen up, and dinner will be nice. My apologies."

Major Jericho gestured for Lieutenant Herd to start hauling out their gear. "That's a very generous offer, Mr. Jackson. The lieutenant and I would be delighted to join you." He sighed. "Look, it's been stressful for all of us. But we're safe here. I have every confidence that the Ersidians will not allow any harm to come to members of their honor family, and those three are honorary members of Clan Stonetalon. The Ersidians take that very seriously. You can relax. You're in good hands. I understand the situation in the Sol System is very scary and highly inconvenient, but it cannot affect you here."

Jenny hugged her mother and kissed her cheek. "Have a rest. I have schoolwork to finish. I'll get you up in time to get ready for dinner, yes?"

"Yes, thank you." Amélie regarded her new roommates. "I'm sorry."

She retrieved her bags from the pile and carried them into the room vacated by Major Jericho. He bade them all farewell as he helped Lieutenant Herd with their gear, leaving Jenny alone in the room with Ix, Zack and his parents.

Lucy held out her arms as she approached Jenny. "We've heard so much about you, I'm so sorry this is how we finally meet."

Jenny accepted the hug with a smile. "It's good to meet you both. I'm glad you're here."

Carlos clasped his hands together. "Do you really have schoolwork, or can you all tell us exactly what happened?"

Jenny chuckled and took a seat next to Zack. Ix joined her on the couch. "I do have schoolwork, but we should probably tell you before you have dinner with Major Jericho, right Zack?"

He nodded, even as his smiled faded. He shrank back into the couch for a moment before taking a breath, and Jenny could see a flash of dread cross his face. *Maybe I'll tell them about Coulson, so he doesn't have to do it.*

Chapter 26

While Zack paused to consider where to start their tale, his mother excused herself to get drinks for everyone from the kitchen. He waited until she returned to begin.

"I guess it started during this Junior Ranger thing when we were using VR-controlled robots to walk around on Venus." Zack looked down into his lap and picked at a fingernail while he spoke. He told them about the odd panel he found, and then finding the iron star fragment in his room broken later that night.

"It was actually some sort of stasis pod for an Athosian baby. Professor Gladstone told me they collected it from the iron star they explored when he was a young man, so I guess he was lying to me? He never responded to any of my messages. He said he was transferring to the school on Vilicus, so I guess I can ask him about it again."

He continued his story, telling them about the hunt for Squishy and how he eventually found the Athosian and decided to keep him in the stream in the arboretum.

Carlos held up his hand. "You named them 'Squishy'?"

Zack shrugged. "It's not like they could talk. They were like a weird cross between an octopus and a jellyfish. I didn't feel right calling Squishy 'it' all the time."

He told them how the Athosian ship revealed itself and of his subsequent trip through the city's maintenance corridors to try to reunite Squishy with the rest of the Athosians. When he spoke of the accident that injured Rio, Zack didn't mention she was a bioreplicant. He said only that she urged him on and assured him she'd be all right until help arrived.

"Major Jericho decided to let us stick around during first contact with the Athosians. They had set up a sort of conference room in their ship for us, and we were all in there, just sitting down talking when the Devorans attacked us. The Athosians didn't have any choice but to run away."

Zack swallowed and glanced at his friends. "When we first got to Athos, we knew it was far away, but we were in a different galaxy, looking back at home. No human had ever seen the Milky Way like that before."

He pulled out his C7 and grinned. "I have pictures! We're the only one who have ever seen our own galaxy from outside like this."

Jenny pushed his hand down before he could show off the pictures. "Let's finish the story so they can clean up before dinner."

Carlos sat back, putting his arm around Lucy. "This is a fantastic tale, Zack."

He felt himself flush. "It's all true, I swear!"

His mother offered him a smile. "We believe you, honey."

"Jenny and I were coming back from exploring the mainland a bit when we got caught in the tide." He looked over as Jenny nodded in agreement. "That's when we accidentally drank the water that wrecked our stomachs and intestines."

Carlos grimaced. "Every time I've ever swum in the ocean, I felt like I drank liters of saltwater."

Ix cocked its head. "Would that not have serious repercussions on your health?"

Zack's father chuckled. "Yes, if it actually were liters. It was probably just a few hundred milliliters. Regardless, it's highly unpleasant, and I can see how if there were actual toxins in the water, it could be very bad. I guess we'll have to talk about this cybernetic replacement they recommended. Zack, will you be all right if we talk to Major Jericho and that doctor fellow first?"

Zack slumped in his seat. "I don't have much of a choice. They won't do anything for me without your permission anyway."

He tried to ignore the twisting, painful feeling in his guts, as if his stomach were trying to digest itself. He understood his parents' desire to talk to the doctor first, but every day he waited, his discomfort seemed to worsen.

"We had a few nights of sickness, and then we seemed fine." Jenny spoke up to cover Zack's brooding. He was glad for her to talk for a bit. "We were all eating the rations Major Jericho's people brought along anyway. It's pretty close to the nutrient paste the Ersidians are giving us. So, we didn't really notice anything wrong at first."

"Everything was going all right until—" Zack choked on the words as the image of the Trilliax shooting Coulson flooded his memory.

"Some aliens that were exploring the ruins found us." Jenny patted Zack's knee. "There was a misunderstanding, none of us could communicate with them, and they killed one of Major Jericho's people, Sergeant Coulson. In the end, the Trilliax helped us finish repairing the ship and gave us the flight recorder from the Devoran ship."

Carlos sat forward and looked at his wife before turning back to Jenny. "There was a Devoran ship there? On Athos?"

Zack couldn't shake the image of Coulson's corpse with its gaping wounds from the Trilliax weapon. He could only nod in acknowledgment.

"It was an Athosian ship the Devorans modified for their use to infiltrate the Athos system in order to launch a genocidal and ecologically devastating attack. The Trilliax provided us with the flight recorder from that ship." Ix stroked Zack's arm as it took over the narrative. "Apparently, they had been sent to deliver a biological and chemical weapon attack against Athos in the waning days of the war. The captain and crew were ashamed of their actions when they realized after the attack not all Athosians were bent on conquest. Indeed, they had learned there was a sizable faction struggling against the ruling government in an attempt to end the war. Rather than face accolades and live a lie for the rest of their lives for wiping out most of the life on a planet, they chose to crash their ship into the dying world and leave their logs as a record of the truth in the hopes that someone would eventually find it."

Lucy covered her mouth with her hands. "The Devorans killed everyone on the planet."

Ix cocked its head. "As near as we could determine, all life larger than microbes and simple plant life died off. Much of the ecosystem adapted in the centuries since, but we saw no indigenous lifeforms other than plants during our time there."

"It seems like that Devoran captain could have done more good by simply coming home and telling his story and the truth, rather than leaving it to an impossible chance." Lucy's eyes glistened as she regarded her son.

Carlos put his arm around Lucy again and hugged her. "There could be any number of reasons why they didn't come back. It's futile to question a ghost."

"Anyway"—Zack shrugged and wiped his nose on his sleeve—"the ship got fixed, and we came back. The Devorans and the EAC were all over the place when we got to Venus, so the Athosians jumped us here. I guess we should be glad they didn't take us somewhere farther away."

"That's for sure." Carlos chuckled.

Lucy stifled a yawn. "We should start getting cleaned up. Can I make you three anything before Carlos and I go to our room?"

"No, thank you, Mrs. Pepple." Jenny stood and stretched. "I'll eat after I finish this schoolwork."

Zack shook his head. "No. Dinner's just a matter of pushing a couple of buttons and making sure you put a bowl under the dispenser first. I haven't messed that up yet."

His father came over and kissed the top of his head. "We're proud of you, Zack. Just remember that."

Zack heard the words, but with the image of Coulson burned into his mind, he wondered how that could possibly be true.

—— 《》 — 《》 — 《》 — 《》 — 《》 — 《》 ——

As Zack's parents retired to their room to rest and freshen up, Jenny excused herself to her own room, leaving Zack to brood with Ix. She sat in front of her terminal and pulled up the assignment she'd been working on for her literature and composition class. The last assignment for this particular module was one that had been giving her trouble: compose a poem.

That's all it requested: a poem. Any subject, any length. When Jenny first read the assignment, she put it aside, assuming she could complete it with little effort.

How wrong she was.

Every time she stared at the blank page; all she could think about was the missing six months of their lives. Being declared dead, then alive again. Coulson. Zack's expulsion. Tension between the Devorans and the EAC. Mostly, she thought about how much she wanted to eat real food again. After a moment, she opened a new composition.

> Time.
> Devours everything.
> A maw in the void.
>
> Empty.
> Featureless. Unfulfilled.
> At what cost comes survival?
>
> Time.
> Everything changes.
> Pain is static.

She sat back and considered what she wrote. *It's technically a poem. A bit bleak, though.* Jenny wanted more time to mull the words over, but she decided the week she'd already spent looking at a blank page proved no amount of time would help, so she saved the file. Just before she submitted it, something else came to mind.

> Desolate planet
> The last victim of a war
> War never changes

She saved the short Haiku-style poem and submitted that one, instead. *Maybe some old Devoran will read that and know what I'm talking about.*

One major disadvantage to the type of class modules she and Zack were provided was that neither one of them had any contact with an instructor. The time-honored tradition of pandering to one's instructor was futile when, for all Jenny knew, an algorithmic artificial intelligence would evaluate their work, instead of a living, breathing teacher.

Jenny shut off her terminal and returned to the common area. Upon finding neither Zack nor Ix there, she exited the suite and headed for the palace gardens. When she reached the exit, she noticed the gardens had grown busier since her earlier visit. She hesitated, slumping. Navigating crowds of Ersidians, Devorans, Kerrolians, and humans did not appeal to her current mood.

She passed by the doors to the gardens and walked toward the palace's spaceport instead. What little traffic the Citadel's spaceport hosted was mostly outbound at this time of day. It occurred to Jenny as she sought solitude amongst the Citadel's staff and visitors, that she could have just stayed in her room to be alone.

Those four walls are getting boring, though. I wonder if I have time to go into the city? She laughed at the absurdity of seeking solitude amongst the crowds. She continued to wander the halls until she saw a sign for the observation tower. Spiral stairs led up, circling the lift shaft. She paused at the base of the stairs, then thought better of it and boarded the lift.

When she realized how long the lift took to reach the top of the tower, Jenny was glad of her laziness for once. A handful of Ersidians occupied the observation deck, some inside, enjoying the expanse from behind glass, and some braving the winds to stand out on the deck for an open-air view.

Jenny had no desire to feel the wind in her hair at the moment, so she found a window offering a view of the city south of the Citadel. With the exception of centers of commerce, most buildings in Taella City stood only two to three stories high and appeared to be made of stone blocks and wood, although Jenny knew most of them were designed merely to resemble old-style buildings. Ersidian architecture sought to mimic traditional styles while taking advantage of the superior strength of modern materials. The metal and glass spires of commerce centers stood out like glistening spikes bursting through the stone foundation of their society.

In the distance, beyond the city, grassy plains gave way to a verdant forest and ultimately snow-capped mountains beyond that. The setting sun painted the peaks in orange and rose. Apart from the indigenous population, Ersid reminded Jenny very much of Earth.

From her vantage, individuals on the streets and in the parks resembled insects. Ground transports zipped to and fro, their lights becoming more prominent as darkness fell across the city. Air transports streaked above the rooftops like fireflies.

Jenny stood there watching life in the city from on high until the sun set fully, then she descended the tower via the stairs and returned to the suite. By the time she arrived, her mother and Zack's parents had already left to meet Major Jericho and Lieutenant Herd for dinner. Zack and Ix sat in the conversation pit, facing the holoviewer on the wall. An Ersidian program that seemed to be about angry Ersidians yelling at each other until one of them backed down was playing as the two ate.

"Did you eat yet?" Zack watched Jenny cross the room.

"Just getting food now. I'll be back." She grabbed a bowl and filled it from the nutrient dispenser. Today's dinner resembled not-quite-smooth grey sludge. Jenny dipped her finger in it and tasted the goop. A subtle poultry undertone barely cut through the bland earthy taste at the forefront. Coupled with the soggy pulp-like texture, it made for a wholly unsatisfying meal, though nutritionally complete and suitable for her ruined digestive system.

She sighed and returned with her dinner. Jenny took a seat next to Ix and spooned the grey goo into her mouth, forcing herself to eat as quickly as possible. As long as she didn't wait too long between bites, the paste was more tolerable than going hungry.

While Jenny didn't find the content of the show on the holoviewer entertaining, it seemed to keep Zack engrossed enough that he didn't try to talk to her while she ate. The program concluded about the same time as she finished her meal. Ix shut off the holoviewer. A screen showing Citadel events and alerts appeared in the viewing area.

Zack turned to Ix. "I only understood about half of that. They were talking too fast."

"We could replay it." Ix fidgeted with the spoon it had used to eat.

"Please no." Jenny leaned back and cradled her bowl. "If you want to try to understand them, find something where they aren't yelling at each other all the time... or talk to Mungus. I'm sure he'd be happy to speak Ersidian with you."

Zack rested his head on his hand as he leaned on the armrest. "That's a pretty good idea. I think he's coming around tomorrow."

"Did my mother say anything before they left?"

Zack glanced at Ix then shook his head. "Not to us. She didn't say anything at all that I remember."

"Did you two hang around here all day?"

"Yup." Zack leaned forward to look at Jenny. "Why? I've already been to the gardens. I've looked at all the tapestries. Once my parents got here, I didn't want to just leave. You know, in case they needed me."

Jenny shrugged. "I was just curious. I'm getting a little bored, but every time I go somewhere I smell food I want to eat but can't."

"Perhaps the doctor will come by tomorrow and you can finally schedule the appointments to get your cybernetic nutrient extractors." Ix took both Jenny's and Zack's bowls and put them in the recycler in the kitchen. When it returned, Ix settled in between them. "Would you mind if I put something on the holoviewer?"

"I don't mind." Jenny reached over to an adjacent seat and grabbed one of the extra pillows.

"Me neither." Zack pulled his legs up into his seat.

Ix turned on the holoviewer and selected a less shouty show. Subtitles appeared in Jenny's ocular implant allowing her to follow the dialog without having to understand Ersidian. A smile crept onto her lips when she realized exactly what Ix had selected. *It's a sentimental Ersidian melodrama.*

Chapter 27

Despite his lack of enthusiasm for the subject matter of the program Ix selected, Zack admitted to himself the slower pace of the dialog allowed him to understand much more of what was being said than the shouty action-packed show he'd picked earlier.

As the program dragged into its second hour, Zack wondered if Ix chose it more to help him with his Ersidian or because it was genuinely interested in the subject matter. He started to doze about the time his parents returned.

Jenny's mother followed them in and immediately entered her room. Jenny raised an eyebrow before pushing herself up off the bench and following her mother. Zack's parents approached him and Ix.

"I know it's getting late." Carlos regarded the melodrama playing out on the screen. "Do you two have a minute to talk, or do you need to get to bed?"

Ix cocked its head. "I require much less sleep than Zack. I can stay up talking for hours if need be."

Carlos chuckled as Lucy took a seat near Ix.

"We're fine." Zack stifled a yawn, "What's up?"

"How's your school workload?" Carlos leaned forward. "Will it be disruptive to take a couple of days off?"

Zack shrugged. "I don't know. I mean, I'm expelled. I don't know how many more modules they have for us, or if it's even worth doing them right now. What if the school on Vilicus wants me to repeat my second year?"

"If you finish all of the assigned modules," Ix chittered, "there should be no reason why they would make you repeat content."

Lucy folded her legs up underneath her on the seat. "Major Jericho received verification during dinner that Commander Torg and Dr. Zedonkian—"

"Zedokorian, honey."

"Ugh. I keep getting that wrong." Zack's mother grimaced. "Dr. Zedokorian will be coming by tomorrow. If he's okay with it, we want to take you to that other doctor for a consultation right afterwards." She turned to the Valtraxian. "You don't have to come to that, if you don't want to, Ix."

"Then—" Carlos took a seat next to his wife—"we need to talk about our new home on Vilicus."

Zack sat forward. "What about it?"

"Oh, it's nothing bad. There are several configuration options, and since you'll be living with us full-time again while you're in school, we figured we should at least hear your thoughts." Carlos glanced at Ix. "There's plenty of space for Ix, as well. I hope you know you're welcome to continue living with us for as long as you like."

The Valtraxian raised itself up. "Oh. I suppose I neglected to consider whether I would continue to attend Cytherean Academy after Zack's expulsion." Ix slumped, turning to face Zack. "It would be very odd indeed without you in the dorm, Zack."

Engrossed in his own angst over having been expelled, Zack had not stopped to consider that Ix would continue at Cytherean Academy without him. His stomach knotted, and he felt himself flush. "You can't just quit school, Ix. I guess you'll stay with us between terms or something."

Ix clacked its mandibles together. "I will have to give the matter careful consideration."

Carlos sighed. "Well, there's still time. There's no telling how long the Ersidians will want you to stay here."

Zack frowned and sank back into his seat. "You think it might be years? That I might have to finish school here altogether?"

Lucy's eyes widened, and she looked at her husband. "I can't imagine it would be that long. Carlos, you don't think we'll have to relocate here, do you?"

Zack's stomach churned at the thought that his actions would make his family have to move to Ersid after giving up the family home in Wyoming for one on Vilicus.

"We're not there yet." Carlos chewed on his lip for a moment. "Let's just take things a day at a time for now. We'll focus on Zack's health and safety and deal with the other issues as they come up. We just don't have enough information right now for that kind of speculation."

Lucy nodded. "You're right, of course." She reached forward and put her hand on Zack's knee. "Whatever happens, we'll work things out, together."

—— 《》— 《》— 《》— 《》— 《》— 《》——

Jenny shut the door behind her. Amélie sat on the edge of the bed and brushed her hair.

"Well, how was dinner?" Jenny pulled a chair over from the desk so she could face her mother.

"After the food on the ship, it was nice to have fresh food again. Surprisingly, the dessert was especially masterful."

Jenny tried not to be annoyed at her mother's surprise that she could get decent food on Ersid and instead focused on the fact that her mother's reply was not entirely negative.

Amélie stopped brushing her hair and regarded her daughter. "The Ersidian doctor will be by tomorrow. After that,

Zack's parents are taking him to the consultation with that other doctor. Perhaps we should go with them."

"I'll tell you right now, mother, I want that cybernetic nutrient extractor. I want to be able to eat real food again."

Amélie nodded. "Yes, of course. I agree, as soon as possible. Perhaps even within the next few days if the doctors think it's feasible." She narrowed her eyes. "Your other implants? They are still working well?"

"Yes, no problems since replacement after the incident on Bestic." Jenny fidgeted with her ponytail. "I may want the AI in my cortical implant activated, though, since some of my upcoming science classes will rely on VR activities." Turned off by default to help young people adjust to the implants after surgery, turning on the AI feature required only a physician to activate the program.

"I think we can do that at home."

Jenny folded her hands in her lap and sighed. "I've been thinking about Cytherean Academy. How they treated Zack is wrong."

"Probably." Amélie shrugged. "But there is nothing you or I can do about that."

"I feel like there should be."

"Oh, Geneviève," Amélie shook her head and reached out to her daughter. "Sometimes, bad things happen to people, and there is nothing we can do about it. Even if they are our friends."

"We shouldn't be punished for helping." A doubt gnawed at Jenny. It reared its head every time she thought about Cytherean Academy now.

"No, we shouldn't." Amélie tossed the brush on the bed and set her travel case alongside it. She opened the case and rummaged through it until she found a nightgown. "But I think the best thing for you now is to concentrate on getting better, then concentrate on your studies. Wait until you're out of school before you worry about saving the world."

Jenny sulked for a moment, then noticed the vast amount of clothes her mother had removed from her travel case. "Mother, we have a fabricator. Why did you bring all those?"

Amélie looked over her shoulder at Jenny. "Shipboard fabricators never have anything to my liking, and I wanted a selection of clothes I liked for the first few days here at least. Besides, Ersidian fashion is too blocky. The dresses will fit me like a tent."

Jenny fought to keep from rolling her eyes. "This isn't a backwater, Mother. Taella City is a cosmopolitan metropolis. Just about everything you want is available." She looked down at her own drab loungewear. "I just didn't want to dip into my student stipend too much, and you were so far away."

Amélie spun to face her daughter and beamed. "Now, that is a problem we can fix. After your stomach, of course."

Jenny stood and yawned. "I'm going to bed. Bonne nuit."

Amélie threw her arms around Jenny. "Bonne nuit, petite chou."

Jenny left her mother to unpack and bade Zack, his parents, and Ix good night. After shutting her door, she lingered for a moment, listening to Zack's parents discuss packing up their home on Vilicus and kenneling their dog. She found thoughts about Cytherea invading her mind as she changed out of her clothes and got ready for bed, so she pulled up an image of Hiri as she crawled under the covers and let the smiling face of her girlfriend usher her to sleep.

Chapter 28

The next morning after breakfast, Zack, Ix, and Jenny worked on school assignments until Major Jericho and Commander Torg arrived at the suite. Mungus, wearing the uniform of a Citadel guard, accompanied them. Dressed in a newly fabricated uniform, Major Jericho took a seat near the door. As they gathered, Commander Torg gestured toward the conversation pit. "Is everyone comfortable if we do this here?"

Carlos and Lucy nodded. They sat on either side of Zack on one of the couches. Ix found a spot near them, while Mungus stood behind Zack, arms crossed.

Amélie glanced at Jenny. "Should the children be here for this?"

The elder Ersidian turned his gaze on Jenny's mother. "Certainly. This concerns them more than it concerns you."

Jenny's mother pursed her lips and took a seat in the chair near Zack's family. Jenny pulled another chair next to her. Zack's mother took his hand and squeezed.

Clasping his hands behind his back, Commander Torg stood facing all of them. "This situation is highly unusual, but I hope we have made your stay here pleasant so far. I hope you all feel comfortable asking for anything you need that we haven't already provided. I must emphasize that all of you are honored guests."

Carlos glanced at Zack and Lucy, then nodded at Commander Torg. "Everything has been fine, thank you. Not quite a vacation, you understand, because of the circumstances, but we appreciate the hospitality you've shown us and especially Zack and Ix."

Amélie shrugged. "It is fine. You are kind to ask."

"I know information coming from the EAC has been sporadic and sketchy. The Sovereignty tightly controls information coming into the palace for security purposes, and you've been victims of it, and for that, I apologize."

Carlos leaned forward. "Can you tell us what is going on? When can we take our children home?" Zack shook his hand loose from his mother's tight grip.

"I understand your concerns." Commander Torg took a breath. "This is what we know: the standoff between the EAC fleets and the Devoran fleet continues in both Venus and Earth orbit. They're not obstructing traffic, and they've not interfered with repairs to the comm relays, so regular communications between the Sol system and the rest of the galaxy should be up and running again within the week."

"That's good news, at least." Jenny offered her mother a smile.

Amélie nodded in response. "But is it safe to travel there?"

"We do not recommend it at this time." Commander Torg turned his gaze on Zack. "Among the Devorans' many unreasonable demands is that both Zack and Jenny be turned over to them to face justice."

"But we didn't do anything wrong!" Zack fought to keep his voice steady. He noticed Jenny lower her gaze to the floor and fidget in her seat.

"I did slap a Devoran soldier."

Commander Torg chuckled. "Yeah, I heard about that. They're more concerned with harboring an Athosian."

Zack's father stood and shook a trembling finger at Commander Torg. "That is not a crime in the EAC, and we're not part of the Confederation yet. Where do the Devorans get the temerity to dictate—"

"I hear you." Commander Torg raised his hands. "The Sovereignty agrees with you, Mr. Jackson. That's why your son has been granted political asylum here."

Lucy tugged on Carlos's arm until he returned to his seat. He patted Zack's knee and sighed, his shoulders slumping.

"Now, we have reliable intelligence that suggests the Devorans are going to withdraw from the Sol System; they're going to be recalled by the Devoran government. We don't have a timetable for this, but our sources believe it will be very soon. I can't say more than that at this time, though I expect when it happens it will be all over the news." He gestured toward the door. "Information restrictions will still be in place in the palace, but we can't stop you from leaving the grounds and hearing news from any number of reputable agencies anywhere on Ersid."

Carlos looked at his wife, then Amélie, before turning back to Commander Torg. "If it becomes safe to return home before our kids recover from their surgeries, will we be able to stay here until they can travel at least?"

"Of course." Commander Torg relaxed his stance. "You can stay as long as you like. At some point after the Devorans withdraw from the Sol system, I expect you'll be asked to find lodging elsewhere in the city rather than here in the palace, but we won't kick you out to fend for yourselves."

Mungus placed a heavy hand on Zack's shoulder. "They will always have a home with Clan Stonetalon. All of them."

"Thank you, Mungaborrarius." Commander Torg clasped his hands together. "Now, transports are available to take you to your appointments or anywhere else you wish to go, for that matter. Please avail yourselves of the many fine things Taella City has to offer. You may not be able to go home just yet, but there's no reason not to enjoy yourselves while you're here."

Zack snorted. "Except we can't eat anything except that paste."

"Well, there is that." Commander Torg grunted. "Dr. Zedokorian is on his way, so you'll be able to get the medical stuff out of the way soon. In addition, at the behest of Goreborrarius Tonnarvassas and with the consent of His Superior Ferocity, King Gruncikammer, Zack will be assigned a permanent bodyguard."

Carlos laughed. "What?"

Commander Torg regarded Jenny. "It is felt at this time that Geneviève DuBois is not a high priority for the Devorans. Zack Jackson, however"—he returned his attention to Zack's family—"has had extended contact with the Athosians, and, to put it lightly, they're not happy about that."

"Well, that's ridiculous." Lucy crossed her arms. "Zack's just a child."

"I'm fourteen, Mom." Zack glared at his mother. "I'm not a child."

"Due to his honor-debt to your son, Mungaborrarius has been granted the honor."

Zack craned his head back to look at his friend. "You're going to be my bodyguard now? Cool!"

Mungus chuckled and put his hands on Zack's shoulders. "I swear by my ancestors, no harm will befall him while I draw breath."

"Mungaborrarius has been briefed on what his duties entail, and we have every confidence in his abilities." Commander Torg took a breath. "If there's nothing else, I must be going."

Carlos stood. "Now wait a minute. You said we were safe here, but now you say Zack needs a bodyguard?"

"You are safe, here." Commander Torg gestured toward the door. "Out there, in the city? Reasonably safe. Probably safer than any other city in the Confederation. But once you leave Ersid? This is the only way we can fulfill our obligation to keep your son safe."

Lucy rose and stood at her husband's side. "But we're not even supposed to leave until it's safe to return home."

"That's right. There will be no Devoran fleet to capture or destroy your transport when you leave. But covert agents of Devoran State Security? They could be your neighbors or co-workers for all you know."

Commander Torg held up his hand to stave off further questions. "Major Jericho can tell you all about the DSS. I must go meet with the king." He looked at Jenny, then Zack. "I hope your doctors' appointments go well. It'd be a shame if you came all this way and couldn't try any of our food. Good day, now."

Commander Torg turned and left. Major Jericho shut the door behind the Ersidian and held up his hands as Carlos and Lucy bombarded him with questions. Zack slouched in the couch as his elation at having a bodyguard turned to angst. *Are the Devorans going to send assassins after me?*

—— 《》— 《》— 《》— 《》— 《》— 《》 ——

Jenny rubbed her forehead as Zack's parents interrogated Major Jericho. She glanced over to see Mungus smiling at her. "Don't worry, Jenny. If you hang out with us, I'll protect you, too."

"Oh, well, thank you, Mungus. Are you going to go to school with Zack now on Vilicus?"

Zack's eyes widened. "Hey, yeah, that's right. You have to follow me wherever I go, right?"

The Ersidian grunted. "Pretty much. Any classes I can take with you, I will, but I won't be taking all the same classes as you, Zack."

Ix clambered off of the bench. "I believe I shall return to our room and continue my schoolwork." It touched Zack's arm. "I hope the doctors have good news for you."

"Thanks, Ix."

Jenny watched the Valtraxian depart. *Maybe I should—*

Just then, the door opened, Dr. Zedokorian pushed his way past Major Jericho and Zack's parents. "I'm in a hurry, so if everyone could gather please, so I don't have to repeat myself."

Zack's parents returned to their seats next to Zack. Amélie took her daughter's hand and leaned over to whisper. "Is this the doctor you've been seeing?"

Jenny nodded. Dr. Zedokorian pulled a tablet out of his satchel. "Since your cubs are human, I'll spare you the lecture about keeping your bodies pure and free from cybernetics. Once you sign off on these forms, I can refer you to a surgeon who can implant the cybernetic nutrient extractors."

"Well now"—Carlos glanced at his wife—"Zack's pretty young. We probably need to talk this over."

The doctor thrust the pad at Carlos. "Talk all you want but sign the form so I can transfer his care to a human doctor. No matter what you decide about the implant, he should receive care from someone more knowledgeable about human physiology."

Carlos took the tablet, read over the form, and signed it. The physician took the tablet from him and submitted the form before passing the tablet to Amélie. Jenny scanned the form. It appeared to be a simple release and consent for referral.

Once Dr. Zedokorian had the tablet in hand, he worked at the screen for a moment. "If you have time today, I can schedule your consultations this afternoon."

"So soon?" Carlos glanced at his wife and Zack.

Jenny nodded. "Yes, please. The sooner the better."

The doctor grunted. "His specialty isn't much in demand around here. When it's an emergency, you don't want to wait, but humans don't come to Ersid to get cybernetic implants. And if we need them, well, we have our own doctors who are willing to do such distasteful things when medically necessary."

Jenny looked up as a low rumble emanated from Mungus. Zack squirmed and slapped at the Ersidian's hands as they tightened on his shoulders.

"All right. Appointments are set. After lunch. You'll receive confirmations momentarily."

Jenny's appointment confirmation arrived before Dr. Zedokorian finished speaking.

The doctor pressed his hands together and bowed his head. "I hope things go well for you. You should have little trouble adjusting and will probably be back to eating whatever you want within a week of the surgery, I would think. Take care now."

Major Jericho opened the door for the doctor, then addressed everyone. "You can take the provided private transports or public transportation. Commander Torg will see to your needs now. Lieutenant Herd and I ship out tonight."

Jenny stood and hugged Major Jericho. "Thank you. Things would have gone very badly if you hadn't been there with us."

He patted her on the back. Once she returned to her seat, Major Jericho turned and offered a hand to Zack. "Good luck. Don't let the Devorans push you around. Things will get better, I promise."

Jenny examined the appointment confirmation as Zack said his goodbyes to Major Jericho.

She shared the information with her mother. "Looks like we can go after lunch. I was going to work on some school assignments before, unless there's something you need me for."

Amélie possessed the distant look of someone concentrating on reading something in their implants. "That's fine, Geneviève. I'm investigating this Dr. Cruz."

"Fine, mother." Jenny chuckled as she excused herself. She appreciated her mother's diligence in looking out for her, but Jenny's desperation to eat real food again overcame any concerns about Dr. Cruz's reputation or competence.

Chapter 29

The waiting room at Superlative Enhancements Cybernetics Clinic resembled every other doctor's waiting room Zack had seen with one exception: instead of displaying general health advice on the various holodisplays situated around the room, they showcased various cybernetic implants and enhancements. Thinly padded chairs surrounded each of the displays, so patients could sit comfortably while they read. Wall space in between static displays featured artwork showing Earth landscapes. Zack recognized an image of Yosemite Valley with El Capitan and Cathedral Rocks towering above a landscape full of autumn colors and evergreens.

In addition to implants to replace damaged and failing organs, the clinic offered cybernetic limb replacement. According to the adverts Zack read, these performed just as well as natural limbs, but they provided greater durability. The organs, of course, outperformed biological organs by a large margin. The only thing that kept most Earth natives from seeking them out was the perception that replacing bits of oneself with machines chipped away at one's sense of self.

Jenny and her mother sat near the registration desk, chatting about her father. While his father sat with his head resting on his hand, staring forward at nothing in particular, Zack's mother cast askance glances at the informational displays, fighting to keep her lips from curling in disgust.

Just as Zack started to examine a display that detailed the process by which nanotechnology helped construct cortical and ocular implants, an Ersidian nurse called him back to an examination room. His parents followed along behind him. They all stopped at a station just inside the door so the nurse could take Zack's vitals. Then the nurse ushered Zack into an exam room.

Zack hopped up onto the exam table while his parents sat in the chairs. He noticed a terminal atop a cabinet and a small holodisplay that hung from the ceiling on a mobile swing arm. The door opened, and a slight human with dusky skin and straight hair cut into a bob entered the room.

"Good afternoon, I'm Dr. Cruz." The doctor glanced around the room and their eyes settled on Zack. "You must be the patient, Zack Jackson."

Zack nodded. "That's me."

"We're his parents, Carlos and Lucy." Zack's father stood and offered a hand to Dr. Cruz.

"A pleasure. So, please tell me about the problem that requires my assistance." The doctor smiled, and they gingerly grasped Carlos's hand.

Lucy's spine straightened and narrowed her eyes. "Didn't that Ersidian doctor send Zack's chart over?"

Dr. Cruz waved their hand. "Of course, but Ersidians don't particularly approve of what I do here, so I like to hear from the patients what they think their problem is, compare it to notes I get from the referring physician, especially if they're Ersidian, and develop a treatment plan from there."

Zack didn't wait for his parents' response. "I accidentally drank some toxic water on an alien planet, and it messed up my stomach and intestines. I want a cybernetic nutrient extractor to replace my guts so I can eat real food again."

Lucy cleared her throat as she pursed her lips and glared at Zack. "We also want to hear about organic replacement options."

"Hm, yes, you're from Earth, right?" Dr Cruz faced Zack. "We can grow a replacement digestive system from your DNA and transplant a new stomach and intestines. Organ growth will take anywhere between nine and twelve standard months."

Zack groaned. "Mom, I don't want to wait that long to eat real food again."

Carlos rubbed his forehead. "What's the recovery time for a cybernetic replacement?"

"He'd— you use 'he,' yes?"

Zack nodded.

"He would spend a night or two in the hospital for post-surgical observation, then he can begin reintroducing certain foods as soon as we complete our final system check prior to discharge. Most patients are back to eating anything and everything they want within a week post-op."

"A week, Mom." Zack stared at his parents. "Dad... don't make me wait another year to eat real food again. You haven't been living on that nutrient paste for months."

Lucy took her husband's hand. "You know how I feel about cybernetics."

Carlos squeezed her hand. "I know, but I think we need to support Zack in making this decision. This is not the same as someone who replaces perfectly functional body parts out of vanity or the desire to be more than they were born to be. This is a quality-of-life issue."

She wiped a tear from her cheek and nodded. "You're right. It just... it's hard."

Zack turned to Dr. Cruz. "I really want the cybernetic nutrient extractor."

Doctor Cruz pulled the display toward themself and activated a graphic that showed the implant. They turned the display toward Zack and his parents. "It's much smaller than your stomach and intestines, so don't be shocked when you weigh less coming out of the surgery. Now, some of the space will be taken up by the power source, and of course, the tubing that will replace the majority of your alimentary canal. That is, your esophagus and rectum, and pretty much everything in between."

Dr. Cruz used the display to show how the system fit within a body in relation to the other organs. "Now, to save time and future trauma, it is standard procedure to include a cortical processor and the nanite packs that can construct ocular, auditory, and olfactory implants. These nanites are also responsible for essentially wiring the cybernetic nutrient extractor to the nervous system."

Lucy grimaced. "Does he have to have all of that?"

Zack bit his lip. *Maybe I want all of that.*

"Here's the thing: if we install it now, he won't have to undergo a subsequent surgery in the future should he need ocular implants for any reason. This is a standard package, even though most people never activate the olfactory implants, and the auditory implants are regulated by Confederation law."

"We're EAC citizens." Carlos leaned forward to examine the information on the screen.

"The EAC regulates them, too." Dr. Cruz changed the display to show an animation of nanites traveling along the spinal cord on their way to access the optic nerve and assemble a cybernetic enhancement on the back of an eyeball.

"The cortical implant, of course, will remain on standby until you activate it. You can choose to live your whole life without it, as trillions of people do. But if you ever want it, or need it, you won't have to have another surgery to implant it, and that avoids the risk of complications."

Lucy pointed at the display. "What sort of risks does this cyber-stomach thing have?"

"No surgery performed under anesthesia is entirely without risk. Zack is a relatively healthy youth, so his risk of adverse effects from the medications and the procedure itself are minimal. The most common risk factor with these cybernetic nutrient extractors is carelessness."

"How do you mean?" Carlos sat back and took Lucy's hand.

Zack felt himself flush. His friends often told him he was careless.

"Well"—Dr. Cruz swung the display to the side—"with a cybernetic nutrient extractor, Zack will be able to ingest and extract nutrients from almost any organic substance. Meats, fruits, dirt, garbage, feces."

Zack's stomach lurched and he recoiled.

"Basically, if he can put it in his mouth and swallow it, and it's not, you know, a rock or a steel bolt or something, then the system will break it down and distribute the nutrients. Waste products will be stored until the reservoir is full, and he will void it much as he does now. He could eat rotten food and as long as he got past the taste, he'd be fine. But if it's toxic and the toxins can be absorbed through the mucus membranes of the mouth, it will still affect him. If the toxins have to be absorbed through the stomach lining or intestines, however, the system will neutralize them and they will pass through without affecting him."

"That's kind of cool." Zack smiled at the thought of being able to eat anything his friends dared him to.

Dr. Cruz's lips became a thin line. "Some people get a little too complacent. But if you stick to proper food, you'll be fine."

Carlos pointed at the now blank display. "I saw something about nutrient retention?"

"The system will dispense only what Zack's body needs to maintain his nutritional requirements. He literally will not be able to overeat. Nutrients will be stored for a couple of days, and anything not needed will be expelled. I don't want to get graphic, but if you make a habit of stuffing yourself at every meal, you'll be spending a lot of time in the lavatory. Usually if someone overindulges at a party or something, then they don't feel as hungry the next day. But there are people who never really learned to listen to their body's cues and habitually stuff themselves, regardless of whether they're hungry."

Zack thought of the pizza he planned to consume after the surgery and decided he would eat a whole sausage and onion pie by himself.

"So, he won't be able to tell if he's full or not?" Carlos shared a glance with his wife.

Doctor Cruz shook their head. "That first week post-op is crucial for easing into the system." They faced Zack. "Exercise moderation, perhaps even less than you normally would eat, and slowly build back up to a normal diet. The signals from the system should be indistinguishable from what you feel now when you're hungry or sated."

The doctor raised an eyebrow. "If you gorge yourself every day after you're released from the hospital, then your body won't receive the correct information from the system, and it will make moderating your intake much more challenging."

So much for the whole pizza. "I can be careful for a week."

Dr. Cruz chuckled. "We'll give you guidelines and complete information about the system, of course."

"Right, of course." Carlos sighed and leaned into his wife. "If this is what Zack wants, I think we should go ahead and sign the consent and get this underway."

Lucy sighed and nodded, then looked at Zack. "Is this what you want, honey?

"Yes." Zack bounced in his seat atop the exam table. "Please, Mom."

"All right." Carlos put his arm around Lucy. "Let's get it done."

—— 《 》 — 《 》 — 《 》 — 《 》 — 《 》 — 《 》 ——

Jenny pulled the neck of the hospital gown tighter and pulled the covers up higher. The hospital room in which she waited for Dr. Cruz to check in with her felt far too chilly for her taste, like a blast chiller.

Her mother sat in an adjacent chair, poring over the technical specs of the cybernetic nutrient extractor scheduled for installation in her daughter. "This appears to be the same model your father received."

"They're not clothes, Mother. I think there's only one kind per species." Jenny clenched her jaw to keep her teeth from chattering. "How is he getting along with it?"

Amélie shrugged. "He eats well, doesn't complain about it."

"I guess it if it does what it's supposed to, you don't really notice it." Jenny looked up as the door opened and Dr. Cruz entered, wearing a surgical cap to cover their hair.

They rubbed their hands together. "Your friend is in recovery. He did quite well. Now, since you already have some implants, your surgery is slightly more complex. We'll have to be careful not to sever any existing connections. How are you holding up?"

"I'm cold." Jenny suppressed a shiver.

"Yes, that's one disadvantage of operating out of an Ersidian hospital: it's kept cooler than we'd find comfortable because of Ersidians' fur." They perused her vitals on the readout at the end of her bed. "I'll have them adjust the temperature in here while you're in surgery. It should be more comfortable while you recover. Do you have any questions?"

Jenny glanced at her mother. Amélie shook her head. Jenny shrugged. "I guess not. This is the same implant my father has. I'm as ready as I'm going to be."

"Very good." Dr. Cruz regarded Jenny's mother. "I'll take good care of your daughter, Mrs. Dulac. She'll be back and resting comfortably in no time. If you need anything during the surgery, feel free to use the call button."

"Thank you, Doctor."

"A nurse will be in to transport you down to surgery shortly." Dr. Cruz tapped the end of the bed as they exited the room.

Jenny laid back and sighed. *It'll be over soon, then ramen, ice cream, cake, cheese...*

"Try not to worry too much, Geneviève. They talk about this being more complex for you than Zack, but any halfway competent surgeon will have no trouble working around the implants you already have. I'm certain Dr. Cruz is just being cautious."

She turned her head toward her mother. "I'm not worried, just hungry."

Amélie chuckled. "That, too, will pass."

"Maybe, while I'm in surgery, you could check in on Zack and his parents?" She hoped her mother would at least try to be more sociable toward Zack's family since they were going to be living in close quarters for so long.

"Yes, fine. Just think, soon you'll be back at Cytherean Academy with your friends."

"Not Zack." Jenny frowned and picked at her fingernails. "I think..."

"I'm just glad you didn't get yourself expelled. You'll go back to school and be able to put this whole unpleasantness behind you."

The nurse, a hulking Ersidian with black fur, entered the room. Her nose twitched in front of her deep-set brown eyes as she examined the readout at the end of the bed. "It's time. Ready?"

"I'll be here when you get back, Geneviève."

Jenny didn't expect her mother would go see Zack and his family while she was gone. She nodded to the nurse, who grunted as she swung the bed around and pushed it out of the room. Jenny put her head back and closed her eyes. *May Dr. Cruz's hands be steady and swift.*

Chapter 30

Zack's eyes fluttered open. His heart raced as, for a moment, he found himself surrounded by unfamiliar light grey walls with strange machines scattered about. Then, he remembered he lay in an Ersidian hospital. He rubbed his eyes and tried to sit up, but a pain across his abdomen convinced him to remain prone. Zack turned his head to look around the room and saw his mother sleeping in a reclining chair. He didn't see his father, though a second chair sat vacant near the one occupied by his mother.

He lifted the sheet and peered underneath it. Upon seeing his midsection wrapped in bandages, he prodded the area with a free hand. The area around what he assumed was the incision remained tender, but no more so than he expected. As long as he didn't touch it, he experienced no pain at all.

"Mom?" Zack rasped a harsh croak. He swallowed and tried again.

Lucy sat up. "How do you feel, honey?"

"Thirsty. Hungry." Zack felt the less he spoke, the better.

His mother stretched and stood. She pressed the call button on Zack's bed. "I'm sure they'll bring you some water. They might want you to wait a bit before you eat."

"Did they"—Zack propped himself up on his elbows—"move me?"

"No, honey. This is where you started this morning." Lucy brushed hair off Zack's forehead. "You woke up briefly in the recovery room, remember? Maybe that's why you're confused."

"I don't remember that."

An Ersidian nurse with grey-flecked black fur entered the room. His pale blue smock strained to contain his furry bulk. "Oh, he's awake."

"Just now." Lucy returned to her seat. "He's thirsty and hungry."

"Good, that's normal." The nurse retrieved a glass of water from the dispenser and raised the tray table attached to the bed. A small holoviewer activated on the table and filled with text in Ersidian. "The doctor has restricted your menu for tonight. Do you need me to switch the language to Galactic Standard?"

Zack understood enough Ersidian to find the option to do that himself. He shook his head. After he tapped the screen, the menu reverted to text he could read easily. The instructions he understood, but none of the menu items sounded familiar.

"I don't know what these...garla-tagi... things are." He pointed to the list of food items, all with Ersidian names.

The nurse stepped around to read the menu. "It's a selection of nutrient supplements—high-protein, nutrient-rich chilled beverages. The first three are"—he paused to remember the word in Galactic Basic—"dairy-based? That's the closest I can think of. The rest are not."

"They're probably like milkshakes or smoothies, Zack." Lucy squinted to read the screen from afar.

"Oh!" Zack perked up and read the descriptions. They provided no insight. "What's the closest thing to a chocolate milkshake? Have you ever had one of those?"

The nurse grunted. "The cocoa bean. Too bitter." Sighing, he perused the list again. He pointed at the middle of the dairy options. "That's probably the closest, but it might be too sweet for you chocolate-lovers."

Zack stabbed at the entry. His throat burned from talking. "Gotta be better than that paste."

The nurse moved to the end of the bed to check his vitals on the display. "Someone will bring your nutrient supplement by shortly. Dr. Cruz is going to stop by, as well, as soon as they're finished cleaning up from your friend's surgery."

"How is Jenny? Did her surgery go well?" Zack's mom beat him to the question.

"Yes, fine. She's in recovery now. If you both have a good night, you'll be leaving us sometime tomorrow." The nurse left Zack and his mom to wait for his food. Lucy stood and hugged Zack.

"Your father went for a walk while you slept. I'm going to find him and get some dinner. You'll be all right until we get back?"

Zack nodded and pointed at the holoviewer where he pulled up a program on the entertainment network. Lucy smiled and departed in search of Zack's father and food.

—— 《》 — 《》 — 《》 — 《》 — 《》 — 《》 ——

As Jenny waited for her dinner to arrive, she tuned the holoviewer to a program about daredevil cloud gliders. The narrator, who sounded Devoran to her ears, seemed skeptical of the wisdom of cloud gliding in the skies of planets like Jupiter and Saturn. When the program advanced to feature cloud gliders tackling the skies of even more massive, hotter planets that were closer to brown dwarfs than gas giants, their tone became contemptuous of the risk-takers.

Jenny found the disdainful monologue of the program's narration soothing, and her eyelids grew heavy. She didn't want to sleep more necessarily, but lying in bed passively absorbing holoshows hardly seemed like a better alternative.

Just as she dozed off, an orderly entered her room with her dinner. The tawny-furred Ersidian set the tall cup on Jenny's tray table. "Need anything else?"

Jenny peered into the cup. The thick, frozen liquid resembled a green mint milkshake. She shook her head. When she stabbed the provided straw into the goop, it felt like a milkshake to Jenny. She sipped it tentatively. Exertion from pulling the viscous frozen liquid through the straw made her sides hurt.

"Maybe a spoon?"

The orderly retrieved one from the cabinet across from the bed. Jenny tasted the g'ral-tagyn. The cold soothed her raw throat as bright citrus and sweet fruit notes danced across her tongue. She closed her eyes and moaned at the first taste of something that didn't resemble warm, wet cardboard in what seemed like a lifetime.

"Are you all right?"

Jenny's eyes snapped open. The orderly stared at her over his shoulder from the doorway.

"Have you ever tasted nutrient paste?" Jenny savored another spoonful of g'ral-tagyn.

"Yes. It's... adequate. Nutritious."

"Nasty. I've been living on it for a long time. This"—she pointed at her dinner with the spoon—"is heaven."

The orderly chuckled. "I understand." He turned to leave. "Oh, looks like you have a visitor."

Jenny craned her neck to look around the orderly. He stepped aside to let a uniformed Ersidian pass, then exited and closed the door behind as Jenny smiled and greeted her friend.

"Mungus!"

"Hey, Jenny. How are you?" Mungus ran his hand through the disheveled mane of hair on top of his head, then dragged a chair over to sit next to the bed. "Are you here alone?"

"My mother was annoying me, so I sent her home." Jenny spent a lot of time reading up on cybernetic nutrient extractors in between school assignments, and Dr. Cruz explained things thoroughly. The last thing she needed was for her mother to reiterate everything she already knew with an additional helping of how her father's doctor explained things differently.

Mungus grunted. "I just left Zack. He kept falling asleep on me, and his parents looked like they could sleep for about a week too. I hear they're releasing you tomorrow?"

Jenny nodded as she savored another spoonful of her fruity frozen dinner.

"When can you eat regular food?"

"Now, but my throat hurts, and the doctor wants us to take it easy and not gorge ourselves right away."

Mungus scratched his head. "Hm, that must've been why Zack was grunting so much and not actually talking."

Jenny held up her cup. "This helps."

"What is that? Zack said it was a milkshake, but we don't have those. I didn't push him because he was obviously having trouble talking. More than you, anyway."

"G'ral-tagyn."

Mungus laughed. "That's what he was trying to say! I gave up trying to understand some of the stuff he was croaking. I spent most of the time talking to his parents."

Jenny felt like her vocal chords were being dragged over sandpaper, but if she spoke only right after a spoonful of g'ral-tagyn, she could tolerate speaking a sentence or two.

"So, you're going to be living with Zack now?" Although Jenny understood why Zack had been assigned a bodyguard, she didn't think she'd enjoy having Mungus around all day, every day.

"I'm his bodyguard, but I doubt I'll actually be living with him." Mungus shifted in his seat. "I think they're more worried about when he's out in public without his parents than if he's just hanging around at home."

Jenny smiled. "You think he's going to tell you every time he goes out?"

Mungus smacked his palm with his fist. "He'd better."

She laughed and continued eating while Mungus caught her up on his activities since they'd last seen each other on Valtra. School for him at the Citadel seemed to parallel Jenny's experiences, except Mungus enjoyed several classes of a more martial bent, suitable for one whose family comprised generations of soldiers and royal guards.

She let him talk as she contemplated school. Seeing Hiri again remained the only positive to returning to Cytherea now that the school's administration had shown they were willing to throw students to the wolves for political expediency.

"Well, I guess I'd better get going." Mungus rose from his seat. "You're looking good, Jenny. Once you and Zack are released, I've got something planned for all of us. Let Ix know, will you? I haven't seen it around lately."

"I will." Jenny brought up a message to Ix. "Thanks for stopping by, Mungus."

After he left, she composed her message. Since she could not be sure Zack had given the Valtraxian an update, she started with that, then told Ix that Mungus was planning something for them all once she and Zack were released from the hospital. "I have a question for you, Ix. Don't talk to Zack about this, please. I was wondering, are you still returning to Cytherean Academy? It feels wrong to go back after how they treated Zack. I'd really like to know what you're thinking about it."

Jenny sent the message and finished her dinner, then tuned into another cloud gliding program on the holoviewer. She let the visuals of the soaring gliders carry her off to sleep.

Chapter 31

A few days after being released from the hospital, Zack, Jenny, and Ix met Mungus at the Citadel's transport hub. Their driver, a wiry, speckled brown furred Kerrolian, tipped his cap and held the door for them as they approached.

"Would you like a tour of Taella City, or did you have a particular destination in mind?" The driver spoke Galactic Basic with a crisp, neutral accent, rather like a newscaster determined to make themselves clear and understandable to as many people as possible.

Mungus grunted as he ducked into the rear cabin of the transport, narrowly missing his head on the door frame. "You can take us out of the city, right?"

Zack ducked in, sliding across the seat facing Mungus to sit next to the driver's side passenger window. Jenny took the seat next to him, also facing backwards and Ix clambered in next to Mungus.

"Technically yes, but I am under strict instructions to return you no later than the twenty-first hour." The driver shut the door, then made his way around the back of the vehicle, before returning to the front and taking his seat behind the controls. He looked over his shoulder at the group.

Mungus checked his chronometer. "That gives us plenty of time. Take us to Emberrock."

The driver's eyes narrowed. "You all look very young. Surely you'd rather spend your time someplace more interesting."

Zack glanced at Jenny. "What's in Emberrock, Mungus?"

The Ersidian bared his teeth. "It's a surprise. Just take us there, driver. It's my clan's home."

"Oh." The driver nodded, then scratched one of his ears. "Very well, then."

The transport lurched forward. After a few twists and turns to navigate the exit of the palace grounds, they merged onto a thoroughfare and picked up speed. As he watched the city whiz by, he listened to Mungus deflect a series of questions from Ix about their destination. At the rate they traveled, the stone façades of the Ersidian buildings formed a continuous grey streak outside of the window, broken occasionally by a multicolored sign or a building designed and built to another species' aesthetics.

"Ix, seriously"—Mungus snapped his teeth together—"It's a surprise; therefore, I am not going to tell you anything about why we're going to Emberrock."

"My apologies, Mungus. I did not mean to upset you."

Jenny nudged Zack. "Hey, you haven't complained much about school. Are you okay?"

Of all the subjects Jenny could have chosen to change the subject, she picked the one he neither wanted to think about nor talk about. He curled his lip. "My parents say everything is going to work out. They're actually kind of happy that I'll be living at home now while going to school on Vilicus. I don't know what Ix is going to do, though. It technically still lives with us."

He looked at his friend across the cabin. Ix had largely stayed silent on the matter, for reasons Zack did not understand.

Ix tapped its fingers on its carapace. "I have been... torn. I feel your treatment is unjust, however, I am enrolled in an accelerated program at Cytherean Academy for which there are no accommodations at the school on Vilicus. I do not wish you to think I am disloyal, Zack, therefore, I have not made a decision."

"Oh." Zack looked away. He knew Ix attended a special program but didn't realize it was something only Cytherean Academy offered. "Don't quit your thing because of me. That's not fair either, Ix."

Jenny reached across the cabin to touch Ix's arm. "Vilicus and Venus are close enough most of the year you can talk practically in real time and visit during almost all of the school breaks."

"Yeah, that's right." Zack perked up. "Mom and Dad have space in the new place set aside for you, Ix. And it's not like you'll be alone at Cytherean Academy. Jenny will still be there."

Her lips became a thin line. "Yes."

"We barely had any classes together anyway. I guess it won't be all that different." Zack rested his head on his hand as he resumed viewing the passing scenery through the window.

"Don't worry, you two." Mungus grinned. "I'll be there to keep Zack out of trouble."

Jenny snorted. "That brings me very little comfort, Mungus."

"I don't try to get into trouble, Jenny." Zack slouched in his seat. The buildings of the city gave way to grass and razor shrub-covered rolling hills. He'd read about how different the foliage was from Earth's, but from a speeding vehicle, Ersid looked much like any hilly area he'd ever seen with his parents.

"I know, Zack."

"Danger seems attracted to you, Zack." Ix cocked its head. "Perhaps you have a magnetic personality."

Zack blinked and narrowed his eyes. "You too, Ix?"

Jenny laughed. "I don't think that's what that means."

Mungus leaned forward, his black nose twitching just centimeters from Zack's face. "Don't worry, buddy. Danger has to go through me from now on."

Zack laid his head back and closed his eyes. "Thanks, Mungus."

—— 《》 — 《》 — 《》 — 《》 — 《》 — 《》 ——

It wasn't until Jenny blinked open her eyes, that she realized she'd dozed off as they rode to Emberrock. The rolling, foliage-covered hills that had lulled her to sleep speeding by had given way to a city street. Clusters of foreboding blocky, angular buildings towered over them, forming a sort of permacrete canyon. Most buildings featured muted colors that accented the natural grey tones of the construction materials, though Jenny spied several painted with murals or featuring large splashes of color. Even at their reduced rate of travel, she failed to catch a glimpse to see what the accent colors emphasized.

The buildings in Emberrock appeared larger than what Jenny had seen in Taella City, both in height and width. The physical arrangement of the capital seemed designed to draw attention to the Royal Citadel.

"They like to keep things traditional in Taella City; everything in service to the sovereign. Buildings that need more space go down, rather than up. Out here"—Mungus gestured through the window to the buildings they passed—"things are built to be more modern."

"Everything is so blocky." Jenny stared at a residential high-rise that appeared built entirely of oblique angles.

"They're strong and tough"—Mungus pounded his chest with a fist—"like Ersidians."

"You didn't bring us here just to drive us around these buildings, did you?" Jenny didn't mind the drive, actually. It was good to get out of the suite with her friends and away from the adults for a while.

"Of course not. I gave the driver instructions while you were dozing. We're almost there."

The transport pulled up to a towering construction. Massive permacrete pillars surrounded a central, circular structure. The pillars rose up several floors before angling outward. Splayed finger-like supports surrounded additional levels rising up into the sky. The top of the building appeared to host several trees. Any other foliage remained obscured from street level.

The augmented reality tools in Jenny's ocular implants identified the building as the Clan Stonetalon Arcology. The arcology they visited on Valtra easily dwarfed Clan Stonetalon's, but the information her implant fed her indicated the structure she viewed housed well over a thousand families, as well as schools, businesses, and vital community services. Clan Stonetalon's arcology appeared to be a self-contained, self-sufficient city within Emberrock.

The driver spoke to them over the transport's internal comm system. "Once you get out, I'll go park someplace safe, then I'll wait in the market center. Just send me a message when you're ready to leave, and I'll meet you right here. I'll ping you if you start bumping up against the time limit. I'm at your service, but I'm not willing to lose my job if you all want to skirt the rules and be late returning to the city."

Jenny checked the time. It had taken them just over an hour to travel from Taella City, so she set a reminder in her chronometer to alert her half an hour prior to their departure time. Since her side of the transport opened into traffic, she waited for Mungus and Zack to exit before sliding out their side.

Banners flapped in the warm breeze coursing through the city streets. Pedestrians, mostly Ersidians with a quadrupedal Uurt here and there, crossed in front of them as they stared up at the brutal, blocky behemoth towering above. Jenny noticed she and Zack appeared to be the only humans in the area, and Ix the only Valtraxian; everyone else seemed to be Ersidian or Uurt.

"What is this building, Mungus?" Zack leaned back to look up toward the top of the monolithic building.

"We call it Stone Talons." Mungus put his hands on his hip. "It's been my clan's home for centuries."

Ix chittered and stepped back to allow a pair of Uurts walking side by side to pass. "If this arcology is clan Stonetalon's home, who are all the others who live in Emberrock?"

"The clanless, those who have moved away from their clan homes for jobs, marriage, family problems, whatever. Plus, workers from off-world and immigrants, unless they're members of a clan, like you three. You'd have space here in Stone Talons, if you wanted it." Mungus put his arms around Zack and Jenny. "Of course, not all Ersidians want to live in their clan's arcology, and not all clans have one to call their own. Not yet, anyway. Every clan has a star cruiser, though. Even ones that don't have an arcology."

"Cool. Can we see the Stonetalon clan star cruiser, Mungus?" Zack goggled at the immense building towering over them.

"I think it's cruising around right now." Mungus shrugged. "There's probably pictures on the holonet. Maybe a holovid tour of the ship."

"So, why did you bring us here, Mungus?" Jenny thrust her hands in her pockets.

"Well, you can't come all the way to Ersid without visiting home." He strode toward the entrance. "Let's go inside."

Chapter 32

They passed through the doors into the stone-tiled foyer of Stone Talons. Zack marveled at the green-veined black stone floors and walls, polished to a mirror-finish. The foyer opened into a central plaza. Shops bordering quadrants of green space and clusters of tables and benches all surrounded a lift shaft that ascended to the upper levels of the arcology. In between the exposed levels above him, he noticed a staircase that wound around the interior of the building, behind the shops.

The aroma of roasting meat wafted past them. Zack chuckled. He knew from experience such a smell should set his stomach rumbling, particularly since they ate breakfast several hours ago, but his new cyberstomach made no such spontaneous demands upon him.

Still, he liked fresh roasted meat. "Mungus, can we stop to get whatever they're cooking? It smells great!"

Jenny snorted. "Heading straight for the food. That's proof that everything is back to normal for you."

"Ha! We could, but maybe on the way out." The Ersidian pointed toward the lifts at the center. "Your surprise is in the rooftop park. Unless you'd rather take the stairs."

Zack shook his head. "The lift is just fine."

The central shaft featured half-a-dozen lifts arranged in a circle. Indicator lights set in the floor directed passengers to arriving cars and displayed the floor number upon which each lift stopped or passed. Mungus led them to wait for an approaching lift.

As they waited for the car to finish its descent, Zack watched the residents milling around the plaza. The scent from nearby teal and orange blooms hung thick in the air. A pair of cubs chased each other as their parents trailed behind and growled for them to stop. Zack caught snippets of conversation between a pair of maintenance workers, wearing khaki-colored jumpsuits over grease-matted white fur, who emerged from a hatch between two of the shafts. He understood enough of the Ersidian language to learn they had just completed some routine maintenance.

When the doors slid open with a soft hiss, a group of young Ersidians exited, grunting greetings at Mungus as they passed. Mungus stepped forward and held the door long enough for Zack, Jenny, and Ix to enter the lift.

The lack of music inside the car struck Zack as odd. Only the sounds of the hoisting mechanism penetrated the walls, and that alone did not dampen the sound of Mungus's breathing or the clacking and clicking of Ix's exoskeleton.

"Can you give us a hint, Mungus?" Zack looked over his shoulder at his friend. The Ersidian didn't seem as tall as Zack remembered. *Hm. Maybe I am growing.*

"It's nothing much." Mungus grinned. "Just a homecoming party."

"Who came home?" Jenny shifted her weight as the door slid open.

Pounding electronic music filled the air. Multicolored lights hung from the trees and dim amber lanterns illuminated the paths winding their way through the foliage. The effect, lessened by the midday sun, reminded Zack of the decorations strung up in Ishtar Plaza during Cytherean Academy's myriad events.

Mungus faced them and walked backward as he led his friends out of the lift, his arms spread. "You did. My honor family. Welcome home."

Zack struggled to take it all in. To his left, he saw large hunks of meat sizzling in the flames of several large grills tended by smock-wearing Ersidians. Beyond that, he saw several roped off areas in which folks wrestled. On the other side, to his right, he viewed a platform upon which an Uurt band played. Through a grove of trees, he caught glimpses of a stone structure of some sort.

"Does any of this have a significance, Mungus"—Jenny glanced toward the trees—"or is it just a big party?"

Making introductions Zack would never remember as they went, Mungus led them through the crowd toward the grills. "Well, we like to hold a celebration when members of our honor family come visit Ersid for the first time. Normally, we'd have it right after you got through customs at the spaceport. I had to wait until your quarantine was over before I could even plan anything, plus, I was in the middle of some intense training."

"What's that over there?" Jenny pointed toward the large structure visible through the trees.

Mungus waved his hand. "Some museum or a temple or something. After we eat, we should take a moment at the Shrine of the Ancestors, at least, Zack and I should."

Zack looked up. "What? Why?"

"I figure I should say a prayer to my ancestors if I'm going to be your bodyguard from now on." The Ersidian shrugged. "It can't hurt, right?"

Zack nodded. "Sure."

They continued to follow Mungus toward the food. As they navigated the crowd, Zack noticed Jenny seemed to lag behind, and he caught her stealing glances at the structure behind the trees. He stopped long enough for her to catch up while Mungus and Ix moved ahead.

"Is everything all right?"

Jenny frowned and shook her head. "I'm not feeling much like crowds or food right now. I'm going to check out that museum. You go on ahead with Mungus and Ix and get something to eat. I'll be along shortly."

── 《 》 — 《 》 — 《 》 — 《 》 — 《 》 — 《 》 ──

Jenny slipped away, leaving the boys to enjoy their contests of strength. She sent a quick text message to Ix letting the Valtraxian know she sought a quiet place to be alone with her thoughts and she'd catch up with them shortly. The cacophony of guttural cheers by Ersidians as they watched their champions wrestle and compete faded into the background as she distanced herself from the pit.

Ahead, through a small copse of red-leafed trees, Jenny spotted a stone structure with smoother curves than most of the other buildings and façades she saw in Stone Talons, or anywhere else on Ersid. Lines of green and blue highlighted the building's design, drawing her eyes to a giant bird perched on top of a column depicted in a spread-wing pose. Its wings cast shadows on the ground below. Half-a-dozen Ersidians and Uurts wearing gold-trimmed green robes tended the grounds.

A tall, tawny-furred Ersidian woman wearing green robes trimmed in silver approached Jenny. Her long braids, streaked with gray at the roots, hung past her waist. The woman gestured toward the giant bird looming over them. "Come to pray to the Great Bird of the Galaxy?"

Jenny crossed her arms and gazed up at the sculpture. It reminded her of a cross between an eagle and a hornbill with its long, down-curved beak. "I thought Ersidians prayed to their ancestors."

The woman smiled, revealing her canines. "Ah, but the Great Bird *is* our ancestor." She put her arm around Jenny's shoulder and guided her toward the entrance of the structure.

Gesturing to the tapestries and paintings within the gallery, she directed Jenny to a faded tapestry that depicted a farmer leaning on her rake whilst looking up at the sky.

"You may call me Xuth. I am the Grand Shelzot of the Grae-nay Shay-tal." She snuffled. "It doesn't translate well into Galactic Basic. The closest that makes sense is 'Keepers of the Lore of Inspiration.'"

"I'm Jenny. I'm here with Mungaborrarius Tonnarvassas." She admired the fine needlework of the tapestry before her. "I don't understand how a bird can be your ancestor."

Xuth's smile faded. "Did Mungaborrarius explain none of this when he gave you that braid?"

Jenny snorted. "Mungus doesn't explain much of anything. He just is."

Xuth rubbed her muzzle. "Malus faan. I should not be surprised."

"How did you know Mungus gave me this braid?" Jenny reached up and ran her fingers along the honor braid she had woven into her own hair.

Spreading her hands, Xuth gazed toward the ceiling. "Your coming was foretold." She grinned at Jenny. "We were all told you were coming today and why."

Jenny pointed at the tapestry of the farmer. "My people make artwork like this, too, but I don't remember seeing tapestries about farms."

"Ah, but you see, these"—Xuth gestured toward the tapestries hung along the walls of the circular chamber—"tell the story of how Ohamakanaar, the Great Bird, inspired Ersidians and Uurts to reach for the sky and the stars beyond. Without the Great Bird's story, we'd still be bound to the land, hoarding resources and squabbling over territory."

Xuth enveloped Jenny's shoulders with her hands and stood behind her in front of the tapestry. "Day after day after day, Ohamakanaar toiled in her fields. And so it was, year after year. But always, she looked up. In those days, the sky seemed impossibly far away, impossible to reach, impossible to touch."

They moved to the next tapestry, which featured a farmer gazing toward a faraway mountain, her blade raised. Xuth pointed toward the Ersidian figure at the center of the tapestry. "Ohamakanaar's toil seemed endless, the drudgery of existence, but always she looked up. One day, she decided the land could wait. It had been there before she was born and would be there after she died. The sky called to her." Xuth's finger moved to the peak. "She resolved to climb Ersid's highest mountain, in whose shadow she'd lived her whole life. There, she would, at last, touch the sky."

Jenny raised an eyebrow as she focused on the central figure in the tapestry.

"Such a concept may seem absurd to us"—Xuth raised a black-clawed finger—"but remember this was a pre-industrial society."

"And it's just a story, right?" Jenny and Xuth moved to the next tapestry. The colors seemed more vibrant than on the previous two. It depicted Ohamakanaar climbing the mountain and featured a group of Ersidians clustered at the bottom of the mountain watching her ascent.

"Perhaps. Here, we see Ohamakanaar's ascent up Naargonth, the Black Peak. She climbed and climbed until her claws wore down to nubs and her fingers bled.

They moved to the fourth tapestry. The threads, their colors vibrant, looked almost new to Jenny's untrained eyes. "This one looks different."

"Hm, yes, we just received this one. These aren't the originals, of course. Every clan home has a shrine to the Great Bird of the Galaxy. The originals are kept in a sealed vault under Naargonth. No one on Ersid should be deprived of a chance to share in this vital part of our history, so the Loremasters ensure it is available to all."

Xuth stood quiet for a moment and gazed at the tapestry with Jenny. On the left side, Ohamakanaar knelt at the peak, her head thrown back as she gazed upward. In the middle, she stood atop the mountain, her arms, now great wings outstretched. Finally, on the right side, the scene featured Ohamakanaar flying upward. The Ersidian's hand stretched toward a shining silver bead Jenny assumed depicted a star.

"When Ohamakanaar reached the top, she stretched her arms, but still could not touch the sky. It seemed just as far away as it had on the ground. But night was coming, and she saw the first stars, so far away. She summoned all her energy, all her will. So great was her desire to see beyond, her arms transformed into wings, and she flew up and away, into the sky and beyond to the stars." Xuth huffed. "At least, that's what the story says. Realistically, she probably had brought some sort of rudimentary glider up the mountain with her and flung herself from the peak, then fell to her death someplace far from her village where no one ever found her. But, in this case, the truth is less important than the myth."

Jenny stroked her braid, then crossed her arms. "I've never heard a myth that Ersidians can fly."

Xuth threw her head back and laughed. "Ancestors, no. The myth is what I've just told you. Her story, however, it came about, inspired Ersidians and Uurts to look beyond their personal material needs. We came together, worked toward the common good, and, eventually, we reached the stars."

Jenny recalled what she learned in school about human spaceflight. "I think most of our rocketry came from wartime innovations."

Xuth put her hand on Jenny's shoulder. "We had our share of terrible, bloody wars. And from them came great leaps in technology, that is certain. We learned sometimes the right road is the hardest to travel. But surely, humans know that already. You are here, alone, instead of with your friends. What troubles you?"

Jenny had not wandered away from her friends hoping to find a counselor among the throngs of Ersidians she'd never met. She chuckled. "It's complicated."

"Well, I could tell you another story." Xuth guided Jenny over to a set of paintings that ran parallel to the tapestries of Ohamakanaar. "How my people and the Uurts first came to know each other and realized we were closer than our appearances suggest?"

A nearby bench offered a view of the first painting in the series. Jenny sat, slumping, and crossed her arms. "Eventually, we'll all go back home. But, Zack got expelled from Cytherean Academy, so we're really splitting up. Again. It's not right, he didn't do anything wrong."

Jenny heard a low rumble in Xuth's chest, a barely perceptible growl. "Yes, I've heard. I do not care for Devoran politics."

"You seem to know a lot about us."

Xuth reached out and ran a finger down Jenny's honor braid. "Mungaborrarius is my nephew. His mother, my sister, tells me everything. We're very close, though I don't see them as often as I'd like. And what they don't tell me, I read about. Your story, the Devorans, your voyage to Athos and then here, it's been in the news."

"I don't know how I can go back to Cytherean Academy after the way they treated Zack. But, I have a friend there who"—Jenny closed her eyes and thought of Hiri—"well, she's more than a friend. I feel like I'd be abandoning her."

Xuth stroked Jenny's hair. "If your friend cares for you the way you care for her, then she'll support your decision."

"Is this the part where you tell me I'm still young and that I'll find someone else who can make me just as happy?"

Xuth snorted. "Certainly not. Though you may be inexperienced in affairs of the heart, and I certainly don't know enough details about your life to make that judgment, your inexperience doesn't invalidate your feelings. You should talk it over with your friend before you decide. Though, I suspect you've already made the decision and you're weighing the best course to lessen the consequences."

Indeed, Jenny already knew what she had to do. She just hadn't admitted it to herself yet. She wanted to discuss her decision with Hiri, though, not just send a message from a hundred light years away. *Who knows when we can go back home? Maybe we'll all be finished with school before that even happens.*

Jenny stared at the speckled stone floor, focusing on nothing in particular. She struggled to prevent the enormity of the situation bury her under a mountain of despair. Xuth put a heavy arm around Jenny's shoulder and pulled her to her side. She held Jenny while the young woman contemplated the wisdom of that which she knew she must do.

Chapter 33

Zack took care to pile his plate only as high as he would have at one of his family cookouts back in Wyoming. Unfortunately, that meant choosing between large servings of the food he wanted most or smaller servings of all the different foods he wanted to try.

Some of the dishes he recognized, like roasted glommy bird. Others resembled Terran dishes like mashed potatoes and grilled vegetables, but their brilliant jewel-tone hues and odd shapes felt exotic and new to his palate.

Eating proper food again felt like heaven. Moaning in gustatory pleasure, Zack savored every bite.

"You're not going to break that cyberstomach, are you, Zack?" Mungus nudged his friend while keeping his voice low.

Zack shook his head as he finished chewing, then gestured at his plate. "This isn't any more than I would consume back home. I might wait a bit for dessert, though."

Mungus grunted. "We'll go to the shrine first, then get dessert."

While Mungus and Zack headed for the shrine, Ix went off to experience the museum and find Jenny. Zack dumped his dishes in one of the many recycling bins scattered about the dining area, then hurried after Mungus.

They sauntered down a path of black crushed stones toward a squat, truncated pyramid constructed of red-and-green speckled stone. The shape of the structure reminded Zack of the arcology they had visited on Valtra.

On their way to the entrance, they encountered an Ersidian who staggered and tipped his hat before belching and going on his way.

Mungus grunted and snarled. "There's always one who has to get liquored up before facing the ancestors."

Murals depicting some of Clan Stonetalon's most famous members adorned the doors. Zack tried to keep up with the pace Mungus rattled multisyllabic names. The doors slid open as they approached, interrupting Mungus's makeshift introduction.

"Bah, you'll never remember their names anyway." Mungus gestured for Zack to follow him.

The inside of the shrine, a single room, muffled the sounds of the party outside. Dim flickering light illuminated dozens of nooks lining the walls. A sharp-eyed bird with a downward-curved bill overlooked three pyramidal pillars at the center of the back wall. Atop each pillar sat a gleaming, brilliant-cut red gemstone the size of Zack's fist. The gems glowed from within, undoubtedly lit by some source within the pillars.

"The Shrine of Clan Stonetalon." Mungus crossed his arms over his chest, clasped his shoulders, and bowed. "Here we honor all of our ancestors."

Mungus motioned for Zack to do the same. He mimicked the Ersidian's motions.

After Zack bowed, Mungus gestured toward the mat in front of the three pyramids. "Now we kneel."

After Mungus lowered himself onto his knees, Zack followed suit. The Ersidian began a prayer of which Zack understood only a few words.

After a moment, Mungus glanced at his friend. "Sorry, there's an invocation at the beginning in the Old Tongue. You're probably not learning much of that at school, huh?"

Zack shook his head. "I caught a couple of words."

"The rest I can do in Galactic Basic." Mungus closed his eyes and bowed his head. "Goreborrarius the Stone Talon, namesake of my clan, namesake of my father; honored ancestors, give me the strength, skill, and wisdom to see my duty through; the courage to guard my honor-brother Zack Jackson with my life, if necessary. May our days together be free of danger, but grant him the good sense to keep his head down if the krunk hits the turbine."

Zack tilted his head. Furrowing his brow, he regarded Mungus through narrowed eyes. "It seemed all formal until that last sentence."

Mungus grinned. "Hey, it can't hurt, right?"

"I guess." Zack smelled a toasty, woody scent on the air before he saw the thin plumes of smoke drifting up from a grate at the base of the wall. His eyes felt drawn to the bird bust overlooking the shrine. "What's that big bird thing?"

Mungus glanced up. "Oh, that's Ohamakanaar, the Great Bird of the Galaxy."

"Never heard of it."

Mungus stood, then placed his hands on his hips. "It's a moldy old myth about an Ersidian who wanted to touch the sky, so she climbed a mountain, grew some wings and jumped off into space. Supposedly our inspiration to put our differences aside and explore the universe or something like that."

Zack thought for a moment. "My mom told me about an old myth like that. Some guy and his son wanted to fly, so they made some wings. One of them flew too close to the sun and his wings melted or burned up or something and he fell into the ocean and drowned."

"That's inspiring." Mungus laughed.

"I guess the lesson is"—scratching his head, Zack followed Mungus out of the shrine—"Huh, I'm not actually sure what that's supposed to inspire me to do. Don't fly with wings I made myself, I guess."

"That's a good lesson, I suppose." Mungus chewed on his lip as he considered the story. "Of course, if you're an engineer, you could build your own wings to fly with. Maybe he was just a bad engineer."

"Mom said that story is an Ancient Greek myth. People still believed the gods lived on a mountain around there and came down to mess with people just for fun. I'm not sure they even had things like wheels and roads back then." Zack found some of the mythology stories that his mom told him entertaining, like the one about the snake-haired lady who turned people to stone. However, a lot of the stories reminded him of those silly family drama shows where the characters didn't talk to each other and just made assumptions until they all became angry and yelled at each other.

He followed Mungus back toward the pounding music and dancing Ersidians. As he approached the dessert table, he spotted Ix and Jenny leaving the museum and heading their way.

—— ⟪⟫ — ⟪⟫ — ⟪⟫ — ⟪⟫ — ⟪⟫ — ⟪⟫ ——

Jenny spotted Zack and Mungus near the dessert table. Outside the museum, the deep baseline groove of the music rattled her spine. Ix tapped fingers in time to the beat as they headed toward the others.

"I am glad to see most Ersidians are not as... excitable... as Mungus." The Valtraxian skittered alongside Jenny. "The tapestries are quite nice and tell an interesting, if implausible, story."

"He has that implant now." Jenny had always wondered if Mungus's temper was typical of Ersidians. "Mungus said he's calmer."

Ix chittered a moment. "I understand why a perfectly healthy Ersidian would not want cybernetics, but I do not understand their reluctance to use them when it is medically necessary."

Jenny shrugged. "You'll have to talk to Mungus about that."

They rejoined their friends alongside a long table full of pastries, cakes, and jellied fruits. Jenny found the wide array of unfamiliar treats in the spread overwhelming.

She regarded Zack's plate, filled with what looked like some of everything. "You're not overloading yourself, are you?"

The young man glanced up at her with his mouth full of pastry. He shook his head. "I don't think so." Zack struggled to talk around the mouthful of food. "And if I do, I just won't eat as much tomorrow."

"What's good?" Jenny craned her neck to examine the dessert lineup.

Zack turned to look over his shoulder at the table behind them. "All of it?"

Mungus snorted and stood. "I'll bring you something, Jenny. I know just the thing."

For a moment, Jenny considered stopping him, but she realized he might interpret her refusal as a sign that she distrusted him. Of course, she trusted him with her life, but with her taste buds? That was another matter altogether.

She regarded the Valtraxian at the head of the table. "Not having any, Ix?"

Ix shook its head. "I am neither hungry, nor do I have a sugar mouth."

Jenny laughed. Zack froze with a sporkful of cake halfway to his mouth and stared.

"I think Ix means 'sweet tooth.'" Jenny touched Ix's arm. "That's all right, Ix. I think Zack ate enough for both of you."

Mungus returned with a slice of a dessert composed of alternating layers of pure white fluff and colorful berries. "Here, try the summer berry cloud cake. I think it's right up your alley, Jenny."

Upon tapping one of the white layers with her spork, Jenny realized it wasn't cake, but something more akin to meringue. Breaking through the outer crust revealed a fluffy, marshmallowy interior.

The berries burst in her mouth with a clean tartness that complimented the sweet, white confection. Jenny closed her eyes and sighed. "I was wrong to doubt you, Mungus. This is divine."

Ix cocked its head. "Perhaps the divinity is an homage to Ohamakanaar, the Great Bird of the Galaxy."

Mungus snorted in his drink, spraying foamy caramel-colored liquid across the table. Jenny snatched up her plate of cloud cake to protect it.

"It's just an expression, Ix." Jenny used her napkin to help Ix wipe Mungus's drink from its carapace.

As she finished off her summer berry cloud cake, Jenny noticed the sun sinking in the sky. Upon checking her chronometer, she realized they had only a few hours left before they needed to head back.

She noticed Mungus checking his chronometer as well, and when he suggested they all go watch the traditional drummer dance, she felt confident he would not keep them past their curfew.

At the far side of the rooftop terrace, past the wrestling ring, tiered seating stood facing a running track that followed the edge of the roof. A crowd of Ersidians in traditional hunting garb gathered in front of an array of drums affixed to the outer wall of the arcology.

The dance started slowly, with each hunter striking each drum once in turn as they passed them. When each had had a turn, they reversed their march and struck the drums again, this time twice each. On the third pass, they introduced a variance into their cadence. Jenny thought the rhythm of the drumbeat resembled a heartbeat.

With each subsequent pass, the drumbeat tempo grew more frantic as the hunters leapt and tumbled past each other. Always, underneath the rapid-clip drumming, Jenny heard the slow, steady drum of the heartbeat.

The Ersidians watching the dance stamped their feet in time to the heartbeat rhythm, never faltering.

Jenny leaned over to Mungus. "What's this all for?"

"Back in the day, a village would perform a simplified version of this prior to hunts for good fortune." Mungus shrugged. "No one really hunts anymore, so it's been amped up to give a good show. It looks exhausting."

"It's amazing!"

The drummer dance continued for another twenty minutes, ending in a flourish that shuddered their seats and brought the crowd to their feet. At the conclusion of the spectacle, Jenny found her heart pounding. Even Zack and Ix seemed worked up by the excitement of the crowd around them.

As soon as the performance ended, the drummers wasted no time gathering up their equipment and breaking down the stage. Mungus led his friends back toward the lifts.

He gestured toward the food tables. "Now's your chance if you want to grab anything to-go."

For a moment, Jenny pondered if her mother would appreciate anything from the impressive spread but decided against taking a dessert for her. Amélie rarely indulged in treats between meals, even on special occasions. Zack, on the other hand, filled several containers to take back to his parents.

"Shouldn't we say goodbye or something?" Zack nudged Jenny as they waited for the lift to arrive.

Mungus shrugged. "Go around if you want. They'll keep you long past our curfew. Besides, if you think their names are hard to remember, just consider: they think yours are, too, because they're so short. Besides, folks come and go from these types of celebrations constantly, even if they're the guests of honor."

Jenny snorted. "Then what's the point of having guests of honor?"

The Ersidian shoved his hands into his pockets. "Well, it's more important to be a guest of honor than it is to make sure everyone knows where you are and what you're doing at these parties all the time. We actually find it kind of rude when a guest of honor makes a big show of leaving."

"Oh." Zack scrunched up his face. "So, by just quietly ducking away, we're doing it right?"

Jenny nodded. "Sounds like." She preferred a quiet exit than a prolonged series of goodbyes and farewells with folks she'd only just met. She spotted Xuth perusing the dessert table. The elder Ersidian turned and waved to them just as the lift doors opened.

Mungus noticed Jenny waving to Xuth. "You met my aunt, did you? I'll bet she had some things to say about me, huh?"

The lift doors slid shut, and the pod began its descent with a slight shudder. Jenny shook her head and smiled. "We didn't talk about you much at all. She told me about the Great Bird of the Galaxy, mostly."

"She's good at that." Mungus turned to Zack. "Sorry, I should have sent you to her when you had questions."

"Well, we can come back here, right?" Zack leaned against the back wall of the lift pod.

"Sure, any time you want. This is where I'll bring you all, and your parents, too, if they decide you need to leave the palace." Mungus sighed. "I hope they don't kick you out too soon. I love having a room at the palace."

Jenny suspected the amenities in Stone Talons' flats were similar to their palace suite, though perhaps on a smaller scale. Each family would get their own flat to live in, rather than a multi-room suite to share.

By the time they found their transport and returned to the palace, Ersid's twin moons had risen high into the sky. Mungus accompanied them to their suite, but he said goodbye at the door, declining to come in.

Zack's parents greeted them as they entered. A quick scan of the room showed Jenny her mother had not waited in the common area for them.

"Your mom went out, Jenny." Carlos sat with his arm around his wife. "She wanted to check out some of the shops in the commerce district, I think."

Jenny nodded. "Thanks, Mr. Jackson. I'm going to turn in, maybe do some reading."

She bade everyone a good night, leaving Zack and Ix to tell his parents all about the party at Stone Talons.

Chapter 34

The main problem Zack had with the remote learning program that kept him from falling behind in school was that he didn't get to attend class with any of his friends. Still, he found the distraction-free environment of his room allowed him to complete the coursework more quickly. By the end of the first month of remote classes on Ersid, Zack was able to complete most day's assignments by lunch time, leaving his afternoons open to explore the palace gardens or take trips into the city with his folks.

He caught snippets of the news only while with his parents. The stand-off continued above Venus and Earth. Given few new developments, the crisis received only brief mentions interspersed with other news coming in via the Galactic News Network.

Zack soon believed Jenny, Ix, and he would finish their school year remotely on Ersid, so it was no surprise when his parents approached him one morning to talk about school. He paused the 30th Century Literature video presentation to let them into his room.

Carlos and Lucy sat on the edge of Zack's bed, facing his school terminal. Lucy frowned as she shoved the messy pile of blankets and sheets aside to make room.

His father rubbed his thighs before he spoke. "Well, you probably figure you're going to finish out this term here, right?"

Zack's head bobbed. "Yeah. It's fine, though. I think I'll be done early." He scrunched up his face. "It feels early. It's hard to keep track of when it is back home."

"Still a couple of weeks until midterms for the spring term." Lucy fidgeted with the braid hanging over her shoulder.

"Huh. This independent study stuff doesn't have us do midterms. We just keep going at our own pace until we're done." Zack glanced over at Ix's pile. The Valtraxian chittered to itself, immersed in a VR program. "I think Ix is actually finished for the year."

Zack's parents glanced at the Valtraxian seemingly oblivious to the conversation occurring around it before they returned their attention to Zack. Carlos sighed. "If we stay into next term, I think we should consider having you attend a local school, rather than remote classes."

Zack nodded. "I was thinking that, too." He shrugged. "It's fine. I'm going to have to make new friends no matter what, so I don't care if it's here or on Vilicus."

For a moment, Zack thought his mom was going to lunge forward to pull him into a hug, but she took his father's hand, instead. "Hopefully, we'll be able to go home before the next term starts."

Carlos squeezed Lucy's hand. "We can hope." He looked at Zack. "Well, we won't keep you from schoolwork any longer."

"I was pretty much done for the day." Zack spun around and closed out his terminal. "I was thinking about going out to the palace gardens, maybe grabbing a snack."

His parents stood to leave. "All right, don't eat too much. We found a pizza place downtown."

Zack sat bolt upright. "Pizza? Here?"

Carlos laughed. "Yeah, can you believe it? This will be an adventure, huh?"

Lucy shook her head as they left. "I hope they don't put glommy bird on it."

Zack sent Ix a message from his C7 to let the Valtraxian know where he was going. He reviewed the rest of the messages waiting in his inbox. *Still nothing from Rio, and Dravs hasn't heard anything either.* He sighed, put away his C7, then headed out. He waved to his parents making tea in the kitchen.

As he headed toward the palace gardens, he sent another message to Mungus, to tell the Ersidian where to find him. Mungus became tense if, when he showed up at their quarters after school, Zack wasn't around. Before sending the message, Zack changed his mind about where he wanted to go, and he changed the message to let Mungus know he would head to the docks first, and then the gardens. He wanted to look at the Athosian ship some more. With any luck, one of them would finally be outside and he could ask about Squishy.

To his dismay, apart from several shuttles, no ships berthed at the royal docks; the Athosian ship was gone. The Ersidian dockworkers refused to answer his queries, saying only they had no answers for him.

He noticed a human wearing a uniform standing at the end of one of the docks watching ships pass the royal space dock. As he neared the end of the platform, Zack recognized Major Jericho. He called out to him, "I thought you left."

Major Jericho looked over his shoulder and beckoned for Zack to join him. "We were supposed to, but things got complicated. I've been asked to liaison with the Athosians for the time being."

"Where'd they go?" Zack peered over the edge. He didn't see the Athosian ship anywhere.

"They moved to a more secure docking facility."

Zack grabbed the rail next to Major Jericho and peered down at the forest floor under the space dock. Deep shadows shrouded the verdant canopy as leaves swayed in the breeze. Each time a low-flying ship flew near, the trees would violently shudder, dislodging dozens of birds, which then returned to their perches once the ship passed.

"I assume you've heard the news from Devorus?" Major Jericho raised his eyebrows as he regarded Zack.

Zack shook his head. "No, what's going on? I've been trying to find my friend in Cytherea. The girl I was with before all this happened."

Major Jericho's brow furrowed. "Oh. I don't know anything about that. I'm talking about the trouble in the Devoran capitol. Apparently, Valianna is making a play to overthrow the military government."

When Zack met her, the Devoran princess didn't seem interested in retaking the throne, but she was the first proper politician he'd encountered. According to Jenny, when Valianna learned about the Athosians on Venus, the Athosians he awakened, her attitude changed.

Feeling his chest tighten, Zack peered down into the forest. "I feel like it's my fault. Like I should do something."

"Like what? You don't want to be anywhere near there if the shooting starts." Major Jericho sighed. "The Devorans have been heading down this path for a long time. Your actions might have been a spark to light the flames, but someone or something else would have come along in your absence. If you want to do something, contact your Devoran friends at school. This will be more frightening for them than it is for you."

Zack furrowed his brow as Dravs came to mind. He wondered what sort of stories the Devoran government would tell about his involvement and whether or not his friend would believe them.

Light from the setting sun flooded in, casting a warm orange glow over the trees below. Major Jericho turned around, putting his back to the sun. "You look troubled."

"I was just thinking." Zack followed suit. "I'm worried about my friend Rio. No one has seen or heard from her since we left. Plus, when I go back to school, I'm probably going see a friend again, a Devoran. He goes to school at Cytherean Academy, but he lives on Vilicus with his family between terms."

"Wow. Full plate already." Major Jericho chuckled. "This Devoran is a classmate, right? Not a mentor or anything like that?"

"Yeah, we started Cytherean Academy together. His sister is a year or two ahead of us, but Dravs and me are the same age, I think."

Major Jericho shook his head. "Well, no, you're not. Keep in mind, Devorans live about a thousand years. He spent his first thirty in a nursery, then maybe ten years in schools similar to what you attended on Earth before transferring to Cytherean Academy."

"You mean, Dravs is, like forty?" Zack's eyes widened and his hands slipped off the rails. He grabbed hold again and propped himself up. "He's old enough to be my dad!"

"It's not that simple. If you'd been born the same year, right next to each other, he'd still be a toddler eating his own boogers." Major Jericho grinned.

Zack laughed. "It's so weird."

"Devorans spend a prolonged time as infants and toddlers. Their"—Major Jericho made an air quotes gesture—"'teenage years' are about like ours, but they end up spending a lot more time drifting, trying to figure out what they want to do with their lives, and are probably close to a hundred years old before they settle on a career. Most don't even think about starting a family until they're well into three or four hundred years."

"Wow..." Zack tried to imagine what it would be like to be Devoran.

"It can be a lot to wrap your head around. The first time I took my wives and husband to Devorus, it blew their minds that all my Devoran friends had been around since our great-great-grandparents were kids."

Zack squinted while he tried to figure out just how many wives and husbands Major Jericho was talking about. "Husband and wives? How's that?"

He laughed. "Like many families on Rigel Kent, we're a polycule. We live in a commune, Aaru Delta. My first wife, my second wife, my husband—he's their second husband—our kids. We're all one big happy family." Major Jericho's smile faded. "I can't imagine what they went through when they heard I'd been killed. I haven't seen my kids since Valianna came to Cytherea. Obviously, they're all relieved I'm still alive, but it must've been rough."

Zack wondered the same thing about his parents. "I had a lot of weepy messages from my parents too."

The major put his hand on Zack's shoulder. "During one of my first assignments as a liaison on Devorus, I was assigned to assist this sheltered noble Devoran who'd never really been around a human before. She became, well, we were more than friends. Don't let all this nonsense wreck your friendship with the Devorans you know. They're good people."

Zack huffed. "He may not even want to talk to me anymore after this. I mean, he liked Princess Valianna and all, but I don't think he expected me to start a civil war."

"Maybe not, but if he's still talking to you, I think it'll be all right. There are going to be more challenges to endure, Zack. No one can tell you how to handle them simultaneously. I'll make some inquiries about that girl, but don't get your hopes up. No one is keen to talk to any of us about anything. However, I'll leave you with this, something someone much wiser than I once said." Major Jericho scratched his chin. "'Never be cruel. Never be cowardly. Always try to be nice, and never fail to be kind. Hate is always foolish.' Love and truth are worth fighting for until your last breath. You're already pretty good at living that way, but it's easy to stray from the path. Your friends, even your Devoran friend, can help keep you from getting lost."

Major Jericho patted Zack on the shoulder. "We probably won't get a chance to talk again before I or you leave. Take care, be careful. I think you'll do all right." He winked at Zack and walked away, leaving the young man to contemplate his words as the setting sun splayed its warm glow over the royal forest of Taella City.

—— 《》 — 《》 — 《》 — 《》 — 《》 — 《》 ——

Jenny squeezed her eyes shut and stretched, counting to ten before looking at the school assignment again. She scanned over the essay once more, and upon seeing no egregious errors, she submitted it.

School was finished for the term.

Now all I have to do is wait for the evaluations to come back, but at least I've finished all the assignments. Jenny shut down the terminal and contemplated flinging herself into bed for a long nap.

Her mother entered the room, forcing Jenny to reconsider. "Bonjour, petite chou."

"Hello, Mother." Jenny leaned back in her chair. "I've just finished the last of my school assignments. I'm done for the term."

Amélie sat on a bed across from Jenny. "So early? Well done!"

Jenny sighed. "Now what? I spent so much time working on this schoolwork, I don't know what to do with myself now that I'm finished for the term."

Her mother thought for a moment. "We could visit some of the local sights. Aren't your Junior Ranger friends coming here soon?"

Ugh. The Junior Ranger excursion. I forgot about that. She hadn't intended to join her troop on that particular excursion, even before all the trouble with the Devorans and Athosians started. So, when the troop leader, Bariss, distributed permission slips, she put hers aside and forgot about it.

Jenny pinched the bridge of her nose. "I'm already here, and I've been stranded on two different planets already without proper preparation. The thought of spending two weeks in the Ersidian wilderness with them does not appeal to me. Not that it ever really did. I want my bed. I want a roof over my head. I want hot food, not half-warmed rations badly cooked in a portable cooker."

"Geneviève, are you saying you wish to quit the Junior Rangers?"

That thought had crossed Jenny's mind. She usually didn't mind the weekly meetings, although they occasionally conflicted with other things she wanted to do. Plus, the meetings were often the only times she'd get to see Zack and Ix at school.

It would be easy to quit now. If I go through with this... She offered her mother little more than a non-committal shrug. "I don't know. So much has changed."

"Well, why don't we go out to eat, hm? Just the two of us?" Amélie reached forward and patted Jenny's leg.

"That sounds nice." Jenny stood and stretched. She and her mother entered the common area where Zack's parents were watching the news.

"Jenny and I are going out. Good..."

A newscaster's voice cut through the silent space left by Amélie. "We have confirmed reports that the Devoran fleets have left the Sol system. Their departure coincides with reports of an attack on the Devoran capital of D'Vana-Ko."

Jenny found herself staring at the screen as she slid into one of the plush seats surrounding the conversation pit.

The GNN news announcer's voiceover continued as holoimages of ships translating out of system appeared. "We have confirmed reports that the violence in D'Vana-Ko appears to be an attack on the government itself. We go now to footage we've received from our Devoran correspondent on the ground in the Devoran capital. This footage is unedited, fresh from the comm relay network and may not be suitable for small children."

The images flickered and switched to a view of the Devoran city skyline. The clean, swooping lines and arcs of Devoran architecture stood in contrast to the pastel lavender sky. Columns of smoke rose from a cluster of domed buildings on the right side of the image. A pale green-scaled Devoran stood in front of the vista and nodded. "Virkin Gran, Galactic News Network. Just moments ago, explosions served a frightening wake-up call to the inhabitants of D'Vana-Ko."

"What is going on, Carlos?" Zack's mother grabbed her husband's arm as she laid her head on his shoulder.

"Madness."

Jenny glanced at her mother who stared wide-eyed at the images.

Virkin Gran looked over his shoulder at the smoking domes. "Bombs blew the doors off government center buildings and armed partisans rushed the guards. Our verified sources have informed us that the attackers are loyalists of the former Imperial family of Devorus and their intent is to restore power to the remaining living member of that family, Valianna Hallox."

Jenny gasped. "I met her. On Cytherea. She was there with us."

"We've been told to expect a statement from Valianna Hallox shortly. Until then, all we can do is watch safely from a distance. Everyone is being kept away from the government center and—" Virkin Gran's brow furrow just before his eyes widened and the feed went dark.

After a few seconds, the holovideo of the GNN newscaster returned. A middle-aged human with graying hair, he licked his lips and smoothed the front of his suit jacket before clearing his throat. "That appears to be all we have at the moment. We'll keep you apprised as this situation develops."

The GNN logo appeared before the broadcast switched to local weather. Lucy muted it. "Is it terrible that I can only think that maybe we'll all get to go home soon?"

Jenny didn't think it sounded terrible. She had the same thought.

Chapter 35

Zack and Ix sat on a stone bench in the palace gardens, watching visitors wander while they awaited appointments or just took in the sights. An Ersidian couple passed them, vigorously discussing something in a dialect that did not sound familiar to Zack, despite the classes he'd taken on Ersidian language.

With school essentially over for the term, he found it boring to simply sit in the gardens but preferred it to lounging around the suite. His parents and Mungus agreed Zack shouldn't leave the palace grounds without his Ersidian bodyguard. Keeping busy kept Zack's mind off of troubling topics, and fortunately, Ix's company helped in that regard.

A young, tawny-furred Ersidian wearing an emerald and black school uniform steered a powered wheelchair toward them and parked it before opening a container of food. He sat munching, transfixed by a pair of birds darting in and out of a nearby tree.

"I have been investigating my school options, Zack." Ix touched the young man's arm to get his attention.

"You figured out a way to transfer to the school on Vilicus?"

Ix cocked its head. "I am not certain that will be possible. One of the stipulations of my emancipation was that I would specifically attend Cytherean Academy for my education."

"Does it really matter?" Zack slouched and shifted to find a more comfortable position on the unyielding stone. "Isn't one school basically the same as another?"

"Perhaps from an academic standpoint. Legally, however, Cytherean Academy is mentioned specifically, and since it is in-part funded by the Confederation and the schools on Vilicus are not, that creates complications." Ix cocked its head. "Yet, the school on Vilicus uses a Confederation curriculum, whereas Cytherean Academy does not, which does not make sense to me. But, there is good news."

Zack turned to regard his Valtraxian friend. "What's that?"

"Our idle time here has enabled me to work far enough ahead on my engineering and applied science studies, that I am almost finished. Perhaps, another full term at Cytherean Academy and I will be able to apply to join the workforce on Vilicus, assuming I do not have to finish remotely from here."

Zack thought for a moment. The birds flitting about the tree settled on a branch and the young Ersidian eating lunch next to them grunted in disapproval.

"If they're letting you learn remotely here with us, why can't you just continue remote classes from Vilicus?"

The Valtraxian chittered. "I inquired about that possibility. I have been granted an exception because the Ersidian government has granted us asylum. Once we are cleared to return to the Sol system, the exception ends, and I must return to Cytherean Academy, or I will be found in violation of the terms of my emancipation and will be expected to return to the hive."

"Oh." Zack frowned. *A year isn't so bad, I guess.*

"Do you think your father would be able to help me with job placement once he has returned to Vilicus? He is an engineer, is he not?"

"Yeah, a civil engineer." Zack nodded. "I'm sure he'll help."

"Krunk!"

Zack looked over at the Ersidian student. The container with his half-eaten meal lay on the ground in front of him. He leaned forward, clutching at his armrest while reaching toward the container with a shaky hand, swearing.

"Would you like some help with that?"

The uniformed youth growled. "I would not like that."

Zack shrugged and turned to face Ix.

"But I would appreciate it."

The student's lunch consisted of a roasted glommy bird leg with individually packaged sides. Bits of dirt and pebbles covered the partially eaten leg, but the other containers seemed to have weathered the spill with no ill effects.

One by one, Zack handed the containers back to the boy, then held up the dirt-covered leg by two fingers. "What do you want to do with this?"

The Ersidian snatched the leg from Zack's hand, then brushed the dirt off it. "It's still good. A little dirt never hurt me." As he chewed, he waved a greasy finger at Zack's honor braid. "What clan?"

Zack looked down at his belt and ran his hand along the braid. "Um, Stonetalon."

The student grunted. "Thank you, Stonetalon."

A commotion near the palace entrance drew Zack's attention. Visitors and workers alike clustered near information kiosks. "What's going on over there?"

Ix cocked its head and chittered. "The news feeds are all talking about an attack at the Devoran capital. Some sort of coup, they're saying." The Valtraxian scrambled off the bench. "We should probably go inside."

Just as Ix suggested it, Zack's C7 pinged with a message from his parents asking him to come to the suite right away. He stowed the device in his pocket and nodded to the Ersidian youth. "Enjoy your lunch."

He shrugged. "Glommy bird is always good."

Zack chuckled. "It sure is."

He followed Ix back toward the palace, weaving their way through the crowd straining to get a closer look at the newsfeeds. Even the guards at the palace doors paid more attention to the breaking story than Zack and Ix struggling to push their way through the rowdy crowd.

As their progress slowed, Zack sent a text response to his father letting him know they were on their way. He took advantage of the crowd blocking their way to try to make sense of what the newsreaders reported, but the noise of the crowd drowned out enough of their words that the overall meaning eluded his grasp of Ersidian.

"Ix, can you understand anything they're saying?"

The Valtraxian rose up on its hindmost four legs to peer above the crowd. After a moment, Ix lowered itself back down to Zack's level.

"They are mostly making baseless speculations at the moment. They are expecting statements within the hour from the Devoran government and also from Princess Valianna, for some reason."

The doors slid open, relieving enough congestion to enable Zack and Ix to slip past. The guards, recognizing them, ushered them past the checkpoint they had established to keep the outside mob from overwhelming the interior corridors.

The pair made their way through the maze of corridors in the public-access area to their suite in the residential wing. Zack saw Mungus loping down the corridor toward them as they approached the suite.

"Hey, did you hear what happened?"

"Sort of? Some kind of attack on Devorus?" Zack opened the door and the three entered the suite. Zack's parents sat with Jenny and her mother watching the news on the holoviewer. As Zack sat down alongside his parents, Carlos caught his son and Ix up on the events unfolding on Devorus.

"So, if the Devorans left Cytherea, does that mean we can go home now?" Zack glanced over at Ix before looking at his mother and father. The Valtraxian settled in between Jenny and Zack's parents while Mungus paced the floor behind them.

Carlos put his hand on Zack's shoulder. "Well, they haven't said why the Devorans left. We don't have a confirmed timeline that the two events are connected yet. We may know something concrete in a day or two."

Zack considered other reasons the Devorans might suddenly leave the Sol System so close to an attack on their capital. Widening his eyes, he realized they might be coming for him on Ersid.

The newsfeed shifted to a podium set before the animated backdrop of the Imperial Devoran seal on a colorful starfield. After a moment, a statuesque Devoran with scales of blue strode into view. She wore a shell-and-feather headdress, and glittering beads dangled from the tips of her frill.

Jenny lifted her head off her mother's shoulder and sat upright. "Princess Valianna."

The noblewoman stared into the camera for a moment. "Citizens of the Confederation, the Earth-Alpha Centauri Alliance, and allied systems, I am Valianna Hallox, and I have returned from my family's exile to assume my rightful place as sovereign of the Devoran Empire." She emphasized the word "empire" and took a breath before continuing. "For too long a government fronted by the military leaders who deposed my mother and father have bullied their way into exerting unearned influence over galactic affairs. They have unjustly interfered with regional affairs of a Confederation petitioner, harassed citizens of that petitioner, and finally, circumvented due process by committing an act of war upon that petitioner."

Zack realized she referred to the events on Cytherea that stranded Jenny, Ix, and him on Athos.

"Not only did they attack an EAC facility without provocation, but also they injured and killed EAC and Confederation citizens alike in their unsanctioned attack. They blamed the fallout on the enemy of a conflict that has been resolved for nearly one thousand standard years."

An image of Captain Drellex Fon appeared on the backdrop behind Valianna. "Captain Drellex Fon, lauded as the hero of the Devoran/Athosian War chose to sacrifice himself, his ship, and his crew after it became clear to him that he'd been sent on a genocidal mission. Devorus has spent generations cheering his success in bringing the Athosians to their knees when we should be recoiling in horror at the destruction of an entire planet's biosphere and the extermination of trillions upon trillions of noncombatants of species we've never encountered. People who lived and worked on Athos, not involved with the war effort, people with friends and families. Killed, no, murdered. Unjustly, by us."

The room remained silent, save for the click of Ix's fingers on its exoskeleton. Zack glanced at Mungus. Even his burly Ersidian friend stared at the holoviewer, hanging on Valianna's words.

The backdrop behind the princess reverted to the Imperial seal and starfield. "Twenty minutes ago, I accepted the surrender of Grand Marshall Hannut Maxis and dissolved the Devoran Supreme Council. I have recalled all our ambassadors and advisory staff. We will reorganize our government into one which views, as a top priority, the equity of all our citizens and guests from across the Confederation and our allies."

She licked her lips and lowered her head. "I beg your tolerance and your patience as the Devoran Empire reckons with a very difficult past that the previous government outlawed even mentioning. We have amends and reparations to make and much work to do. This government is not entitled to your respect and subservience, but we would like to earn your trust once more." Valianna crossed her left arm over her chest, clasped her shoulder, and bowed her head. "May our ancestors swimming in the boundless Sea of Serenity watch over you all."

The newsfeed returned to a GNN newscaster who stared wide-eyed for a moment before clearing his throat. "Well, a shocking new development from Devorus. We expect statements from the Confederation President and other heads of state soon. Stay tuned to the Galactic News Network for the latest..."

Carlos muted the feed. "Well, they didn't outright say it, but I think it's clear those ships left Sol to head home."

Lucy gripped her husband's hand. "That means we'll be going home soon too."

Zack slouched and bit his lip to keep it from trembling. His mind raced. *Is this all because of me and Squishy? What about Dravs? Is Cytherean Academy going to let me back in? Are the Devoran military guys still mad at me?*

An alarm blared, interrupting Zack's thoughts. Stiffening, Mungus crossed the room and stood in front of the door.

Amélie stood. "What is going on, Munches?"

"Mungus, Mother," Jenny growled under her breath.

Mungus's ears twitched as he listened to orders shouted from the hallway. "Sounds like the palace is going on lockdown. None of you will be able to leave the suite without clearance." He gazed at Zack. "Especially you."

Lucy took her son's trembling hand. "It'll be all right, Zack."

—— 《》— 《》— 《》— 《》— 《》— 《》——

As Jenny waited for her heart rate to return to normal after the unexpected alarm, she pushed herself away from the couch and approached Mungus.

"Can we shut it off? We've all heard it."

Mungus shook his head. "It runs until it's done. It's a big palace, and a lot of guards and workers have to get to their posts."

Jenny grunted, wishing she could silence the blaring klaxon. She wandered into the kitchen and perused the food preservation unit. Dinner out on the town was now impossible during the security lockdown; they would have to make do with what they had on hand.

She found glommy eggs, half a loaf of Ersidian round bread, and a dozen bottles of assorted beverages ranging from Quantum Cola to local beer. She shut the door. "There's not enough food for dinner."

Carlos hopped up from his seat. "That can't be right."

Mungus cleared his throat. "I may have gotten carried away for lunch after everyone started making plans to go out tonight. You all had a lot of leftovers in there. I cleaned them up."

Zack snorted. "You ate all our food?"

"Not all of it. I don't like round bread"—Mungus crossed his arms—"and I wasn't about to cook glommy eggs for lunch."

Jenny leaned on the counter and glared across the room at him. "You're going to get them to let us out for food, right?"

Mungus held up his hands. "Cool those thrusters, Jen-Je... Jenny. I'll just call my father and get him to authorize us for access to the palace kitchens. They'll bring whatever you want. We just have to eat it here."

The Ersidian pulled a comm unit from his belt pouch. "In fact, I'll ask him now."

Jenny shook her head, then noticed Zack wiping his eyes. She approached him and knelt behind his seat. Reaching over the back of the couch, she put her hand on his shoulder. "People will remember the good you did, Zack. Things will turn out all right."

Zack sniffed and looked over his shoulder at her. "Will they? I have to start all over, find new friends, learn a new school. Plus, Coulson's still dead and it's my fault and..."

Jenny patted his shoulder. "Just give it time. Valianna will get the Devorans to back off, and you're moving to be with your family. It's not starting over." She didn't have words to assuage his guilt over Coulson, but she knew that one decision she made would likely make him feel a little better.

"You won't need all new friends, Zack. Isn't Dravs's family on Vilicus? You'll see him on school breaks. Besides, I'm leaving Cytherean Academy and transferring to the school on Vilicus with you."

Zack started. "What?"

"Geneviève?" Her mother stepped toward Jenny, raising her hand to her mouth.

Jenny straightened up. "They expelled Zack for no good reason. He did nothing wrong. I won't go to a school that treats Zack, or any other student, like that. They're more interested in kissing Devoran tails for funding than supporting their own students. A place like that doesn't deserve students like us."

Lucy clasped Jenny's hand, tears welling in her eyes. Carlos strode across the room and gathered the young woman in a hug. "I'm glad Zack has friends like you."

Ix chittered. "I would quit, too, Zack, but they would send me back to Valtra if I did."

Zack leaned across his mother and took the Valtraxian's hand. "I know, Ix. It's okay." He looked up at Jenny. "Thank you."

Amélie gestured to her daughter and pointed at their bedrooms. "I wish to speak to you in private, Geneviève."

Huffing, Jenny circled the conversation pit, then waited for her mother at the door to her room. Once Amélie entered, Jenny closed the door.

"Geneviève, I know you are upset, but do you really think dropping out of school is the answer?"

Crossing her arms, Jenny regarded her mother. "I didn't drop out. I transferred. Dr. Bernard Harris, Jr. School has already accepted my application and all the credits from Cytherea. They said they'd accept all the work I completed here, as well, so they're not making me repeat the last year of school."

Amélie sat on the edge of the bed, shaking her head. "I wish you'd spoken to me first. Your father is almost well enough to return to *Messier Habitat*; we were planning on doing so at the first opportunity. You could have finished school there."

Jenny sat next to her mother. She gazed at her hands folded in her lap. "Of course I could have, but I wanted to support Zack." She put her head on her mother's shoulder. "I don't appreciate the trouble he's brought my way, but I couldn't stand by and do nothing while Cytherean Academy blamed him for everything that happened. They didn't even give him a chance to defend himself."

"It is very commendable, Geneviève." Amélie put her arm around her daughter and squeezed. "I am proud of you. Your father will be too."

Jenny drew a shaky breath, bit her trembling lip, and wondered if Hiri would be equally proud. Choosing to leave her girlfriend on Cytherea and follow Zack to Vilicus felt like a betrayal. She hoped Hiri would understand.

Chapter 36

Zack rarely watched the news; however, over the next several days, he endured hours of talking heads analyzing every detail of the Devoran coup and waited for any mention of Cytherean or Devoran withdrawal from the Sol System. Even though the security lockdown had been lifted the very same night, Zack dared not venture far from the newsfeeds for fear of missing information from back home.

The news he was waiting for came with the arrival of Commander Torg. The brown-furred Ersidian looked down at Zack when the young man answered the door. "I have news your parents will want to hear. The girl's, too."

Jenny looked up from her seat on the sofa where she'd been reading correspondence from her friends at school. "I'll send for my mother. She's out in the gardens, I think."

Zack let the Commander in, then approached his parents' room and knocked on the door. "Commander Torg is here with news."

He then went to retrieve Ix from their room. By the time he returned with the Valtraxian, all the adults had assembled.

Commander Torg cleared his throat. "I'll be brief. In our opinion it is safe for you to return to the Sol System. The Sovereignty will arrange for your passage back to Earth or wherever you want to go on one of our cruisers. However, we will also accept any petitions to extend your political asylum, should you so choose."

Zack didn't wait for his parents to respond. "I'm ready to go home"—he glanced up at his father—"to Vilicus, I guess, right?"

Carlos nodded. "That's right. Ix too. Unless you have to head back to Cytherean Academy right away."

The Valtraxian shook its head. "I do not need to return there until the fall term begins. There should be ample time for me to accompany you to Vilicus and arrange transport to the school from there."

Commander Torg made a notation on his tablet before turning his attention to Jenny and her mother. "And you two?"

Amélie regarded her daughter. "Geneviève and I will return to Vilicus with them. Thank you."

"Very well." Commander Torg noted that on his tablet. "I suggest you pack up, then. *Sovereign's Hammer* will dock here at the Citadel tomorrow. It won't leave without you, but as we're diverting it from its scheduled patrol route to transport you back to Sol, we'd appreciate your promptness."

Carlos nodded. "We'll be ready, Commander."

The Ersidian left them to their preparations.

Zack scrunched up his face as he thought. *I probably only need one change of clothes for the trip. All my stuff from home is already on Vilicus.* "How long was your trip here, Mom and Dad?"

"Our travel time or elapsed time?" Lucy guided Zack toward his room. He brushed her hands off his shoulders.

"I'm just trying to figure out how many changes of clothes I should pack and what I can recycle. I only have one small bag; I didn't plan to leave Cytherea."

Carlos pulled Lucy away from their son. "We were only onboard the ship about a day and a half. The Ersidian cruiser might be faster than the transport we took. One change of shirt and pants and a couple of pairs of socks and underwear ought to do it. If you have new clothes you want to keep, we can probably fit them in our bags."

"Okay." Zack followed Ix into their room. The Valtraxian dug through its pile, tossing out things it intended to recycle and setting things it wanted to keep in a separate pile.

Zack watched for a moment. "You collected a lot of junk while we were here, Ix."

The Valtraxian stopped and turned to face Zack, cocking its head. "It occurred to me I would likely not be able to participate in the Junior Ranger outing, so I decided to learn as much as I could using the *Junior Ranger's Guide to Ersid*'s guidelines. Fortunately, it is a much more up-to-date resource than the *Junior Ranger's Guide to Bestic*."

Zack laughed. "That book was useless."

"Especially as an electronic resource. If we had had a physical copy, at least we could have burned it for warmth."

"I'm glad you're able to come home with us." Zack put his hand on the Valtraxian's shoulder. "But I'm going to miss you when you have to go back to school."

Ix stroked Zack's arm. "We will speak often. I promise."

—— 《 》 — 《 》 — 《 》 — 《 》 — 《 》 — 《 》 ——

If Zack had been unprepared for an unexpected trip away from home, Jenny was even more so. The suitcase she'd acquired through the palace's fabricators lacked many of the amenities she enjoyed from her DeForest Lux-Stor travel bag, but she managed to discard and recycle enough clothes to make it work.

She laid out on the nightstand the next day's clothes and decided that what she wore today would go into the recycler. She noticed her mother's door open and took a moment to stand in the doorway and watch her mother sort her clothes and toiletries into her luggage and her overnight bag.

"You packed too much, Mother."

Amélie glanced up at her daughter. "I had to pack quickly and did not know what to expect. No one told me you were staying in Taella City at the royal palace. Still, it does not hurt to be prepared."

What about over-prepared? Jenny bit back her retort as a message from Hiri pinged her comm implant. The same night she told everyone she had transferred from Cytherean Academy in support of Zack, she finally summoned the fortitude to send Hiri a message to tell her, then she promptly focused on ignoring her anxiety about her girlfriend's response.

"Mother, I'll be in my room for a bit. Could you give me some privacy, please? I just received a message I need to see."

For a moment, Jenny thought her mother might refuse, but then Amélie nodded. Jenny returned to her room, closing the door behind her. She opened Hiri's message. The young woman had changed her hair and was now wearing it in a shoulder-length shaggy bob that faded from her natural dark colors to a light lavender ombre pattern.

Hiri smiled and pressed her hands together. "First, I'm going to apologize if this message is rambly; I'm just going off-the-cuff here, because I didn't want to wait to respond to your message."

Hiri paused for a moment. "I admire you very much for standing up to Cytherean Academy for how they treated Zack. I mean, I'm sad you're not coming back to school, but I'm really just happy that you're all right and you get to come home. Vilicus isn't that far away, so I can probably visit during school breaks."

She looked down for a moment and bit her lip. "Look, there's no way I want to break up, even if we're not going to the same school. I know long-distance relationships are hard, but Venus and Vilicus practically have real-time communication all year, I think. Even if they don't, it's nothing like what we're doing now while you're on Ersid, so it probably won't be that bad. School's going to be really busy for me next term anyway, so maybe this will help me concentrate on classes and we'll just see each other at breaks."

Jenny wiped a tear from her cheek, even as she found herself smiling. Hiri continued to ramble, essentially reiterating what she'd already said. *I guess I worried for nothing. Maybe everything really will be all right.*

She dried her face and checked her appearance in the mirror before opening the door. Her mother was still in her own room, sorting the myriad outfits she'd brought. Jenny approached her. "I can help you pack."

"Is everything all right?" Amélie looked into Jenny's eyes as she reached out to touch her daughter on the shoulder.

"Yes, Mother, fine." Jenny smiled. "Everything is fine. Shall we?"

Working together, they finished packing Amélie's luggage in less than twenty minutes, then adjourned to the conversation pit to await their suite mates. Carlos and Lucy were already sitting there, talking quietly while Galactic News Network played on the holoviewer in silent mode.

"You packed quickly." Amélie sat in a seat adjacent to Zack's parents. Jenny took the seat next to her.

Carlos shrugged. "We never actually unpacked. We've mostly been wearing clothes we had fabricated shortly after we arrived and just recycled them all."

Lucy chuckled and shook her head. "I hate traveling. I had just gotten everything unpacked in our new home on Vilicus when we got word that we had to prepare to come here. It was a mad scramble to find someone to watch after our dog. We don't really know any of our neighbors yet."

"How is it? I know Zack's been worried." Jenny suspected the housing units on Vilicus offered more space and greater variety of layouts and customization options than those on *Messier Habitat* because Vilicus was much newer and larger.

Carlos glanced at his wife and smiled. "Oh, I think he'll like it. He has a bigger room; we all have more space."

"I'm not even really missing all the land we had in Wyoming." Lucy pulled a small holoprojector out of her pocket and brought up an image of a ranch-style home surrounded by farmland. "We have a hydroponic garden adjacent to the kitchen that's open to the habitat ring."

She swiped her hand and the image switched to that of an array of containers with sprouts suspended in a framework. Beyond, Jenny saw the gentle curve of the habitat, the ring of Vilicus, rising in the distance overhead like the inside of an impossibly huge tire.

Amélie furrowed her brow as she regarded Lucy. "So, you just stay home and grow plants all day?"

Lucy laughed. "Certainly not. They don't need my constant interference. I'll be teaching life skill classes at several of the primary schools. Zack still thinks I might be one of his teachers, but I decided to stick to younger children until we're more settled. It's quite a different environment on Vilicus than I was used to in Wyoming."

"After that horrible accident, Geneviève's father and I have spent our entire recovery on Vilicus, and I admit, it is very nice. But Messier will always be home to me." Amélie sighed and slumped in her seat. "François will probably never be the same, and his job has retired him early."

Jenny sat up, staring at her mother. "Papa lost his job? You never said anything about that!"

"Oh, I didn't want to worry you, Geneviève. He worked there long enough that it isn't going to affect us much, except he'll be home more." She shrugged. "Who knows, maybe we'll travel more. On big ships, of course, cruisers, not tiny shuttles like the one that crashed."

Zack bounded out of his room, followed by Ix. "Done! Anything going on?" He looked around the room. "Hey, where's Mungus?"

Leaning back in his seat, Carlos looked over his shoulder at Zack. "He had to go talk to his father about something. He said to send him a message if we needed him. Speaking of which"— Zack's father leaned forward and rubbed his hands together—"why don't we all go out for one last dinner here in Taella City?"

Jenny turned to her mother. Amélie smiled and nodded. "Yes, that sounds lovely."

Chapter 37

After dinner, Zack's parents and Jenny's mother boarded one transport, leaving the kids to enjoy the second transport for themselves on the ride back to the Royal Citadel. The city at night became a blur of lights as they sped along the highway.

The passenger compartment featured four reclining seats, two facing front and two facing back. Ix sat curled in an awkward position facing backwards next to Jenny while Zack and Mungus sat in the forward-facing seats.

Zack rubbed his stomach. "There's a downside to this cyberstomach. I already don't feel stuffed. I kind of miss it."

"You sure packed it away, though." Mungus popped the top button on his uniform shirt.

"We probably won't need to eat tomorrow at all." Jenny leaned back in her seat and closed her eyes.

"You know, this was kind of like the best Junior Ranger trip we've ever had, except there were less adults telling us what to do all the time." Zack nudged Mungus.

"I guess." The Ersidian huffed. "Probably not going to be doing any of that stuff anymore, huh? I mean, what's the point? Me having to be your bodyguard is going to put a cramp in their style and besides, you three have been to a planet outside of the galaxy. What could the Junior Rangers do to top that?"

"It's true." Zack chewed on his lip for a moment. "I don't think my parents are going to let me go on any trips for a while anyway. They thought Valtra was too dangerous, and after Athos, I had to have whole organs replaced."

Ix chittered. "On the bright side, Vilicus is large enough you could probably spend years exploring the completed sections without seeing everything."

Zack sat up. "Yeah, that's right. It's like a whole new world to explore, except I'll get to go home and sleep in my own bed every night."

Groaning, Mungus slammed his head against his headrest. "I forgot to arrange for quarters there. Krunk." He rubbed the end of his muzzle. "Oh well, maybe they've already taken care of that for me."

Zack thought about that for a moment. "So, you've got to pretty much follow me everywhere, but you're not living with us. How's that going to work?"

Mungus shrugged. "I guess I'll be getting up early and escorting you to school. We might have a few classes together, but half of my days are probably going to be spent training while you're learning book stuff. Then I get you home and go with you anywhere else you have to go."

"For how long?" Jenny cracked one eye open to regard them.

"My father said it's at least a year. See if the Devorans settle down. If there's credible threats against his life, maybe longer. They're taking this very seriously." He scrunched up his face and sniffed. "I think the king likes to stick it to the Devorans whenever he can, and any on Vilicus who are loyal to the old military are definitely going to be grumpy about Zack having an Ersidian bodyguard." Mungus stuck his elbow in Zack's ribs. "You know they're talking about the coup being your fault?"

Zack's chest grew tight. "What? I wasn't even... I didn't do anything!"

Mungus laughed. "They shot at you from a frigate, and you ended up on Ersid seeking political asylum. Now they're just flinging mud to see if it sticks." His smile faded and he leaned close to Zack. "Nothing is going to happen to you while I'm around, Zack. I swear it."

"I believe you, Mungus." Zack slumped in his seat. "I just wish they'd forget all about me now."

Jenny opened her eyes. "They probably will. I've been watching the news from Devorus. Valianna waited until she had overwhelming support before launching her coup, and once she gets their government reorganized, she's not going to let them do anything to you. They're saying it'll be years before the Devorans really involve themselves in galactic politics again, and they haven't even dealt with the fallout from that information we brought back from Athos."

"I hope you're right." Zack sighed. "I've had enough excitement for a while, I think. And I don't want anyone else to get—" He swallowed as he couldn't decide between "hurt "and "killed." His chest ached every time he pictured Rio, lying on the storeroom floor, the flesh of her legs split and peeled away. He remembered her azure bio-replicant blood splattered all over the room, like spilled paint. Then he recalled Coulson's chest lying open, a gaping, bloody, and smoky chasm in which Zack felt he could see his own death.

"Rio... Coulson..." Zack's voice broke as the consequences of his decisions hit him full force in the scant moment he dared relax, thinking it was all over.

Ix unfurled and reached across the cabin to stroke Zack's arm. "You cannot change what has happened. Dwelling on what you could have done differently will bring you nothing but pain and further uncertainty."

Zack sniffled and wiped his nose on his sleeve. Mungus put his arm around his friend and hugged him.

Jenny stared at Ix. "That's... I'm surprised, Ix."

The Valtraxian turned to look at Jenny, cocking its head. "Despite the melodrama and occasional shouted dialog, there are lessons in many of the Ersidian entertainment programs I have been watching."

Mungus snorted. "Life advice from Ersidian melodramas, filtered through a Valtraxian."

"Ix isn't wrong, Mungus." Jenny patted Zack's knee. "I'm sure a counselor would tell you all these things you're feeling are normal, Zack. I mean, we've all been through a lot, and you seem to have gotten the worst of it."

She leaned back and placed her hand on her stomach. "I probably would have gotten a cybernetic nutrient extractor at some point anyway. Try to do the best you can with today, and don't worry about yesterday."

Zack nodded and wiped his face again. Through the window, he saw them pull into the palace garage. *One last night on Ersid, then finally, I get to go home.*

Once they exited the vehicles, Zack waited for his parents, then fell in line behind them. His mother swayed, humming and giggling, as she walked with her arm entwined with his father's.

Why is all this bothering me so much now? Why can't I just forget about these terrible things? The weight of Coulson's death, coupled with renewed memories of Rio's terrible injuries, felt like carrying a backpack overloaded with schoolbooks. Zack bit the inside of his cheek to distract himself from the flood of despair that threatened to overtake him. By the time they reached the suite, Zack felt more in control of his emotions. Just to be safe, he bade his parents goodnight and hurried off to bed, eager to put the evening behind him.

—— 《》 — 《》 — 《》 — 《》 — 《》 — 《》 ——

Following behind Zack toward the suite, Jenny watched as his shoulders slumped lower and lower. She imagined the full force of everything he'd been through since that last day on Venus finally bearing down on him with the weight of a thousand worlds.

He seemed to stand up straighter by the time they reached the suite, but he headed into his room with only a perfunctory "good night." Jenny considered checking up on him, but she decided to leave that task to Ix, who followed him.

Zack's mother paused by the sofa, propping herself up with both hands while Carlos steadied her. "Feeling all right, dear?"

"I don't think of myself as a lightweight, but I suspect that Ersidian wine was a bit stronger than I'm used to." She covered her mouth and giggled.

Amélie nodded and patted her stomach. "It is. That's another advantage to cyberstomaches, Lucy. They filter out the worst effects of alcohol."

Lucy blew a raspberry. "I will remain *au naturale*, if you don't mind."

Jenny snorted and stifled a laugh.

Carlos whispered something in her ear. Her eyes widened, then she burst out laughing. "I meant I don't want cybernetics. I'm going to keep my clothes on, thank you very much."

Amélie shook her head and covered her mouth with her hand. "I think we should all go to bed. Tomorrow will be a busy day. Good night."

Jenny waited for her mother to leave the room, then approached Zack's parents as Carlos steered his wife around the conversation pit.

"Before you go..."

Carlos stopped Lucy and turned to Jenny. "Hm? What is it?"

"I think Zack never really processed everything that happened, with Rio being hurt and Coulson dying. Now that we're all going home and things are settling down, I think he's finally realizing how bad, how dangerous things really were for him."

Lucy staggered and started for Zack's door. Carlos took her arm and shook his head. "Let him sleep."

"I just wanted you to know. In case we get private cabins in the cruiser home. I know he gets embarrassed if he cries when there are other people around." She offered his parents a smile.

Carlos put his hand on her shoulders. "Thanks, we'll talk to him. Thank you for being a good friend to Zack."

"After all this—" Jenny chuckled—"he's like the little brother I never had. Good night."

She left Zack's parents and retired to her room

Just as she changed into her nightshirt, the door chime rang. Her mother, ready for bed, regarded her with a furrowed brow. "Is everything all right?"

Jenny nodded and pulled the band out of her hair, letting it fall down around her shoulders. "Zack is finally coming to grips with how close this all was for him. I just wanted to let his parents know that he would probably need some help dealing with it."

She brushed out her hair while her mother made small talk about dinner. Eventually, they bade each other good night, and Jenny crawled into bed and fell asleep.

She awoke to a knocking at her door. Bleary-eyed, she opened it. Her mother, already dressed, entered and gathered up the previous night's clothes. Jenny checked the time on her implants and groaned when she realized the time was even later than she normally woke up.

"Is anyone else awake?" Jenny rubbed her eyes.

"Carlos and Zack are. I haven't seen Ix. Carlos said Lucy was 'sleeping it off.'" Amélie pointed toward the bathroom. "You should shower before we go. These are nicer than any shipboard showers will be. I was thinking of getting breakfast from a vendor in the gardens. Shall I wait for you?"

Jenny shook her head and yawned. "No. I'm not hungry. I'll be all right on my own. Have you heard anything about when our ship is supposed to arrive for us?"

"It docked last night. They asked us to board at thirteen hundred hours."

Jenny checked the time again. *Just under three hours from now.* "Fine. I'll be ready."

As she showered and dressed, Jenny debated whether she was at all hungry after last night's indulgent dinner. Once she finished, she gathered up all the clothes she still needed to recycle and headed toward the recycler.

Zack and Ix were seated in the kitchen, eating some sort of filled pastry. While it looked and smelled appetizing, Jenny noted that neither seeing nor smelling it triggered any sort of hunger response.

She stood there, staring at Zack as he ate. "How can you actually be hungry? Is your implant malfunctioning?"

He shrugged. "I wasn't not hungry. I saw they had these, what did the guy call them, Ix?"

"Parmoose pockets."

"Mungus said they were really good, but if we could even find them on Vilicus they wouldn't taste the same because the Ersidians don't export some of the ingredients." Zack took another bite and nodded, then held up his half-eaten pocket. "Want some?"

She shook her head. "No, thank you."

I guess some things never change. Jenny chuckled and shoved her clothes into the recycler. She grabbed her bag out of her room and doubled checked the information from Commander Torg to make sure she knew where the ship waited, then headed for the gardens to catch up to her mother.

Chapter 38

After Zack and Ix finished eating, they put their trash in the recycler and checked in with Zack's parents. Carlos and Lucy were all packed up and ready to go, waiting in their room and enjoying the quiet.

Together they made one final pass through the suite, checking for forgotten items, then headed out. Mungus, dressed in a sharply pressed uniform, awaited them in the hall and escorted them through the hallways.

No one they passed paid them any mind. For them, today was just another day. For Zack, it was the end of a journey that started the day Squishy fell out of the ceiling on top of Ryll Bob in the cafeteria at Cytherean Academy, the day he met Rio.

Sovereign's Hammer was docked at the same berth from which they first stepped foot on Ersid. Apart from the regular dockworkers, Zack saw no one he recognized.

He tugged at Mungus's jacket. "Isn't your father going to see you off? Or your mother?"

The Ersidian grunted. "We already said our goodbyes. They've both... what is that?" His hand dropped to the knife strapped to his waist.

Zack turned to see a hulking, bullet-shaped environmental suit topped with a clear, fluid-filled dome hovering toward them. "It's one of the Athosians!" Zack dashed forward, ignoring Mungus's protest. He noticed a smaller, jelly-like shape attached to the top of the Athosian's dome. "Is that Squishy?"

The Athosian stopped in front of Zack. "It is the polyp you call 'Squishy.'"

Zack recognized the intonations of Alpha Primus. "Oh, I was wondering if it was you. It's hard to tell you all apart since your environmental suits all have similar markings." Taking a quick glance over his shoulder, Zack noticed his parents and Mungus coming up behind him.

"We heard of your impending departure and felt it would be appropriate to once again convey our gratitude for your assistance." A tentacle protruded from the suit, waving toward the people behind Zack. "Are these adult humans your progenitors?"

Zack glanced back. "They're my parents."

"Lucy and Carlos." Zack's mother stepped forward with nervous laughter. "You're actually an Athosian."

"We are." Alpha Primus reached up and let Squishy crawl onto their tentacle. "Your spawn was instrumental in caring for and returning this polyp to us. He is compassionate and considerate, and you are to be commended for teaching him those traits."

Carlos cleared his throat. "Well, thank you."

"Zack Jackson, it is unlikely we will encounter each other again. There is much to do." Alpha Primus's eyes blinked in sequence. Squishy wiggled their tentacles toward Zack.

Zack swallowed. "I'm glad I finally got to meet you. What you left behind in this galaxy has been part of my life for so long, it feels like it's always been there."

"Your curiosity and compassion are great assets, Zack Jackson. We hope you continue to share them, as well as share the truth of what happened to Athos. Refute the lies of the Devorans. It is a worthy endeavor." Squishy continued to reach for Zack. Alpha Primus held the polyp out toward the young man. "This polyp wishes to speak to you. Do you consent?"

Zack nodded and reached for Squishy. Alpha Primus moved closer and Squishy slapped a tentacle onto either side of Zack's face.

A flood of emotions poured into Zack. Gratitude. Affection. Curiosity. Squishy closed their eyes. *Goodbye, friend.*

They withdrew from Zack, then scampered up Alpha Primus's tentacle to rest on top of the dome of the environmental suit once more.

Zack blinked back a tear. As Alpha Primus turned toward the palace, the young man stepped forward and called out. "There's something I've been wondering about. Can you answer one more question for me?"

Alpha Primus spun to regard Zack. "Ask your question."

"The Devoran that tried to kill me on Bestic, the one who was part of the Cult of Athos, he told me the stars were alive and talked about horrors in the void and how we're just like bacteria to them. Is it true?"

Alpha Primus bobbed silently for a moment. "The unknown in the vast void of the interstellar and intergalactic mediums can seem like horror to many. The Conquerors cultivated a belief in their most fervent followers that the stars and the galaxies were part of a vast cosmic organism so immense that any life like us would be as insignificant to them as we regard a bacterium. If that were true, we would be incapable of perceiving such an organism, much as a single bacterium is incapable of perceiving the biological organism in which it lives. Those who believe in such a cosmic lifeform accept this truth based on no empirical evidence, only faith. We must each find our own truth and determine how much of that truth will rely on faith, rather than evidence."

"Oh, uh..." Zack hoped for a "yes" or "no". He couldn't be sure he understood the answer he received.

"Be well, Zack Jackson." Alpha Primus turned and hovered way.

Zack's father put his hand on his son's shoulder and gestured toward *Sovereign's Hammer* at the end of the dock. "Come on, son. Let's go home."

Zack Jackson will return in
Zack Jackson & the Ringworld of Sol

www.ingramcontent.com/pod-product-compliance
Lightning Source LLC
Chambersburg PA
CBHW060438180626
46817CB00007B/2869